TRANCE

TRANCE

Derek Lambert

Arlington Books
Clifford Street Mayfair
London

TRANCE
first published 1981 by
Arlington Books (Publishers) Ltd
3 Clifford Street Mayfair
London W.1.

© *Derek Lambert 1981*

Set in England by
Inforum Ltd, Portsmouth
Printed and bound in England by
Billing & Sons Ltd
Guildford, Worcester and London

British Library Cataloguing in Publication Data
Lambert, Derek
Trance.
I. Title
823'.914[F]   PR6062.A/

ISBN   0 85140 549 5

For Mrs Roslyn Kloegman
who over the years has immaculately typed
more than a million words for me.

ACKNOWLEDGEMENT

Heartfelt thanks to Steven. A. Martindale, the Washington, D.C. lawyer, who helped with the legal details.
Any mistakes are mine, not his.

Part One

I

The nightmare began during the early hours of Christmas Eve.

She was walking along Fifth Avenue and snow was brushing against her face; thinking that the snowflakes were feathers, she absent-mindedly brushed them with one hand. Her mink jacket was white with the snow, but underfoot it wasn't yet deep enough to muffle the impact of her stiletto heels on the sidewalk.

She waited at a DON'T WALK sign, watching the snowflakes turn pink as they drifted past the red light; when the flakes turned green she crossed the steet, shrinking inside the mink as the wind blowing in from the East River caught her.

From time to time as she walked, she took her gloved hands from the pockets of the jacket and rubbed them gently together as though reassuring herself about some quality they possessed. When the cold found them she thrust them abruptly back into the pockets.

In the windows of the stores, lights glittered on sleighs and elegant trees, and stars beckoned above cribs. Taped carols flowed from a doorway between Fifty-Sixth and Fifty-Seventh Streets, only to be lost in the falling snow.

Outside Tiffany's she paused to gaze at their display, a robin perched among sparkling, silver holly leaves, each berry a ruby. She smiled as a memory stirred and walked on.

9

But despite Christmas, Fifth Avenue had a lonely air about it, the loneliness accentuated by the occasional pedestrian.

These night-walkers glanced curiously at the long-legged girl in the gold evening shoes striding past them. Why, she wasn't even wearing a hat or a scarf and her long, blonde hair was sprinkled with snow. Odd – foolhardy, in fact – to be alone on the streets of New York at this hour. However, it was none of their business.

Traffic was sparse, the cars leaving wet, black trails behind them. The driver of one pulled up beside the girl, opened the window and called out: "Hi, pussy-cat. Want a ride? Pussy-cats shouldn't be out in the snow." He was middle-aged, cigar stub between his lips. But she walked past him. "Hey," he called out, "I was speaking to you . . ." The words died; she hadn't even seen him. He tossed the wet-tipped cigar butt into the snow and drove away.

She was opposite the Rockefeller Center now. Cradled among the high-rise in the Channel Gardens, leading to the Lower Plaza and the giant Christmas tree, stood a group of angels with wings of radiant light and, above them, a star trailing a glittering plume.

She frowned. She had seen a display with a similar theme somewhere else. For the first time she felt the cold aching in her ears and she touched them.

The blue and white police car stopped just ahead of her in front of St Patrick's Cathedral. A policeman in plain clothes – snap-brim hat and black topcoat – climbed out and waited for her while his partner spoke on the car radio. There was aggression in the hunch of his shoulders, the set of his lean features, but when he noticed the expression on her face his voice was gentle. "Excuse me, ma'am," he said, "but this is a helluva time for a girl to be out alone in New York."

She stopped and stared at him and he had the feeling that he had suddenly materialised in front of her at the snap of a magician's fingers. "Who are you?" she asked.

"Detective Kessler, ma'am." He showed her his shield. "We wondered if you were in some kind of trouble."

"Trouble?" She took her gloved hands from her pockets

and massaged them together. "Trouble? Why should I be in any trouble?"

Blue eyes stared at him. There was a trace of unseasonal tan on her face. Class, he thought, and said: "It's kind of a rough night to be walking the streets. And you not dressed for it."

She glanced down at her white, ankle-length skirt and the gold evening shoes. "It is very cold," she said.

"Have you got far to go?"

"I don't know."

"You don't know?" He wondered if she was on a high and whether they would have to take her home or to the precinct or Bellevue.

She shook her head.

"Have you got any ID?"

She searched her pockets and produced an American Express credit card. Her name – if it *was* her card, the police-man in him thought – was Helen Fleming.

"Where do you live, Mrs Fleming?" he asked, watching her reaction to her name.

"Miss," she said. "Miss Fleming. And I live on Sixty-First."

Class all right. "That's quite a walk from here." She began to shiver and he said: "You'd better get someplace out of the cold. Try and remember where you were going, Miss Fleming."

"I wasn't going anywhere," she replied.

Jesus! he thought. "Maybe we should run you home."

"I'm so cold," she said.

From the police car his partner called out: "What's going on out there?"

"So how about it?" Kessler said to the girl.

"Are you a police officer?"

"That's right, ma'am. I showed you my shield, remember?"

"Of course," she said. "I'm sorry."

"Do you remember anything?" he asked suddenly.

"Anything?"

"About tonight. Why you are walking along here at this time of night." He glanced at his wrist-watch. "It's three o'clock."

"I'm trying to remember," she said. She frowned and bit her lower lip; when he looked into her eyes he saw that the pupils were dilated.

The snow was falling more thickly now, muffling their voices, and he knew he had to get her off the sidewalk.

"Did you have a date?"

"With Peter."

"Peter who?" His partner was climbing out of the car, fleshy features disgusted.

"Peter Lodge," she said.

"Didn't he take you home?"

"No," she said and, after a pause: "Peter didn't take me home."

"Some other guy?"

"No-one took me home."

"Where is he, this Peter Lodge?"

"At home, I guess. In the Village. He's got a couple of boutiques there."

As his partner joined him, Detective Kessler took the girl's arm gently and said: "You'd better get in the car with us and we'll take you home."

"What's going on?" his partner asked.

"We're taking this lady home."

"We are? Why, what's wrong with her?"

"She's a little distressed," Kessler told him.

"Yeah? A little distressed, huh?" Kessler's colleague bent down and peered into the girl's face. "Been to a party, lady?"

It was then that the girl screamed.

II

A soft light, clean and exciting. A snow light, a childhood light.

Helen Fleming let the light reach her through half-closed eyelids. Outside the snow would be untouched, except perhaps for the tracks of birds, and the Adirondack Mountains would be white and pink in the dawn light, and there would be envelopes of snow on the pointed, wooden roofs of the houses.

But there would only be time before school to scoop up a few handfuls of snow and throw them; late afternoon was the time to play in the snow, to build a snowman with charcoal eyes and a top-hat without a crown, before the light to the west turned a chill pink, and your hands, despite the mittens, ached with the cold.

In the schoolroom they gazed longingly through the windows at the snow while Miss Whelan, who had grey hair with yellowish streaks at the front and wore tweed skirts and twin-sets, wrote with squeaky chalk on the blackboard.

Half way through the English lesson, she summoned Helen to the front of the class and told her to write her name on the board.

"Now that's what I call handwriting," she told the class as Helen finished the last 'g' with a slender loop. "I want all of you to write your names on the first page of your exercise

13

books and see if you can write them as well as Helen Fleming." Before allowing Helen to return to her desk, she held one of her hands. "You have beautiful hands, my dear," Miss Whelan said. "Take care of them."

Which was the first time that Helen became aware of her hands as anything more than implements. She took them from beneath the sheets and looked at them. "What time is it?" she asked.

"Three o'clock," Peter Lodge said. "You've been out for ten hours."

"She said I had beautiful hands."

"Who said you had beautiful hands?" His voice was soft and patient.

"Miss Whelan."

"Who's Miss Whelan?"

"She was my schoolteacher at Glens Falls in Upper New York State."

"Okay," he said, "she was your teacher, what, ten years ago?"

"Fifteen, I guess."

"Okay, fifteen. But you're not at Glens Falls now. You're in your apartment on Sixty-First Street and you're twenty-two years-old and it's Christmas Eve and we're all very worried about you."

She closed her eyes again because she wanted to be in Glens Falls with the snow waiting outside; but Miss Whelan and the rest of the class had departed.

He took her hand. "Tell me what happened," he said.

She opened her eyes and let her hand lie in his and said: "You tell me what happened."

"You were found wandering down Fifth Avenue at three o'clock this morning."

"Who found me?"

"The police found you. They took you to Bellevue, but you were discharged because there wasn't anything wrong with you except that you didn't know what had happened to you."

"And do you?"

He shook his head. "That's what we are trying to find out."

14

"*We?*"

She heard another voice, vaguely familiar. "I'm glad you're feeling better, Miss Fleming." Behind Peter she saw Dr Bowen, handsome in a jowly sort of way with prematurely thinning hair and the beginnings of a paunch.

He smiled at her, a bedside smile. "We were worried about you for a while. You were very cold and confused." The smile broadened. "But now you're home and you're warm –"

"And everything's going to be all right," she interrupted him. Bowen was Peter's doctor and his manner irritated her.

"We hope so," he said.

Always *we*, she thought. "So I was found wandering on Fifth Avenue," she said. "Can you think of a better place to be found wandering?" She adjusted the pillows and sat upright; she was surprised by her hostility. "Why was I taken to Bellevue? Why not straight home? All right, so I might have had too much to drink but it was two days before Christmas . . ."

"You weren't drunk," Peter said patiently.

"Then what was I?"

Dr Bowen said: "You were suffering from amnesia, probably caused by some sort of shock. The hospital called me and I drove you home. I gave you a shot to calm you down and make you sleep. Now we want to find out what that shock was."

"How can I tell you if I'm suffering from amnesia?"

"You *were* suffering from amnesia, Helen," dropping the *Miss Fleming*, she noted. "You aren't necessarily suffering from it anymore."

They looked at her expectantly.

"I don't know what shocked me," she said.

Peter leaned back in his chair, an antique. She thought it might break under his weight; not that he was overweight but he was tall, over six foot, although with his limp his height was deceptive.

He asked her if she remembered what had happened after he had picked her up at eight the previous evening. Did she remember where they had eaten?

15

Certainly she remembered. At the Indian Pavilion on East Fifty-Fourth. Good, but chapatis and pompadons were hardly Christmas fare.

"And then?"

"Are you from the DA's office?"

"I'm serious, Helen."

"And then we went to a party."

This time the scream was never uttered but she heard it and its force closed windows and doors and, as it reverberated inside her, blinds slammed shut, creating darkness in which there were areas of faint light, the size of thumb-prints, like weaknesses in a silk screen.

* * *

The party in the block in the upper Fifties between Fifth and Madison had been a predictable affair. Models, designers and fashion-writers, and the usual smattering of laymen who liked to be part of a trendy scene, fashion, theatre, movies, books . . .

The setting had been predictable, too. The apartment, owned by a male model, was exquisitely furnished and yet, in her opinion, a mess, half salon and half den as though he had suddenly decided to assert his masculinity. Dusky-pink drapes, easy chairs upholstered with Regency stripes, alcoves with concealed lighting and on the wall above a zebra skin, a rifle as though he had been on safari.

The Christmas decorations were exquisite, too. Spun-glass baubles hung from the ceiling, spinning blurs of coloured light around the walls and on top of the television, on which, unwatched, a video recording of a Gucci fashion-show in Rome was being shown, stood a host of angels gazing at the Star of Bethlehem. Wistfully, Helen remembered Christmases in the north with roaring log-fires and heaps of presents piled underneath a real Christmas tree.

From the moment she entered the room she was aware of tensions and she was thankful that Peter was beside her, thankful for his reliability in company in which, although she was

16

already a star – at least her hands were because that was what she modelled – she was still a stranger.

Well, not reliability exactly because that had a dull ring to it, and dull Peter certainly was not. He wasn't out-going but he had presence; and when a smile broke up his features it was a revelation because they were normally so watchful, so contained. His hair and eyes were brown and he liked to dress casually but not modishly. Tonight he wore a brown suit with flared pants that had gone out of fashion a year or so back.

Friends had confided to Helen that they thought Peter's limp was romantic. Peter did not share their view. He had been a college athlete, tipped for Olympic honours, until a car with a drunk driver at the wheel had crashed into his sports car, smashing his kneecap and the bones of his shin. When Peter was introspective and short-tempered Helen blamed the drunk driver.

Three years ago he had opened a boutique in the Village selling jeans from Hong Kong and shirts from Pakistan; as soon as he had sold sufficient denim and cheese-cloth he had changed his image, and his half dozen, trend-setting, all-male boutiques were snapping at the heels of Ted Lapidus.

"What can I get you two to drink?" asked the owner of the apartment. His name was Daniel York and his cleft-chin, combined with a devastating smile (not spontaneous like Peter's), had helped to sell millions of dollars worth of male cosmetics. Tonight he seemed ill at ease.

She asked for a glass of Chablis, Peter a Scotch on the rocks.

"He seems to be on edge," she said while York was fetching the drinks.

Peter shrugged. "Temperament. They all suffer from that. Plus the fact that he's committing the unforgiveable."

"What's that?"

"Growing old."

"Then he can model for older men."

"There isn't much call for that. Older men have either made it or they've fallen by the wayside. Either way they're not interested in ads for after-shave. Ads for hairpieces are what they're more interested in. Can you see someone like Daniel

17

York modelling a rug?"

"Clothes?" Helen suggested.

"No way. Men don't want to be reminded that all they're fit for is cardigans and carpet slippers. Nor do your Daniel Yorks want to see pictures of themselves dressed up like a favourite uncle. Movie stars are allowed to grow old; models aren't."

"It's terrifying." She looked at her hands, symbols of the transience of her profession. "Are they all haunted by growing old?"

"Not if they're sensible, no. But not many of them are. They hang onto their youth too long, try and pull it back on a thread of vanity."

"And if they're sensible?"

"They invest the bread while they're making it. Set themselves up in business. But not many make it. Where are the faces that ten years ago sold a billion cans of beer?"

She considered this while Daniel York handed them their drinks. The trouble with all of us, she thought, is that we are all dependent on superficial characteristics for our living. On a muscular torso or a saint-like face; on outdoor Californian beauty or aloof refinement.

And we are all aware that we have made it by the grace of God, without recourse to our brains. Which wasn't to say that models weren't intelligent. But when their packaging had faded, what had they got?

Where would I be if it wasn't for my hands? she wondered, as she watched Daniel York talking. Teaching, probably, in Albany. Which would have been satisfying and worthwhile and maybe that's where I should have stayed. But no, this was the life, every girl's dream.

"And where have those hands been today?" Daniel York was asking without interest, his bright blue eyes flicking from one guest to another.

"In gloves," she said. "One off, one on."

"Beautiful hands," he said. "Just beautiful."

She wished that more people would comment on her face which wasn't so bad – forehead a little too high perhaps and, so she had once been told, eyes questing – or her figure, which was long-limbed, breasts a little too full for modelling clothes.

"What have you been doing today?" Peter asked Daniel York. "Persuading us poor sweating males to smell clean and wholesome?"

"Today? Nothing today, Peter. In fact, I haven't done anything all week. Resting on my laurels, I guess. You know, I did that Paco Rabanne thing last week."

On the defensive, Helen decided. He was of medium height with curly black hair, the grey at the temples accentuated with a rinse so that it didn't appear in isolated strands. The famous smile had left a crease in one cheek and she noticed that the hand holding a vodka and tonic was shaking.

"Do you know Carl?" he asked, nodding towards a sleek, young man wearing a blue blazer with brass yachting buttons and a white, silk shirt open at the neck.

As Daniel York took her arm and guided her through the other guests, Peter whispered to her: "Carlos, in fact, but he likes to be called Carl. Carl Cortoni. His father's got a lot of clout. Mutal funds, real estate."

Daniel York was introducing Cortoni and she thought she noticed some sort of understanding between them. Or was she being hyper-sensitive this evening? After the introductions York backed away with practised ease.

Cortoni nodded politely and said to her: "Are you a model, Miss Fleming?"

"Hands," she said.

He frowned. "I don't quite –"

"Anything that goes on hands I model it. Anything from nail lacquer to soap powder."

"I follow. Peter and I, of course, are old sparring partners."

"Carl's in the boutique business too," Peter explained.

"We had been thinking of going into partnership," Cortoni told her.

Helen turned to Peter. "You didn't tell me."

"It fell through," Peter said.

"But it could pick itself up again," Cortoni said.

Again the sense of tension. She examined Cortoni over the rim of her glass. Shiny, blond hair, exuding good health

19

probably maintained by squash and sauna. Self-assured and yet ill at ease . . . he looked . . . *protected*, that was it.

Peter was saying that he would be interested to hear just how the deal could be revived.

"We'll talk about it," Cortoni said. "They're smart properties you've got. They've got style, class." He turned to Helen. "Don't you think so, Miss Fleming?"

"Like their owner," Helen smiled.

"A good name, Lodge. I thought if we got together we might call the boutiques 'Lodges'. You can't do much with Cortoni as a name. Argentinian extraction, by the way, not Italian as most people seem to think."

"But with Italian connections," Peter said.

Cortoni shrugged. "We're in business."

Helen said: "That fair hair isn't Argentinian."

"My father married a Scandinavian," Cortoni said. "But they got a divorce, you know how it is."

Helen did know how it was. Her parents had been divorced when she was fifteen – she couldn't believe it at the time, everything had been so secure and cosy in their home – and her mother had taken her to Florida, and another father. After college she had left home and returned north.

Cortoni said: "Can I get you another drink?"

Helen looked at her glass with surprise: it was empty. "Chablis," she told him.

"Smooth," Peter remarked while Cortoni made his way to the bar in the corner of the room. "Like his father but not so tough."

"I think I've heard of his father. Miguel?"

"There was a big case a couple of years back. Using clients' cash invested in his mutual funds to finance his own companies. When the value of his companies was falsely inflated he sold them."

"Did he go to prison?"

"No," Peter said, "he was acquitted."

"Was he guilty?"

"Oh, he was guilty all right but the main prosecution witness disappeared."

20

"Was Carl Cortoni involved?"

"Not in court he wasn't. Daddy wouldn't allow that to happen."

"You seem to know a lot about the Cortoni family," Helen said.

"I made it my business to. Carl's been trying to buy me out – with papa's money, of course."

"But he didn't succeed, obviously."

Peter was silent.

"Why," Helen asked, "didn't you tell me about it?"

"Why should I? It was just a business deal that didn't come off."

"Not according to Cortoni. He seems to think you might still get together."

"In a partnership?" Peter shook his head. "Carl's ideas of equality are something like eighty-twenty in his favour. No, all Carl wants are my shops and my know-how. Still I'll talk to him. He might even make it seventy-thirty."

"But you wouldn't sell?"

"No way. I'm doing very nicely thanks, without Carl or his father's money."

"Supposing . . . Thank you," she said, breaking off as Cortoni rejoined them and handed her a glass of wine.

Cortoni raised his glass – beer – and said: "Happy Christmas."

"Happy Christmas," she said, drinking.

"So, how long have you been modelling, Miss Fleming?"

"Not long. Eighteen months or so, I guess. Peter discovered me." She took Peter's arm. "He was thinking of opening up a boutique in Albany and we met at a party there."

"Do most models specialise like you? You must forgive me for asking all these questions, I have a very inquisitive nature . . ."

He had a curiously stilted way of speaking, as though he had taken elocution lessons to iron out any lingering traces of Argentinian.

She told him: "Some are lucky enough to be able to model almost anything. You know, girls who have got everything in

21

the right place. But most of us concentrate on our one asset. Eyes, legs, hands . . ."

"I think you should branch out," Cortoni said.

"How do you mean, branch out?"

"Whoever told you that hands were all you had going for you needs a white stick," glancing at Peter. "I figure you could model almost anything. Don't you agree, Peter?"

"Anything except centre-folds," Peter replied.

"But you said –" Helen began.

"Come on, honey," Peter said. "Look, there's Earl Winters," pointing at a plump man with a monkish fringe of hair who had just entered the room and was being greeted effusively. "You'll have to excuse us, Carlos," he said to Cortoni, as he led her away.

The room was crowded now and, as the second and third drinks were consumed, so the noise increased. The talk was intense, excited, theatrical. It was mostly shop but the guests weren't dressed with the elegance they portrayed professionally: when relaxing they discarded fashion as servicemen discard uniforms. Someone had switched off the television and 'Sleighbells' was issuing from hidden speakers, but no-one was listening.

Helen thought she could smell pot. She grimaced; she wasn't self-righteous about the smoking of marijuana – she just didn't like the smell of it. And it didn't go with Christmas somehow. She had never smoked the stuff herself; she supposed it was sophisticated but she was doing fine as far as sophistication was concerned because people remarked about her haughty manner which was, in fact, part shyness. With certain people she could converse easily; with Peter and with Earl Winters . . .

Earl put his arm round her. A paternal – no, avuncular – gesture. "I don't know how the agency survived before I met you." He was her agent; Daniel York's as well. "How are you, Helen? Happy Christmas."

"And to you, Earl."

"What's your poison?" Daniel York asked. "Coke, tomato-juice, a glass of wine, maybe, because it's Christmas?"

22

Earl Winters suffered from some sort of skin complaint – he wore black cotton gloves to cover his hands – and had been told that alcohol aggravated the condition. "Just a tonic water, Danny," he said, removing his arm from Helen's waist and standing with his gloved hands behind his back, his favourite stance.

Helen was very fond of Earl. Not only was he a shrewd manipulator of her talents but he was also a friend; the relationship was confined socially to lunch at the Oyster Bar at Grand Central or an evening cocktail at the Plaza; nothing sexual but not platonic either.

His skin disease was, according to the doctors, an allergy, a nervous condition, but tonight, casually dressed in a brown, roll-neck sweater, tweed jacket and flannels, he looked the least nervous person in the room. Rumpled, as always, but holding court.

"I think we've got some good things coming up for you in the New Year," he told her. "Have you ever been to Rome?"

She shook her head.

"Well, keep your fingers crossed."

Daniel York asked casually: "Any news about that project you were trying to line up for me?"

"Yeah, it fell through. Sorry about that, Danny, I wasn't going to tell you until after Christmas but you asked."

"No," York said, "don't feel sorry. I'm glad, honest. I was planning on taking a vacation to Mexico anyway. No," he said again, gulping his vodka, "I'm really pleased. Acapulco here I come." He smiled brilliantly at Helen. "Where did you acquire your tan?"

"Florida," she said, "visiting my mother. How's that for an assignment?"

"Great for your mother," he said, fidgeting with a gold crucifix he wore at his throat.

He made her feel nervous and when he moved away to talk to a girl fashion writer from *New York* magazine she was relieved.

"Phew!" Earl Winters exclaimed. "Tonight he's modelling tensions. Don't be taken in by the decent way he took the no-job news. He hated it and he blames me. He'll take it out on me later tonight, mark my words."

"I feel sorry for him," Peter Lodge remarked.

"I shouldn't waste your pity," Earl Winters said. "He's mean."

"What I don't understand," Helen said, "is why a man with his looks didn't go into movies. Why modelling?"

Earl Winters said: "Easy. He can't act."

Peter shook his head. "There's more to it than that. You've got to have something in addition to looks. Style, charisma, presence, call it what you like. Anyway, you've got to be different. No good just being pretty, no good just being macho."

"Chemistry," Earl said, "is what you've got to have. Or to put it another way, you've got to sell yourself, not somebody else's product."

Helen watched Daniel York turn down the stereo. He raised one hand and a thick, gold-chain bracelet slid down his forearm. "Okay," he said, "let's eat. Everyone except weight-watchers up to the buffet. Okay?" He turned up the stereo again. "I'm dreaming of a white Christmas," sang Bing Crosby.

"According to the met. man that's just what we'll be getting," Earl Winters said as they headed for the food.

"How lovely," Helen said.

They were joined by a tall and muscular model named Marty Padget. He was deeply tanned and wore a thick, black moustache; he would have been more rugged if he hadn't seemed so well cared for. A sort of indoor-outdoor look, Helen thought.

Marty Padget, also one of Earl Winters' stable, modelled swimsuits. "Hi," he said to Helen, "how's it going?" His voice was soft, decidedly un-rugged.

"It's fine for gloves," she told him. "But swimsuits at Christmas?"

"Don't tell me." He gave an exaggerated shiver. "You get frozen assets. In any case, I want out of them. You know," patting his stomach, "I can't go on holding this in much

24

longer?" He turned to Winters. "Can you get me out of swimsuits and into something warmer?"

Daniel York, who had come up behind them, said: "How about after-shave, Marty?"

Padget pulled at his moustache. "C'mon, Danny, you know I couldn't compete with you. How could anyone upstage that smile?"

"Funny," York said. "I just can't remember inviting you to the party, Marty."

"You didn't," Padget said. "But I can forgive an oversight so I came anyway."

The hostility hovered between them. Helen decided that she wasn't enjoying the party and would leave as soon as possible.

The buffet was cold: turkey and ham and potato and Russian salad; afterwards there were mince pies so hot that tiny jets of steam escaped when you cut into them. Then York cleared the floor for dancing and put a Bony M record on the stereo. Helen danced with Peter, a mild rock number; they kept their distance and, because of his bad leg, he barely moved, but they looked into each other's eyes and they were together. She wondered if they would make love later.

While they danced she became aware of voices raised. Not too loud but loud enough to catch a word here and there. Daniel York and Carl Cortoni. Odd, she thought, because Cortoni wasn't the sort of man to become involved in a scene in public. She didn't hear anything clearly, but money seemed to be the topic. Or lack of it.

". . . No deal," from Cortoni.

". . . More time," from York.

When he became aware that their words were carrying, York grabbed Cortoni's arm and led him into a bedroom.

"What was all that about?" she asked Peter.

He shrugged, spread his hands, still moving them with the music and said: "Search me. A lovers' tiff?"

But that was just Peter getting a low one into Cortoni whom he didn't like because of their professional antagonism. Cortoni didn't look gay and she knew that Daniel York wasn't; quite a stud, in fact, according to the other models.

A lot of the guests who had to work on Christmas Eve were leaving now, giving as their excuses early-morning calls. Daniel York, emerging from the bedroom, said he understood. How many times had he wished as he faced a camera that he had turned in early the previous evening?

Helen looked around for Cortoni. He was standing by the bar. As Peter emerged from the bathroom Cortoni caught him by his sleeve. They began to talk earnestly together.

There were only half a dozen or so guests left and when Helen discovered that some of them were sniffing coke she decided to leave. She crossed the room, waited for a pause in the conversation between Cortoni and Peter and said: "I guess it's time I went home."

Peter looked surprised, a little irritated.

"I've got to be up early," she said and whispered in his ear: "They're sniffing cocaine over there," pointing at two men and a girl sitting on cushions passing a slender, silver spoon from one to the other.

"So?"

For a moment she was nonplussed by his attitude. "So let them sniff away. It's just not my scene, that's all."

"Look," he said, "I'm discussing some business right now."

"With the opposition?"

"Can you get a cab home just this once?"

"I suppose." Anger spurted, then died like the flame of a match. "I'll get the porter to call me one."

"That's my girl." He smiled at her and kissed her lightly on the lips. "I'll call you in the morning."

She considered asking Earl Winters to drive her home. But no, that was outside their relationship. She said goodbye to him without telling him that Peter was staying on.

At the door Daniel York said: "So soon?"

She made the early call excuse and he said: "Anyway, the party's breaking up," as the coke-sniffers, bright-eyed and smiling beautifully, walked past them into the corridor.

It was 1.35 by the lobby clock when she asked the porter to call her a cab. Later than she had thought, surely Peter could have dragged himself away from a man he so clearly disliked.

26

Especially when he had said he had no intention of selling out. She peered into the street through the locked revolving doors; it was just beginning to snow; she wished she could have walked the few blocks home but it hadn't taken her long to discover that you didn't walk home alone at night in New York.

While she waited for the cab, the porter, a middle-aged man with an accent she couldn't identify, and long hair greased across his bald head from one side, gave her his views on Christmas. It was a lonely time, he said, and he was glad he was working.

It was 1.40 when the cab arrived. The porter released the lock on the door. "Goodbye," she said and, thrusting two ten-dollar bills into his hand: "Have the best Christmas you can."

The cab drew up outside her block at 1.52. As the driver, a young man with a Castro beard, turned round expectantly and looked at her through the Plexiglass screen, she realised what she had done.

"Well," said Peter Lodge as he bent over the bed to catch her words, "what had you done?"

"It was what I hadn't done, really."

"Well, what had you or hadn't you done?"

"I've forgotten," she said.

On the other side of the bed Dr Bowen sat back in his chair. In one hand he held an opthalmoscope. "You had us worried again there," he said, stroking his thinning hair. "You seemed to leave us."

"Do you think we should take her to a clinic?" Peter Lodge asked Bowen. "I mean does she need specialised treatment?" Helen was touched at his concern.

Bowen put away his opthalmoscope. "I think she'll be all right. But she should be kept under observation. Can you get a nurse?"

"No trouble," Peter said.

"She should be kept as quiet as possible. You know, no more questions. Not for the time being anyway."

27

"Now I know what it's like to be deaf and dumb," Helen said. "People discuss you as if you weren't there."

"I'll call by and see you tomorrow morning," Bowen said, consulting a gold watch he took from his vest pocket. As Peter escorted the doctor out of the room, he said over his shoulder: "You stay there, honey" – as if she was going anyplace – "while I make a couple of phone calls."

Idly, she wondered who he was calling. She felt curiously calm; perhaps she was still under the influence of the sedative Dr Bowen had given her.

Outside the snow was piling up in the corners of the window panes. A pigeon, seeking the heat from the air-conditioner, landed on the sill in a small flurry of snow and, throat pulsing, peered into the room.

She stretched and sighed. Around her in the small, pink and white room were echoes from the past. A furry animal on the shelf named Dingo, *The Wind in the Willows* and *Little Women*, on top of a chest of drawers a black-and-white photograph of her mother and father just before the divorce.

She would ask Peter to bring the small Christmas tree with the plastic berries into the bedroom. They would put their presents beneath it and tomorrow, when this nonsense was all over, they would take it back into the sitting-room. In the kitchen she had a small Christmas pudding that only needed to be heated, and in the refrigerator a duck which she was going to cook *à l'orange* (cookery-book open beside the oven). She had also bought some crackers containing indoor fireworks.

Had she returned to the party?

Cold touched her as though a snowflake had blown through the window. What had happened between 1.52 and 3 am.? She burrowed deep into the bedclothes seeking childhood. Faintly she heard Peter replace the telephone receiver in the living-room. Of course, he had been calling Daniel York to see if she had returned to the party. She closed her eyes beneath the bedclothes and saw only the face and Castro beard of the taxi-driver.

One hour and eight minutes missing.

"Helen?"

She wriggled up from the bedclothes. He was standing beside the bed looking down at her.

"Did you get through all right?"

He nodded without elaborating. But from the expression on his face, she knew that something terrible had happened.

III

Lieutenant Boyd Tyler of Homicide gazed speculatively at the body of Daniel York.

He guessed that the causes of death were shock and loss of blood due to arterial haemorrhage and he estimated that, judging by the condition of the corpse, York had been killed about twelve hours earlier. There was no doubt, or little doubt – Tyler was a careful man – about the weapon used to kill him: a carving knife with a wooden handle protruded from his back.

York lay face-down on the parquet flooring which had apparently been cleared for dancing. Blood, now congealed, had spilled across the polished wood and been absorbed by a deep-pile, white rug beside the television.

A patrolman was speaking on the telephone. When he replaced the receiver, Tyler said: "Who was that?"

"A guy called Lodge. Peter Lodge." The patrolman, young with sideburns and a moustache, nervously consulted his notebook: Tyler's reputation stalked ahead of him.

"What did he want?"

"He wanted to speak to – to him," pointing at the body. "Why?"

"He didn't say," the patrolman said, clearing his throat. "Did you ask him?"

"Yes, Lieutenant, I did, but he told me it was none of my

30

goddam business. That was even before he knew I was a cop."

"And when he knew?"

"Well, you know, I told him York was dead and he seemed kind of stunned."

Tyler sighed. "Was he at this shindig?" The debris of the party was scattered around them. It included a slim, silver spoon still dusted with white powder which Tyler presumed was cocaine.

The patrolman brightened. "Yes, sir, he was."

"You got his phone number and address?"

"Yes, sir!"

"Then check them out."

While the patrolman called the number, Tyler walked round and round the body like a prizefighter, watching for any sign of life from a vanquished opponent.

He stepped back while the police photographer took pictures, blinking at each bleep of light.

To Sergeant Phillip Saul he said: "Well, what have we got, Phil? Who was this Daniel York?"

Saul's manner with Tyler was easier than the patrolman's; he had worked with him for four years – since Tyler's wife had been murdered by the brother of a man Tyler had charged with murder.

Saul didn't look like anyone's idea of a policeman and that was his strength. He had only just made the height requirement when he joined the force; he was Jewish and laconic, aged thirty-six, with angular features and a deceptively fragile appearance, as though a single blow would break a bone. But he was an expert in unarmed combat.

He told Tyler: "He was a model according to reception downstairs and the maid who found the body."

"Okay," Tyler said, "run a check on him. Anything else?"

"This." Saul handed Tyler a handwritten list of names. "Looks like a guest-list for the party. There's a Cortoni here. Could be a relative of Miguel Cortoni."

Tyler took the list. "Son, probably. Not bad for openers." He ran his finger down the other names. "I know a few of the others, too."

31

"That figures," Saul said.

Because of his urbane manner, his thoroughness and his lack of interest in material possessions – bribes, that was – Boyd Tyler was often assigned to cases on the fashionable East Side. He was believed by some of his colleagues to be bloodless, ruthless even, meticulous to an obsessive degree.

Before May Tyler had died – before Boyd Tyler had stopped living – the two of them had shared a belief that an honest cop, working by the book, could reach the top, chief of the Homicide Bureau maybe, possibly even higher. Now Tyler no longer cared about promotion; in fact, he had turned it down. But, because of May, he still worked by the book and he was still remorseless.

He was always well-dressed in a colourless sort of way. He favoured grey suits, white shirts and plain knitted ties; today he wore a grey, double-breasted topcoat with a herringbone pattern; as usual he was hatless; his hair was short and neat, needled with grey; there was about his pale, honed features a hint of Red Indian, of suppressed violence.

One other aspect of Boyd Tyler irked other senior homicide detectives: he had one of the best records for convictions in the Bureau, taking into account the rarefied areas in which he operated.

The patrolman handed him the telephone. "Mr Lodge?" Tyler asked.

"I guessed you'd call back," Lodge said.

"This is Lieutenant Tyler, Homicide. I understand you were at a party last night given by the deceased man."

"By Daniel York, that's right. This is terrible . . ."

"How was he when you last saw him, Mr Lodge?"

"Fine, just fine. A little stoned, maybe, but he seemed to be in good shape."

"Stoned, Mr Lodge?"

"Drunk. Just drunk, Lieutenant. He was drinking vodka as far as I can remember."

"What time did you leave the party?"

"Around 2.30, I guess. I'm not sure. I didn't make a note of the time. There wasn't any reason . . ." His voice tailed away.

32

"Were there many left at the party?"

A pause. Then: "No, I was one of the last to leave. There were only three other guys left."

"Their names?"

Another pause. "I don't know who they were. Just guests."

Lies, thought Tyler, were more easy to detect on the telephone because you weren't distracted by physical response. Not that he believed shifty eyes meant a damn thing; the most spectacular liars he had encountered had stared at him with unwavering candour.

"We'd like to have a talk with you, Mr Lodge."

"Of course. But not here if you don't mind."

"You're at Miss Fleming's apartment, right?"

"How did you know that?" a new brittle quality to Lodge's voice.

Tyler, who was looking at the name Helen Fleming bracketed with Peter Lodge on the guest-list, said, "Don't you worry about that, Mr Lodge." He beckoned Saul and stabbed one finger at the telephone directory. "How about at your place?"

"Okay," Lodge said. "I'll give you the address."

"Don't worry," Tyler said, reading from the line above Saul's fingernail, "we have that already. See you in one hour." He hung up.

Saul grinned and tapped his nose with one finger.

While Tyler had been talking, Chamberlain from the Scientific Division had arrived; he was plump and baggy-suited and he lectured on his speciality, fingerprints, all over the States. He regarded the knife sticking out of Daniel York's back, with his head on one side. "Possibilities there," he said, "if the killer was an amateur."

"Does this look like a pro job?" Tyler asked.

"I guess not." Chamberlain sounded offended. "It was just small-talk. Okay, so it's an amateur job and maybe there will be some latent prints. Does that satisfy you?"

Chamberlain opened his case, took out powder, transparent tape and cards on which to tape the prints shown up by the powder. "You know," he said, "a lot of people think prints

33

come from secretions in the skin at the tips of the fingers."

Tyler raised his eyebrows at Saul but Saul, who had also heard it all before, said: "No shit. Where do they come from, Harry?"

"From secretions all over the body," Chamberlain said, dusting the wooden hilt of the knife. "Particularly the face and hair. You'd be surprised how often people touch them. But I've got bad news for you," he said, gazing at the knife-handle through an old-fashioned magnifying glass. "It's clean, well almost."

"What do you mean, *almost*?" Tyler asked.

"A couple of traces close to the blade but nothing identifiable." He stood up. "It's been wiped clean. Are you fellas still so sure this was an amateur job?"

"Okay, Harry," Tyler said, "your point. Now try everything in the immediate vicinity of the body."

"Okay, okay." Still smiling faintly from his moment of triumph, Chamberlain knelt down again and began to dust the area of parquet blocks that was free of congealed blood because it wouldn't be the first time a killer had knelt beside a body to wipe prints from a weapon and, unthinkingly, pressed his fingers onto the floor to help push himself upright. Even a professional could do that. But the blocks were clean.

Tyler said: "How about the door?"

"What about the door?" Chamberlain asked. "If you're thinking of prints, forget it. Probably every damn person at the party touched the door."

"Not if he" – pointing at the body – "was a gentleman and opened it for them." Tyler examined the cream-painted door. It had two strong locks, a safety-chain and a peep-hole. "If that were so, there might only be two sets of prints – York's and the killer's."

"Okay, okay," Chamberlain said, "I'll try. But my guess is that he wiped every incriminating print clean. That's the normal pattern once a killer has remembered to wipe the murder weapon. In fact, there have been cases when a guy was busted because he was the only person whose prints weren't in the room. I remember –"

34

"How about doing it now," Tyler said, "before we handle it?"

Chamberlain took his equipment to the door. He dusted the round, metal handles on the locks, the metal block on the end of the safety-chain and the paintwork around them. "Well," he said as he began to tape the prints, "we've got a handful here." He glanced at Tyler and Saul to see if they had caught the joke.

In the background the patrolman again cleared his throat. "Excuse me, sir," he said to Tyler, "but I'm afraid some of those prints may be mine."

Chamberlain smiled at him. "Don't worry, son, we'll soon eliminate those. I remember –"

Tyler beckoned Saul and together they walked out into the corridor.

*   *   *

Tyler looked at John Remick with affection.

Remick was hungrily consuming a quarter-inch T–bone steak in an Irish pub on East Forty-Fifth Street. From time to time manners would intrude upon his hunger and he would slow down his eating, but not for long.

Phillip Saul apart, Remick was the only person in whom Tyler confided. He didn't explore his feelings for Remick too deeply but he suspected they hinged on the fact that Remick was the sort of man he would have wished his son – May had been pregnant when she had been killed – to grow up like.

Squarely built with black hair so dark that it seemed to have blue lights in it (May's hair), he was saved from conventional good looks by a studious air which occasionally erupted into boyish enthusiasms. His eyes were greenish and he needed to shave twice a day.

Remick was twenty-six years old and he was a doctor. But he was that breed of doctor who cannot confine his attentions to human maladies; such doctors turn to research or combine their medicine with another profession; Remick's second profession was law enforcement – he was a police surgeon.

35

He was also a bachelor and so, like Saul who was divorced and Tyler, the widower, they were much in demand at Christmas and other public holidays when, it was felt, other officers would prefer to be with their families and would not give of their best.

Tyler and Remick had first met during a protracted investigation into a rape and murder that had dragged into an even more protracted court hearing. A girl had been sexually assaulted and knifed in an apartment in Tudor City on East Forty-Second, while the girl with whom she shared the apartment had been forced to watch. But the girl witness had been so terrified that she had forgotten most of what she had seen.

Since that case a friendship, sustained and occasionally threatened by argument, had developed. Remick believed Tyler was too restricted by tried and proven theory; as far as Tyler was concerned Remick was too innovative.

Before the rape case went to court Remick had suggested that the girl witness, suffering from panic-induced amnesia, should be hypnotised into remembering all of what she had seen; but Tyler had blocked the move because he believed the girl had remembered enough to get a conviction, and testimony obtained during a trance would be savaged by the defence lawyer.

The case had been thrown out.

As Remick poised himself for his final assault on his steak, Tyler leaned across the red-chequered tablecloth and replenished his glass of Californian red. Like Saul, his own appetite had been destroyed by the day's sandwiches and hot-dogs; their plates had been pushed aside, contents half-eaten, and they were both drinking beer.

A waiter wearing a green apron removed the two plates. Like the pub, which had two shillelaghs on the walls and shamrocks painted over the bar, he was more Irish than the Irish with brawny forearms, curly hair and a breezy manner.

It was just after 10 pm and the three men, sitting in a booth where they couldn't be overheard, were tired.

Saul who had been watching Remick with awe said: "You

know something? You amaze me. How can you spend the day in the company of a stiff and then come out and eat red meat?"

Remick put down his knife and fork, sighed contentedly and drank some wine. "Corpses never bother me," he said. "But living people, crippled or mutilated . . . Now that's another thing altogether." He drank some more wine. "How are you making out with the York killing? As I told you the stabbing was classic. 'To smite under the fifth rib . . .' *The Bible*," he added as they looked at him doubtfully. "Although the Biblical stabbing was in the chest, I guess, and this was in the back."

"Had he been a junkie for long?" Saul asked.

"Three or four years, maybe more. He had probably been able to control it in the early days when things were going well for him. But recently he'd been main-lining a helluva lot. But he could have been saved with treatment," Remick said.

"You're quite a psychologist too," Tyler said. "How do you know things hadn't been so good for him recently?"

"A guess. He was a handsome-looking guy. I've seen his picture all over town –"

"What was he advertising?" Saul interrupted.

"Cigarettes, wasn't it?"

"There you go," Saul said. "You know the guy but not his product. That's advertising."

Remick asked: "What was he advertising?"

"After-shave," Saul said.

"Brand?"

"I forget."

"Anyway," Remick went on, "he was a model and he had been successful, but his face hasn't been around recently. Also he hadn't been taking care of himself" – Remick didn't elaborate – "which is unusual for a model. In my opinion he was staring into a bleak future. At Christmas time, too."

"Hey, Christmas," Saul remembered, "let's have another drink."

"I've got enough wine," Remick told him. Tyler said that because it was Christmas in just under two hours' time he would have a brandy, a Courvoisier.

37

Tyler parted the curtains, red to match the tablecloth and said: "It's stopped snowing."

Saul, deciding on a Christmas rye-and-dry-ginger, gave the order to the waiter, who said: "Oi'll be right back," as though he had just stepped off the boat from Dublin.

"Anything else about York?" Tyler asked.

"Not a lot. If it hadn't been for the dope and the fact that he had been neglecting himself, he would have been in good shape for forty-five. He had taken a shot of heroin some time in the twenty-four hours before he died."

Tyler took a small notebook from the inside pocket of the jacket of his grey suit. "According to the blood analyst the alcohol content of his blood was .10 which isn't so much on Christmas Eve." He picked up his brandy and stared at it.

"Heterosexual?" Tyler asked.

"If he was homosexual, which I doubt, then he was the dominant kind." Looking faintly embarrassed, Remick drank some more wine. "But what did you guys dig up?"

"We saw a man named Lodge," Saul told him. "Peter Lodge. Ring any bells?"

Remick shook his head.

"Owns some boutiques. You couldn't call them a chain yet but they're coming on."

"And?"

"He was a guest at the party," Tyler said. "We ran a check on him but not a hell of a lot showed up. In fact, he seems to be a pretty law-abiding citizen."

"And there aren't too many of those around," Saul said.

It was 10.45. A party of young people came into the pub wearing paper-hats and blowing paper trumpets. The barman scowled at them and they quietened down.

Remick asked: "How did Lodge react to questioning?"

"A little shifty," Tyler replied. "More so because I think he's normally a forthright sort of guy. We fed him some of the facts to see if he made a mistake and supplied a few more."

"And did he?"

"Not a damn thing." Tyler stared at the young people at the bar as though remembering something.

"But he was lying," Saul said.

"About what?"

"He says he was one of the last to leave and yet he can't remember who else was still there."

"Maybe we should hypnotise him," Remick said.

"Don't start that again," Tyler said.

"I was only kidding," Remick said. "You're doing this by the book, right?"

"Don't knock it," Tyler said. "It works. And by the book doesn't mean patient-and-plodding. But any investigation has to have a shape. A triangle if you like. A broad base of evidence, statements etcetera, that tapers off to an apex and that apex is the arrest."

"But not necessarily the conviction," Remick said.

"The rape?"

"Well," Remick said carefully, "the guy walked out, didn't he? But if we'd *helped* that girl to remember he'd be having a not-so-happy Christmas in Sing Sing or Attica. Christ," he said, and he wasn't kidding any more, "it was worth a try."

"And you know what would have happened?"

"You tell me."

"If she'd remembered under hypnosis she might have forgotten when she came out of it. You know, just like they always forgot in the old vaudeville acts. And even if she had still remembered when she came out of the trance, and even if she had testified about what she had remembered, the defence lawyer would have torn her testimony to shreds. He would have claimed – and quite correctly – that what she was saying could have been suggested to her under hypnosis. Did you know they say that a hypnotist can create an honest liar?"

"It depends on the hypnotist and," Remick said tightly, "hypnotism isn't just a vaudeville act any more."

Saul, accustomed to mediating when the discussion turned to hypnotism, took out a leather cigar-case containing three Jamaican cigars and offered it to Remick. "Season of goodwill to all men," he said.

Tyler said: "Except to murderers. Whoever killed York should have had a lot of blood on his clothes."

"Did you check Lodge's clothes?" Remick asked.

"He said he had taken the suit he wore at the party to the tailor's for alterations."

"And had he?"

"His tailor closed up shop this afternoon and went to Miami for Christmas."

Remick examined the cigar Saul had given him, rolled it between thumb and forefinger, pierced it with a wooden toothpick. "You know damn well I'm trying to give up smoking. Doctors shouldn't smoke. You know what the ads say. *The Surgeon General Has Determined That Cigarette Smoking Is Dangerous to Your Health*. And they're damn right," he added, taking the band off the cigar.

"A Christmas cigar won't make any difference," Saul said. "Anyway, you shouldn't inhale cigar smoke." He picked up a book of matches and struck one for Remick.

Tyler who didn't smoke said: "I figure Lodge is covering up for someone."

"Himself maybe," Saul said. He lit his own cigar with loving care and his angular features relaxed.

"And I don't mean just the people he left behind at the party. I got the impression he was trying to sidetrack me. He was somehow too emphatic about the girl he took to the party. The fact that she left early; that she always turned in early because she had to get up early to get to the studios. Everything was *early*," Tyler said.

"Why didn't he leave with her?" Remick asked, blowing out smoke quickly, anxious to be rid of it.

"He said they had an understanding."

"These models . . ." Saul shook his head. "I dated one once. Trouble was she was in love with herself. Reckoned she spent five hours a day looking after her face and body."

"What did she model?" Remick asked.

"Porn," Saul said.

The owner of the pub who looked more Italian than Irish, consulted the gold watch on his wrist, waited a few seconds, hit a brass gong that a waiter had placed on the bar and announced: "Ladies and gentlemen, it's Christmas Day.

40

Drinks on the house."

"Whoopee!" shouted one of the girls at the bar. "Champagne cocktails." She stretched and kissed the man beside her.

"Drink what you like, lady," the pub owner said, making his way back to his table.

"What'll it be gentlemen?" the waiter asked Tyler, Remick and Saul.

"A happy Christmas to you," Saul said.

"And to you, sor."

They ordered the same drinks, drank them quickly and collected their coats. It had stopped snowing. Separately they made their way to their cars.

Tyler walked briskly towards an underground car park on Lexington. His breath smoked on the cold air, frozen slush crackled underfoot.

When May had been alive he had always made a point of getting home early on Christmas Eve, whatever he was working on. It was the only time he broke the rules and they revelled in this one, annual misdemeanour. Around midnight they made love. A few flakes of snow settled on the lapels of Tyler's coat. He brushed them away, brushed away those other Christmases.

Tomorrow – no, today – if he got lucky, and despite his methodical approach Tyler never discounted luck, he might catch a killer.

IV

She awoke as a dream was receding. She tried to halt its flight but its detail continued to shrink until it was the size of a pinhead, and then it was gone.

The light was as fresh and white as it had been yesterday. There was Dingo and *Little Women* . . . It was Christmas Day.

She sat up excitedly. In one corner of the bedroom stood the tree with the plastic berries, and underneath it the presents, each packed with gift wrapping, instant bows of shiny ribbon stuck over the knots. But why was the tree in her bedroom?

She looked at her hands. The cotton gloves that she wore at night were missing and, presumably, the cream she applied before putting on the gloves. She frowned.

She swung her legs out of bed, her feet found her slippers. She put on a robe with a floral pattern over her nightdress and went into the living-room. She smelled coffee and from the kitchen she heard the clatter of crockery.

As she remembered, remembered that she had lost her memory, the nurse in a starched white uniform emerged from the kitchen and said brightly: "Oh, so we're up, are we?"

"Yes," Helen said, "we're up."

"Well, we mustn't stay up too long," the nurse said. "We must do what we've got to do," glancing towards the bathroom, "and then get back to bed."

"Oh no," Helen said, "I'm staying up. It is Christmas Day, you know."

"But Dr Bowen said –"

"I don't care what Dr Bowen said."

"Then I shall have to telephone him."

"You must do as you think fit."

As she went to the bathroom to attend to her hands, Helen could feel the nurse, middle-aged and pinkly clean, staring at her with aggrieved hostility.

Inside the bathroom she locked the door and stared at herself in the mirror in the wall-cabinet. The eyes looking back at her were clear and healthy but they were the eyes of a stranger: they had seen something she didn't know about. Something that Peter *did* know about; she knew that from the expression on his face after he had made the telephone call yesterday.

Faintly she heard the nurse's voice: "Yes, I do know what day it is. But you told me to call you . . ."

She thought: "I must be sensible. I must carry on as if nothing had happened. If I appear normal they – Dr Bowen, the nurse, Peter – will stop treating me like a prisoner."

First her hands. Her assets. It was the only time in months that she had neglected them. She examined the palms and the slender fingers, nails still lacquered red. A man had once told her that he always imagined her holding a rose.

She washed her hands with a bland soap, then removed the lacquer with an oily polish remover. Nails were said to grow faster on the right hand than the left; when she had first heard this she had imagined them having a race.

She cleansed her hands a second time with a mixture of olive oil and sugar. She rinsed them in warm water and massaged each finger; after that she massaged between the fingers with the ball of each thumb.

Since Miss Whelan, and much later Peter Lodge, had drawn her attention to her hands, she had judged other people by theirs; more often than not they told the truth.

Peter's hands, for instance, were well-cared-for and dependable but at the same time, because of the long lean fingers, foraging. They could also be sensitive, she remembered, feeling their touch on her breasts. Dr Bowen's hands were plump and indulged, like Dr Bowen. Miss Whelan's hands had been chalky and overworked.

The nurse's voice reached her again. "Very well, Dr Bowen, I'll see what I can do." A pause, followed by a knock on the door. "Miss Fleming?"

"What can I do for you, Miss . . .?"

"Bulmer," the nurse said. "Might I ask what you're doing in there?"

"No," Helen said, "you might not."

"Dr Bowen says you are to go straight back to bed."

"I don't like his hands," Helen shouted.

"I don't –"

Helen turned on the shower and began to rub lanolin into her nails. Odd how the animosity between her and Nurse Bulmer had been instantaneous and mutual; she hadn't even looked at her hands but she knew they would be mannish, rough-skinned from too much cold water and carbolic.

But this morning, because of what had happened – *Please God! What had happened?* – she was disorientated. She should have taken a shower before attending to her hands. She took off her robe and nightdress, put on a shower-cap and stepped into the pale blue bath.

This time the knocking on the door was louder and more insistent. She stuck her head outside the mainstream of the water and shouted: "I'll be out in my own good time."

"Are you sure you're all right?" Peter's voice asked.

She smiled, instinctively touching her breasts. "Of course I'm all right. I'll be out in a jiffy. Pour yourself some coffee. And a happy Christmas!" she yelled as she switched off the water and stepped out of the bath.

"You're sure you don't mind me doing this?" she asked later as she manicured her nails in the living-room under an adjustable desk lamp. "I can't stand people filing their nails in public."

"You go right ahead," Peter told her as she used an emery board on her thumbnail. "They're your credit cards."

In the kitchen Nurse Bulmer rattled the coffee cups. "She," indicating the kitchen, "says you've refused to go back to bed."

"Why should I? I'm perfectly well. A touch of amnesia is all. It happens to people all the time. Remember when you couldn't remember whether we'd had dinner together one evening?"

"That was different," Peter said. "I was loaded."

"So maybe I drank too much Chablis."

"Maybe." He was silent for a moment and she sensed that he didn't want to discuss it. "No harm in staying up until lunch-time, I guess."

She didn't tell him that, after lunch, *the* lunch, she intended to go for a walk and take him with her. Every Christmas afternoon that she could remember she had walked in the afternoon. She applied an orange stick bearing a ball of cotton wool dipped in oil to the cuticle of the first finger of her left hand.

Peter stood up and walked around the room. He looked at ease in his white polo-neck and tweed jacket but she knew he wasn't. She wished he would sit down on the beanbag beside the 'jungle' – the corner of the room where the rubber plant and the potted ferns grew – because you couldn't look ill-at-ease on a beanbag.

The phone rang. Peter looked at her questioningly. "Go ahead," she said carefully applying a base coat to her nails before the red lacquer.

"Hallo," said Peter to the unknown caller, a man. "Yes, I heard," hurriedly. And: "No I can't . . . Look, I'll call you this evening."

"Who was that calling you at my apartment?" Helen asked.

"Carl Cortoni," Peter said.

"Carl or Carlos?"

"Carl." Peter managed a smile. "He still wants to do a deal. All very boring. That's why I said I'd call him back."

"Good old Carl," she said. When she had applied the last sealer coat to her nails she stood up and walked about with her hands in front of her, waiting for the polish to dry. "Peter will tell me when he's good and ready," she thought as she went into the kitchen. "Or when he thinks *I'm* good and ready." She certainly wasn't going to spoil Christmas Day by quarrelling about it. Perhaps someone had died, someone they both knew.

She said to the nurse: "Really, Miss Bulmer, I don't think there's much point in you staying on here," and regretted the remark immediately. "But why don't you stay as a guest and have Christmas lunch with us," she amended, "maybe help me out in the kitchen. Who wants nail polish in their roast duck?"

All the fight went out of Nurse Bulmer. "That's very kind of you," she said. "Very kind." She took off her starched cap. "Shall I peel the potatoes?"

Christmas was a lonely time, the night porter had said. The bearded taxi-driver had barely spoken until –

Forgetting that her nails were still wet she opened the refrigerator and took out the duck.

When it was crackling and spitting in the oven, she remembered the presents under the tree in her bedroom. From Peter, a rope of pearls; for Peter, a set of ivory chess pieces. She also wrapped a present for Nurse Bulmer – a pair of sheepskin gloves.

The lunch wasn't as bad as it might have been. Although Peter's secret did hang over the table. Nurse Bulmer, feeling wanted, regaled them with her professional experiences.

The duck was mercifully tender and when Peter applied a match to the brandy-soaked Christmas pudding, flames flickered over it like blue moths and for a while the living-room with its modern white furniture, lime-green, wall-to-wall carpeting and Impressionist prints, was almost Pickwickian.

It was while they were letting off the indoor fireworks from the crackers that Helen said she intended to go out that afternoon.

Peter and Nurse Bulmer looked at each other questioningly.

"Look," Helen said, waving a sparkler, "there's absolutely nothing wrong with me. I am my own mistress and I shall do whatever I want to, so why don't you both accept it and then we can enjoy the rest of the day." She placed the spent, still-glowing sparkler in the ashtray.

"Faced with that," Peter said, "there's not a helluva lot we can do. What do you think, Nurse?"

"I agree with you," Nurse Bulmer said placidly.

"And you're coming with me," Helen said to Peter.

"I'll do the dishes," Nurse Bulmer said.

Helen put on a pair of maroon pants, tucking them into black boots, and a snug, old cony-fur coat from pre-modelling days, and was glad she had because it was colder than she had expected.

"So," she said as they emerged onto the street, "where shall we walk?" In her opinion Peter didn't exercise his bad leg enough.

"The park?"

"I don't like Central Park on a Sunday," Helen said.

"It isn't Sunday."

"It's the same thing. Let's go downtown to Battery Park. I like the sea on days like this."

Peter shrugged. "Just as you please," and unlocked the door of his yellow TR 7 parked outside the block.

The streets were still and muffled, their scars covered by snow. High above, sunlight glinted coldly on glass and steel and from the city's vents steam rose in heavy clouds. The diners were crowded, windows misted, but there weren't many people abroad on the sidewalks.

Peter parked the car and they entered the park at Bowling Green. Couples wearing Christmas present clothes walked along the paths while on the white lawns their children played with new sledges, footballs, baseball bats and balls.

Peter walked with a cherry-wood stick, one hand deep in the pockets of his reefer coat, managing to give the impression that he was only out of doors under duress.

When they reached Castle Clinton she breathed deeply of the sharp air blowing in from New York Bay and said: "There, do you see what I mean?" pointing at the boats and the steel-blue water.

"Uh-huh."

"Jenny Lind sang there," she said, swivelling her finger in the direction of the round, sandstone hulk of Castle Clinton. "That's where they used to process immigrants, over there in the garden."

"That was Ellis Island," he said firmly.

"That was after 1800," she said – history was her thing. "Before that it was the castle garden."

"Big deal," he said.

They walked along the promenade and it seemed wrong to her that on a day like this, with the breeze coming in from the sea, there should be this tension between them.

"Peter," she said, "isn't it about time you told me?" She tucked her arm beneath his. "What did Daniel York tell you on the phone yesterday? I know you think that with this amnesia thing you don't want to tell me anything that might upset me. But you're upsetting me more by not telling me, honestly Peter. Is it . . . Has someone we know died?"

He tightened the pressure of his arm against her hand. He said nothing. She stopped walking, jerking him back. To their left a boat was just leaving for the Statue of Liberty.

"Peter, I want to know."

He watched the boat and said: "If you know something's wrong then I guess I'd better tell you. But I thought I'd keep it from you until you'd recovered your memory. I didn't want to make things worse, honey," patting her hand.

"Is it . . . very bad?"

"You were right about someone being dead but not about Daniel York telling me because he's the one who's dead."

Oddly she wasn't surprised. Not even when he told her how York had died.

They retraced their footsteps in silence as the dying sun cast smouldering reflections on the high-rise of the Financial District.

When they got back to the apartment block two men were waiting in the lobby. One was tall and dark-haired with a lean predatory face, the other smaller with spry features and awkward-looking limbs.

Somehow she knew they were detectives but was surprised to find that Peter knew them. As the two men approached them, footsteps ringing on the marble floor, he whispered to her: "They don't know anything about the way you were found on Fifth Avenue." Aloud he said: "Helen, this is

Lieutenant Tyler and this is Sergeant Saul of the New York Police Department. They're investigating what I was just telling you about."

After they had shaken hands and apologised to Helen for intruding into her privacy on this day of all days, Tyler said to Peter: "You mean you only just told her?"

Peter nodded.

"Why was that, Mr Lodge?"

And why, Helen wondered, *had he whispered to her that the two detectives knew nothing about her amnesia?* Was he trying to protect her from something?

"I didn't want to worry her unduly," Peter said.

Tyler said: "But you were both at a party with the guy the night he was killed, for Chrissake. Didn't you think the fact that her host has been murdered might have been of some interest to Miss Fleming?"

"It *is* Christmas," Peter said and added: "I guess I should have told her."

"I would have thought," Tyler said in a clipped voice, "that the temptation to tell Miss Fleming would have been irresistible." He shook his head in wonderment. "Can we go up to your apartment, Miss Fleming?"

"Couldn't it wait?" Peter asked.

Taking Helen's arm, Saul said: "Don't worry, we won't upset Santa Claus," and led her to the elevator.

The door was opened by Nurse Bulmer. "I just finished the dishes," she said, "come on in." And to Helen: "Did we have a nice walk?" She just avoided calling it walkie, Helen thought. "Who would like a nice cup of coffee or tea?" looking at the two detectives and waiting to be introduced.

Peter said: "We've got some private business to talk over, Miss Bulmer. I wonder could you come back in say half an hour?" looking inquiringly at Tyler.

"Why of course, Mr Lodge. Everyone should have a breath of fresh air at least once a day. I'll just get my hat and coat."

"So who is Miss Bulmer?" Tyler asked as the door closed behind her.

"A nurse," Peter said.

"Right, she was wearing a uniform. Even I managed to deduce that, Mr Lodge. What is she doing here?"

As Helen began to explain, Peter interrupted her and said: "She's an old friend. She's on duty at a clinic near Sutton Place this evening and we thought we'd give her a good old-fashioned Christmas before she started work."

"A very charitable thought," Tyler remarked.

"But bullshit," Saul said.

Tyler sat down on the white, uncomfortably-low sofa and settled back with the air of a man who was in no hurry to leave. He crossed his legs, unbuttoned his topcoat.

From the inside pocket of his jacket he produced a photostat of a typewritten sheet of paper. The typing, Helen noticed, wasn't very professional – badly spaced with several erasures.

"Do you know what this is, Mr Lodge?"

"How could I?"

"It's a report from a police officer named Detective Alfred Kessler. He states that at 03.00 hours on the morning of the 24th, Miss Fleming was found wandering on Fifth Avenue apparently suffering from loss of memory."

Tyler took another sheet of paper from his pocket. "And do you know what this is?"

"You tell me," Peter's voice was belligerent.

"Another report. This one from Bellevue. It confirms that Miss Fleming was suffering from amnesia." He replaced the two sheets of paper in his pocket. "Now don't you think it's time you levelled with us, Mr Lodge?" He smiled bleakly at Helen. "And you, Miss Fleming?"

And you, Miss Fleming? What did he mean by that? She took off the old coat, tossed it into the bedroom and sat down. She felt a stab of pain across her forehead, then another.

The detective named Tyler was asking Peter questions but she wasn't listening to them. The other detective – what was his name, Paul? – was examining the shiny-leaved plants in the 'jungle'. Instinctively she began to massage her hands. *And you, Miss Fleming?* Another stab of pain. She tried to concentrate on the questions and answers.

"So there were three or four guests still there when you left?"

50

"That's right."

"But you can't be more specific?"

"I've been thinking about it since you questioned me the first time."

He hadn't told her that the police had questioned him.

"And?"

"I seem to remember that there was a guy named Padget there. Marty Padget. He models swim-suits."

The other detective who was feeling the leaf of the rubber plant between thumb and forefinger interrupted: "Do you stock swim-suits, Mr Lodge?"

"Yeah, I stock 'em. Why?"

"I just wondered. Now's the time to buy them, huh? Before the prices go up with the temperatures?"

"You're a great double-act," Peter said.

"Who else?" Tyler asked.

"I'm trying to think."

"You were right about Padget," Tyler said.

Peter looked startled. "How do you know?"

"The night porter told us. In fact, he gave us all the names of the last guests to leave."

Helen sensed that he was lying; that was the advantage of an observer.

Peter snapped: "Then why the hell are you asking me?"

"Corroboration. Who else, Mr Lodge?"

Peter frowned. Now he's acting, Helen thought. "I think Carlos Cortoni was still there when I left."

"All we need," said the detective named . . . Saul, not Paul, that was it. He left the plants and sat down in a rocking chair that Helen had bought in Fulton Street. It began to creak rhythmically.

If Peter had thought about it he would have wondered at the surprise in Saul's voice: Saul was supposed to know who had left the party last.

"Anyone else?" Tyler asked.

"I'm trying to think."

From another pocket Tyler produced what looked like a list of names. Some had crosses beside them. "Geraldine Walters?" he asked.

51

"No, she left early, I'm sure of that."

Tyler seemed satisfied.

"Paul St John?"

"No."

"Earl Winters?"

"Yup," Peter said, snapping his fingers, "he was there all right."

The creaking of the rocking chair stopped. "Who's Earl Winters?" Saul asked.

"He's my agent," Helen said. "He was also Daniel York's agent. And Marty Padget's."

A pause, then Saul began to rock the chair again.

"Any more?" Tyler asked.

"I thought you knew them all."

Poor Peter, he was just beginning to realise that he had been tricked.

Tyler put away the list of names and turned to Helen. "Now it's your turn, Miss Fleming."

"Do you mind if I get some aspirin?" Helen said. "I've got a headache."

"Sure, go ahead."

She went into the bathroom and stared at those eyes in the mirror, those knowing, not-telling eyes. She opened the cabinet, took two aspirins from a bottle and washed them down with a glass of water.

"As I understand it," Tyler said, trying to get comfortable on the sofa, "you left the party early."

"That's right," she said.

"Any reason?"

"I didn't like the party."

"Why was that, Miss Fleming?"

"They were sniffing cocaine."

"They?"

"A few of them. I don't remember who."

Saul, still rocking, said: "Why didn't Peter take you home?"

"I didn't want him to. He was talking business."

"Who with?"

Peter broke in: "Cortoni as it happens. Look, do you have to put her through this? She's told you she's got a headache."

Saul said: "Daniel York has more than a headache."

"Maybe," Helen said, "if you could stop creaking that chair it might help." The headache was still there but it was subsiding.

"Sorry, ma'am." Saul pulled on the arms of the chair and the creaking stopped.

"So," said Tyler, "you left the party early, you caught a cab home, and the next thing we know is that you're stopped outside St Paddy's suffering, so you claim, from annesia."

Peter said: "I don't like the *you claim* bit."

Tyler ignored him. "What happened, Miss Fleming, between the time you left the party and when you spoke to Detective Kessler?"

"I don't know," she said. "I don't remember."

There was that screen again with the imperfections through which light shone faintly. Poke out those imperfections, punch, punch, punch, and peer through them and she would see.

Tyler stood up and walked to the window. It was dark now. And cruel, she thought.

Tyler was staring out of the window, his back towards them. "You see, Miss Fleming," he said quietly, "we *do* know a little about what happened to you. But only a little."

Peter snapped: "Stop torturing her."

"I'm sorry," Tyler said. "I don't mean to. But I have to know, you see." He turned. "Didn't you know, Miss Fleming, that after you left you returned to the party?"

Silence.

She knew that Tyler wasn't lying now. The ache in her head sharpened again; cold was rising through her body.

They were all staring at her. Staring.

"I can't remember," she said. "Can't remember . . ."

"Try, Miss Fleming." Tyler's voice.

"Can't remember . . ."

A creak. Saul, too, was on his feet. His voice came from far away. "We believe, Miss Fleming, that you may have witnessed the murder."

53

And now Tyler's voice, also far away: "Worse, we believe that the killer may have seen you."

V

She awoke at dawn on Boxing Day. Her bedroom door was ajar and gently she pushed it open further. Nurse Bulmer, whom she had finally asked to stay over the whole holiday, was asleep on the sofa, greying hair down to her shoulders, face tranquil. Beside her on the marble-topped coffee table lay a Jean Plaidy paperback, horn-rimmed spectacles acting as a bookmark.

Helen closed the door again, pursing her lips as the handle clicked. But there was no sound from the living-room.

Hastily she began to dress in the same clothes that she had worn yesterday because they were handy. Today she intended to get away. From them all. Even Peter who had said he would call round at lunch-time. To try and remember.

Holding her boots in one hand she tip-toed across the sitting-room to the bathroom where she washed and attended perfunctorily to her hands; today they would have to wait.

As she made her way to the living-room door, Nurse Bulmer smiled as she was swept away on horseback by a swashbuckling Plaidy hero. Holding her breath, Helen closed the door behind her and ran down the stairs to the next floor so that the noise of the elevator stopping didn't disturb the nurse.

Her blue Honda hatchback was parked a block away under a bonnet of snow. It was light now but the morning didn't have yesterday's fresh glow. There was still snow on the sidewalks but it had been mashed up. On the street itself there was a sheen of ice.

She opened the door of the Honda and sat at the wheel. Where did you go at this hour in New York on Boxing Day? Outside the city, she decided, that was where.

A friend of hers, Katy Tanner, who had breath-taking legs and modelled shoes and stockings, had a cabin upstate, near Bear Mountain; she had been planning to spend Christmas there with her boyfriend; perhaps she wouldn't mind a visitor. Just for half an hour or so before Helen went walking in the forest. Alone. To think.

She put on her driving gloves – "Never go out without gloves, especially in the cold" – started the engine and eased the hatchback into the traffic, what there was of it.

The driver of the old black Pontiac Pan-Am waited a moment before pulling out two cars behind her. He had an acne-scarred face and pale, slicked-down hair and he wore a hearing-aid and light-sensitive glasses. He switched on the radio. Further snowfalls, the newscaster said, were expected in New York and upstate.

He shrugged. That could be good: it could be shitty. He pressed a button on the radio and once again – how many more times? – Bing was dreaming of a white Christmas. Well, he'd got it, the man thought, as he lit a cigarette and settled down for the drive.

Five minutes later Helen Fleming stopped outside a Brew Burger. She ordered orange juice, ham and eggs and coffee, and from a wall-phone called Katy Tanner.

Katy's voice was sleepy. Boy oh boy! she said, what time was it? In the background Helen could hear a grumbling male voice. When Helen told Katy that it was 8.30 am the tone of Katy's voice changed and she said: "What's the matter, sweetie, are you in some sort of trouble?"

Helen told her that Daniel York had been killed and that she had been with him shortly before he died and that she had been having nightmares about it.

"Then you'd better come on up," Katy Tanner said to more grumbling accompaniment and then some whispering while

56

Katy explained. When she spoke again she said: "I'm sorry I forgot, we're visiting this morning. Leaving in about an hour. But you make yourself at home, we'll be back around two. Okay?"

"Thanks, Katy," Helen said.

"I'll leave the key in my usual devillish clever hiding-place – under the flowerpot."

When the ham and eggs arrived Helen didn't feel like eating them. She drank some iced water and some coffee. Then she paid the check and crossed the road to her car.

This time the driver of the black Pan-Am allowed three cars between himself and the blue Honda.

She turned onto the Franklin D. Roosevelt Drive and crossed the Hudson by the George Washington Bridge. From there she turned onto the Palisades Interstate Parkway and headed north, glancing from time to time across the river at the Bronx and Yonkers quilted with snow.

There were times when she felt calm, in command; others when wings of fear beat inside her. She should have connected her flight down Fifth Avenue with Daniel York's murder; but her brain simply hadn't wanted to make that connection. At first it had erased the entire party.

Then the missing period had been the one hour and eight minutes between the time the cab had drawn up outside her apartment block and the moment Detective Kessler had stopped her outside St Patrick's. Now this period had been fractionally reduced because, when Tyler had told her that she had returned to the party, she had remembered discovering the loss of her purse. That must have taken a minute so now only one hour and seven minutes was missing.

She would have to concentrate minute by minute until . . . It was like slotting transparencies into a viewfinder.

She braked sharply as a Jeep Cherokee loomed up in front of her; without realising it she had changed lanes. Horn blaring, an old grey Thunderbird overtook her in her original lane. Behind it, but slowing down, was a black car. She noticed that the driver was wearing tinted glasses and a hearing-aid. She would have to concentrate more on her driving, leave the introspection until later.

There had been more snow out here than in the city, she noted, and the countryside was tranquil with it. The river was the colour of ice and the sky had lost yesterday's polish. As she entered Route 9W it began to snow lightly, the flakes rushing at the windshield before veering away. Half an hour later it was snowing thickly and steadily.

She took an exit to the left. The cabin was about two miles away in forest-land of pine and grey and paper birch. She thought one of the cars behind her had taken the same exit but, because of the snow, she couldn't be sure.

She found the lane winding through the trees and drove along it. The key was under the flowerpot.

Inside the cabin a log-fire was blazing. With its worn leather furniture, half-filled bookshelves and storm-lamps converted to electricity, it had a careless, back-to-nature air about it. But in the kitchen on the other side of the breakfast bar, there was a fridge, a dishwasher, an oven and a rotary grill.

She took off her gloves and warmed her hands in front of the fire. On the table was a note: *Food in fridge, drinks on trolley, back at two. Katy.*

Helen made herself a cup of coffee. It was still snowing but not so thickly now. The quiet woods beckoned; that was the place to think. She called Peter and told him that she wouldn't be back until the evening, breaking the connection when he asked where she was. Then she put on her gloves again, pulled up the collar of the old cony and let herself out of the cabin.

By which time the driver of the Pan-Am had approached on foot to within two hundred yards of the cabin. The lenses of his spectacles were only faintly tinted, but just dark enough to eliminate the snow-glare when he peered through the scope on the .340 Weatherby Magnum he held across his chest.

It wasn't until she had been walking for five minutes that she suspected she was being followed. At first she put it out of her mind. It was ridiculous; no-one knew that she had come out to the cabin. Her brain was playing her up again. She increased her stride and the silence, broken only by the clicking of ice-sheathed twigs and the occasional flight of a bird, closed in on her.

The path led up a gentle hill through the birches to a belt of pine. When she reached it, she thought, she would turn back. She clenched her fists in her pockets and forced herself back to the cab as it stood, engine ticking over, outside her block.

"This is it, lady."

"I'm sorry, I've left my purse behind."

"You mean you haven't got the fare?" Eyes glaring through the screen.

"I mean you'll have to take me back. Then you'll get paid."

"This was going to be my last trip."

"Do you want to get paid?"

The cab jerked forward.

If I can reach Daniel York's apartment block, she thought as she approached the line of pine trees, then there will be only one hour to account for.

Somewhere behind her a twig cracked. She stopped and stared back through the lightly falling snow. Nothing. An animal, perhaps. A fox or a squirrel – no, squirrels hibernated, didn't they?

She shivered. Above her a robin took flight from an over-hanging branch, showering her with snow. She turned and walked on.

The man wearing the hearing-aid had been disappointed when he saw her leave the cabin. It had looked snug in there through a slit in the drapes and, either with the rifle or the Colt Cobra .38 that he carried in the pocket of his topcoat, he would have forced her to strip at gunpoint in front of the log fire.

That would have been great. That snotty, aloof, model-type expression on her face. Well, it wouldn't have been so snotty as he squeezed those big breasts, hurt them, and then screwed her hard, making her kneel in front of the fire. The man who had given him the $2,500 contract to kill her hadn't said anything about not screwing her, so that was his bonus.

And all the while she would have thought it was rape, and she would have been hoping, praying, that when he had

59

finished he would leave and she would never have known that, as he withdrew, he would have been reaching for the pistol; and she would never have known anything more as he placed the snub-nosed barrel at the back of her head and blew her brains out.

Except that he did like to see the expression on their faces just before he pulled the trigger; maybe he would have made her turn over, sit up, plead with him a little before he shot her.

Well, she had spoiled all that for him. But there were compensations. He liked to hunt and it would be good out here, stalking, the rifle sleek and heavy in his hands, getting her in the scope, finger caressing the trigger . . . how bright the blood would be on the snow.

He left the cabin and set off up the winding track leading to the belt of pine trees.

There *was* someone back there.

When she turned to look a second time she caught a slight movement behind a tall holly bush that she had passed a minute or so earlier. And snow had fallen from the branches although no bird had flown away.

She moaned softly to herself. If she could make the pine trees . . . But, no, there she would be trapped in the dark caverns among the tree-trunks, and it would be easy for her pursuer, who had come to kill her – and this she knew with a terrible certainty was what he intended to do – to find her. Her only chance was to confuse him. To run suddenly from the track and lose herself among the birches and the undergrowth; to circle him and get back to the cabin. To a telephone. Even now she might be framed in the sights of a gun.

She walked on until she reached a thicket of brambles. She hesitated, then ducked and, keeping low, ran among the trees. She was making too much noise and, even if he couldn't see her, he would hear her but she couldn't help it. She had to keep running; it was all she could do. At least she was fit. As she ran she prayed. And all the time a part of her asked: "How can this be happening to me?"

When she was a hundred yards from the track she altered

course and began to descend the rise. In the direction of the track she thought she glimpsed a flash of metal. A gun? She ran round a cluster of thin birches. Ahead lay an expanse of undisturbed snow. On it she would be a perfect target.

Please God, please let the snow fall more thickly. Heart thumping, she ran along the fringe of the snow-pasture. She was half way round it when she felt her front foot break through a crust. She lurched forward, fell.

Water began to fill her boots. The crust had been ice. She searched for the bottom of the lake but there was nothing; she was suspended by the ice around her. She tried to pull herself up but the ice cracked. She was sinking.

The sound of the rifle-shot was not as loud as she had expected. There was a noise around her as though someone had hurled a handful of gravel at her. The next shot would get her but, survival instincts still pulsing strongly, she ducked her head as her feet still tried to find an end to the cold, ice-cold water.

When no further shot came, she glanced up. Into the eyes of a dog. A golden retriever. It was wagging its tail.

And through the trees she heard the sound of tearing brambles and breaking twigs and two voices, one a man's and one a boy's. The boy reached her first. Then the man, big and bulky, dressed in a blue and green lumber jacket and leather hat with flaps pulled over his ears.

"Christ!" he shouted, "I thought I'd killed you." He came towards her, sank in the water as far as his knees and held out his hand. He pulled her to the shore, watched by the boy and the dog. Then anger replaced the fear. "Don't you know this is private land? Didn't you see the goddam signs? Can't a guy go out shooting with his son without some crazy dame getting in the way?"

The boy said: "He was aiming at a wood-pigeon. Did you hear the shot scattering?"

"Please," she said, "get me back to the cabin."

The man's anger subsided. "Are you hurt?"

"I don't think so," she said. "Just wet and cold." So cold. "Will you come with me?"

61

"Of course," he said. And to his son: "Go get the gun." The dog followed the boy.

The man took off his jacket and slipped it over her shoulders. "You staying with Katy Tanner?"

Helen nodded.

"She should've warned you."

As they began to walk back in the direction of the cabin, relief washed over Helen. So no-one had been trying to kill her. And maybe the detectives had been wrong about her witnessing a murder – and being witnessed.

The boy caught up with them and handed his father the shotgun. The dog gambolled ahead of them enjoying the snow, until he stopped beside the holly bush where Helen had noticed a movement.

The dog whined, worrying the snow with its muzzle.

"Hey, Jones," the boy said, "what's wrong with you?"

The boy's father said:"Just this young lady's tracks in the snow, I guess."

"No." The boy who had gone on ahead stopped, pointing. "There's some more tracks there. A man's."

The feeling of relief froze.

*   *   *

When she got back to the cabin with the hunter, his son and Jones, she found that Katy and her boyfriend, a scholarly young man named Bob, had returned early because their car had broken down. After the hunters had left Helen sat in front of the fire, drinking a brandy, and told them everything that had happened.

Katy, beautiful, red-haired, out-going Katy, listened sympathetically. Bob listened quietly but Helen got the impression that he wasn't overjoyed to have his Christmas with Katy interrupted; she didn't blame him.

When she told them about the two sets of tracks Bob went outside to look, but when he came back he said: "Too bad, *if* there were two sets the snow's covered them."

Katy asked her to stay the night and Bob said less than

enthusiastically: "Sure, why not."

But she drove back to Manhattan. Back to an infuriated Peter who only calmed down when she told him that she thought she had been trailed through the forest.

"Did you tell the police?"

"There's nothing to tell. I didn't see anyone and it's been snowing ever since."

But he called just the same and left a message for Tyler who was away from his office.

"The terrible thing," she said, as he replaced the receiver, "is that if anyone was trying to kill me because of the murder it would have been for nothing because I still can't remember and I don't think I ever will."

She began to cry. With a handkerchief he gently dried the tears.

VI

That same day Boyd Tyler and Phillip Saul interviewed three men.

The first was Carlos Cortoni. To reach him they had to travel to the fashionable east end of Long Island where his father owned a mansion and, because of the snow, they took the Long Island Railroad.

In the carriage they studied what the computer had come up with about Daniel York. Five years earlier he had been convicted of possessing marijuana and, when in his thirties, he had been investigated on a morals charge involving a fourteen year-old girl, but the case had never reached the courts because the girl had admitted lying about her age.

"Must be that after-shave," Saul said.

"After-shave?"

"That's what he advertised," Saul explained, "or had you forgotten? Wow, these models. Don't let anyone ever tell you they're all fruits. I should know, my old lady went off with one. Poor bastard, I feel sorry for him," he added.

The check-out hadn't revealed much more of interest about the dead man. Caucasian male, weighing 172 pounds, born August 27th, 1937, in Bay City, Michigan, and the usual statistics provided by computer link-ups with other agencies.

"We're indebted to Mr Peter Lodge for Cortoni," Tyler remarked. "Even though he was on the guest-list."

"Do you figure he would have given us those three names if you hadn't given him that crap about the night porter?"

"All I know is you nearly blew it. You looked as though you'd had a cardiac arrest when he named Cortoni."

All the night porter had admitted under interrogation was that, flush with the two ten-dollar bills Helen Fleming had given him, he had unlocked the street doors, abandoned his post and joined a craps game in the basement. Having lost the twenty dollars, he had gone back to the lobby just as Helen Fleming returned.

Tyler and Saul left the train at Bridgehampton. Outside stood a solitary cab. They told the driver to take them to Cortoni's house on the beach and to wait because they didn't expect anyone there to offer them transport back to the station.

The house which lay at the end of an avenue lined with leafless maples and evergreen hedges, was a rambling, mellow-bricked building with turrets and tall chimneys, used mostly in the summer by the look of it, but festive enough today with coloured lights festooning a pine tree on the lawn and decorations at some of the windows. A wind coming in from the sea blew the falling snow at Tyler and Saul as they stood in the porch waiting for someone to open the door.

Finally a manservant wearing a plum-coloured jacket, opened the door and surveyed them, the familiar appraisal of someone who knew you were police officers. "Yes," he said, "can I help you?"

Showing him his shield, Tyler said: "Police. We'd like to see Carlos Cortoni."

"I don't think –" But they were inside.

In one corner of the hall stood a Christmas tree lit with winking lights and overloaded with tinsel and baubles; in the other a suit of armour.

Neither Carlos Cortoni nor his father was pleased to see Tyler and Saul, Cortoni senior less pleased than his son. He was powerfully built but overweight with sleek, grey hair combed around an old-fashioned centre parting; he wore a scarlet dressing-gown, and round his throat a silver chain.

"So what the hell is this?" he asked, his anger enriched by his Argentinian accent. "What gives you the right to come busting in here at Christmas? What will my guests think?" gesturing around the hall with one well-cared-for hand.

"I don't see any guests," Saul said. "Only him," pointing at the suit of armour. "And he doesn't seem to care."

Cortoni's son said: "They're still in bed. It's early. Just because you guys can't sleep. . . Anyway, what the hell *do* you want?"

"A word in your ear, Carlos," Tyler said. "Maybe we could go and sit down someplace."

"You don't sit anywhere," Cortoni senior said. "Speak your business and get the hell out of here."

"Murder is our business," Tyler said.

He and Saul watched Carlos Cortoni closely. His head jerked up and the skin tightened beneath his glossy, blond hair. It could have been surprise, it could have been fear.

"Whose?"

"You mean you don't know?"

"I mean I don't know what the fuck you're talking about."

Tyler told him about the killing. "Can we sit down someplace now?"

Carlos Cortoni looked at his father who said: "*Mierda!* Why my son? There must have been thirty, forty guests at that party, maybe more, huh? But you have to pick on my son. Why? I'll tell you why," before either Tyler or Saul could reply, "because he's a Cortoni is why."

A man with rumpled hair appeared at the head of the staircase and stared down at them curiously. Cortoni noticed him. "Okay," he said to Tyler and Saul, "so we give you five minutes, no more," and led them down a passageway to a lounge.

The room smelled of last night's cigar smoke and the empty glasses hadn't been cleared away. The floral-patterned easy chairs were cold to the touch; through the French windows they could see the bleak sea.

Carlos Cortoni, wearing sharply-creased flannels and a pale blue cashmere V-neck over a white silk shirt, said: "Sit down, gentlemen," and sat down himself. His manner was controlled and yet Tyler got the impression that any strength he possessed emanated from his father. He had recovered from any shock he might have felt.

His father stood with his back to the baronial fireplace. He said: "I was acquitted, right? No need to take it out on my son."

"As I recall it," Tyler said evenly, "the case – fraud, wasn't it? – was thrown out because the principal witness for the prosecution disappeared."

"But I *was* acquitted and this is a free country and you have no right. . . You got a warrant?"

Tyler said: "Look, Mr Cortoni, we're not making any big thing about this and we're sure as hell not searching your house. All we want is some help from your son."

"I seem to have heard that before," Cortoni said, but he was calming down and Tyler asked his son: "How was York during the party?"

"He seemed okay. A little tensed up maybe. You know how these models are. Temperament, I guess. It's understandable. Danny was no chicken."

"Danny? You knew him well?"

"Reasonably. I'm opening up in the boutique business. When I gave a launch I invited him. He was a face in the business. It helped the atmosphere. We got friendly."

"Did he tell you he was upset?" Saul asked.

"Nope. I just sensed it."

"Ever done any modelling yourself, Mr Cortoni?" Saul asked.

"You think I'm the type?"

Saul considered. "No, maybe not. But I can't imagine you with egg on your lapel."

Cortoni looked pleased.

Tyler said: "I believe you were one of the last to leave the party, Mr Cortoni?"

His father interrupted: "You don't have to answer any of their questions, Carlos. . ."

"Who told you that?" Carlos Cortoni asked Tyler.

67

"Peter Lodge."

"Lodge, huh?"

"Do you know him well?"

"I know him," Cortoni said.

"Because you're in the same line of business," Saul said. "Friendly rivals, Mr Cortoni?"

"That's about the strength of it." He nodded, thinking, and plucked at the creases on his pants. "Yeah, Peter was there at the end. And a couple of others."

"Remember their names?" Tyler asked.

"I didn't know their names. No, wait a minute, I did know one of them. An agent. Winters is his name. Earl Winters. Friar Tuck . . ."

"Come again, Mr Cortoni?" Tyler frowned.

"He reminded me of Friar Tuck," Cortoni said.

"Marty Padget?"

"Who's Marty Padget?"

"What time did you leave?" Tyler asked.

"I don't know. Around two, I guess."

"Were you wearing a suit?"

"No, I was wearing a blazer. Why?"

"Where's that blazer now?" Saul asked.

"In my apartment in Manhattan. I only came out here for Christmas."

"Do you mind if we take a look at it?"

His father said: "He does mind. We got rights, you know."

"Do you mind?" Saul asked Carlos Cortoni.

"If my father says —"

"Maybe I should get Dean down," his father said.

"Dean? Who's Dean?" Tyler asked.

"The family lawyer," Cortoni junior told him. He looked inquiringly at his father. "If you think that's necessary . . ."

Tyler said: "I don't think it's necessary."

"Why's that, Lieutenant?"

"Because we're just leaving," Tyler said, standing up. "But we'll take a look at that blazer – before it goes to the cleaners."

Cortoni senior said: "You mean you don't have any more questions?"

"Can you think of any?" Saul asked.

"Well," Carlos Cortoni said, "if I can be of any help at any time."

The two Cortonis looked nonplussed, cops were supposed to ask more questions than that.

In the hallway Tyler paused beside the Christmas tree with its winking lights. "By the way," he asked Carlos Cortoni, "which of this final group left the party last?"

"How the hell would he know that?" Cortoni senior said quickly. "You know, how would he know that if he left first?"

"He hasn't said he did," Tyler snapped, annoyed at the interruption.

"But my father's right," Carlos Cortoni said. "I left first. Of those last few, that is."

The servant in the plum-coloured jacket materialised and hovered beside the door.

"Okay," Cortoni senior said, "let these *gentlemen* out."

The servant opened the door and the cold rushed in. As they stepped out Saul said to the suit of armour: "Don't call us, we'll call you."

*   *   *

Marty Padget lived in a tiny terraced house which he shared with another male model in the East Village. Being a big man he made the house seem even smaller.

"I've been expecting you," he said before Tyler and Saul had identified themselves. "Come on in, I don't want all that cold in the house."

He took them into a room with a legend on the door, MARTY'S PLACE. On the floor was a rowing machine and a set of weights; in one corner stood an exercise bicycle.

Padget nodded at them. "I got to keep fit. No muscles, no job." He grinned at them. "Take a seat if you can find one."

Tyler said: "Why were you expecting us, Mr Padget?" and studied him while he answered. He was wearing a red track suit with white piping; his deep tan emphasised the blue of his

69

eyes – the dead eyes of Daniel York had also been very blue, Tyler remembered –, and his thick moustache had recently been trimmed.

He said: "Why? Because the York killing was on the radio earlier this morning, that's why. I figured you'd have to see almost everyone who was at that party."

"Only the ones who saw him last," Saul said. "Like you." He looked for somewhere to sit, considered the exercise bicycle, then leaned against the wall.

Marty Padget sat on a leather easy-chair beneath a colour photograph of Marty Padget wearing white swimming trunks, poised on a springboard observed admiringly by girls in bikinis. Tyler sat at a desk littered with glossy magazines and letters. Fan mail, he supposed.

"Well," Padget said, "I didn't kill Danny, that's for sure. I loved the guy."

"Loved?" Tyler queried.

"Liked," Padget said. "We'd both been in the game a long time. He longer than me. I've still got a few years to go – provided I work out every day – but he was pretty well washed up. He was drinking too."

"And main-lining," Saul said.

"Is that so? I didn't know that. Poor Danny." He combed at his moustache with his fingers. "You know people don't believe it but this is a hard life."

"I believe you," Saul said. "I mean it."

"I'm thinking of breaking into cigarettes," Padget said. "Swim-suits are *too* much like hard work. One hint of flab and you can forget it. But who notices flab on a cowpoke riding a horse and smoking a low-tar?"

Tyler asked him about the party and whether there was any bad feeling between York and any of his guests. He also asked Padget which of the final group of late-stayers left first, knowing what the answer would be.

"Me," Padget said.

Saul said: "What were you wearing, Mr Padget?"

"At the party?"

"Sure, at the party."

Padget thought for a moment. "A denim suit, I think. It wasn't formal or anything."

"Have you got that suit here, Mr Padget?"

"No," Padget said, "it's at the cleaners."

At the front door as they were leaving Saul asked: "Are you gay, Mr Padget?"

"Sure," Padget said. "Are you?"

*　　*　　*

The third man Tyler and Saul interviewed on Boxing Day was Earl Winters.

"Guess who he'll say left first," said Saul at the wheel of the police Plymouth.

"Earl Winters," Tyler said.

Winters lived in an old-fashioned block on Central Park West. His apartment was spacious but furnished more in keeping with the age of the block than modern-day living. The drapes at the windows of the living-room overlooking the park were lime-green satin and floor-length, with deep folds which looked as though they might conceal moths; the Chesterfield and matching chairs were dark and heavy; the Wilton carpet was worn and the potted palms looked as if they had lived a long time. It was not the sort of apartment you expected a models' agent to occupy.

Earl Winters with his bald head and fringe of hair looked equally remote from his profession. He wore a cream, Arran-knit sweater, baggy golfing slacks and stained sheepskin slippers. But his wife made up for what he lacked in personal pride. She was in her forties, neat and bright, and unlined and expensively perfumed; Tyler could imagine her fund-raising and making a huge success of it. She was just leaving the apartment as they arrived.

Winters led them into the sitting-room where the atmosphere settled heavily on them. Winters said he had heard the news, the phone hadn't stopped ringing. Would they like a drink? And when they said they wouldn't he poured himself a Smirnof vodka and tonic with ice and lemon – the cocktail

71

York was said to have been drinking, Tyler recalled.

"Any ideas, Mr Winter?" Tyler asked, standing at the window and gazing in the direction of the frozen lake in the park. On the street far below a police car, a toy, passed by, siren wailing. Another homicide? Christmas killings were more cold-blooded than any others, perpetrated by people who had no feeling for family togetherness. He thought about May. "I'm sorry, Mr Winters," he said, "I didn't catch your reply."

"I said, no, I hadn't got any ideas. A guy like Danny makes enemies, of course. He was good-looking, successful, he had many admirers."

Saul, who was looking at the Christmas cards on the mantelpiece, said: "But he *was* over the hill, wasn't he?"

"He thought he was. But there was still a lot of work for him if he could accept that he wasn't a juvenile any more."

The phone rang in the hallway and Earl Winters excused himself. They listened to him talking. "Terrible, terrible . . . no, no more than usual . . . highly-strung, sure, but in this profession . . ."

"All this place needs," Saul said, picking up a card and reading it, "is a violinist playing 'In a Monastery Garden'. Did you know that used to be my father's favourite piece of music?" He picked up two or three more cards in rapid succession, then said: "Well, well, what do you know?"

"A card from York?" Tyler guessed.

"You're not human."

"What's it say?"

"A merry Lufthansa Christmas from Danny Lufthansa York."

"Why the Lufthansa?" Saul asked as Winters returned to the room.

"Oh, he did an ad for them once. It was an in-joke," Winters added. He showed no wish to elaborate. The card seemed to have upset him. "I was very fond of Danny. He was a professional, a good scout, too."

Tyler said: "I hope you don't mind me asking, Mr Winters, but why the gloves? I'm sure you've been asked before."

Winters put down his glass and held up his gloved hands.

72

"As a matter of fact not that many people do ask me. It takes a cop to do that." He pressed black-sheathed fingertips together. "I have a skin complaint. An allergy, so I'm told. Dermatitis would be a more accurate description. Do you want to see?" beginning to peel off one black glove.

"No thanks," Tyler said hastily. "I just wondered."

"Sometimes I wear white gloves, but mostly black. I've never made up my mind which is best. Black looks kind of sinister and yet white is more surgical, more obvious in a way."

The phone rang again. "I'm sorry," Winters said. "Everyone is pretty shocked. At Christmas-time too . . ." His voice broke a little as he made for the telephone.

Saul read some more Christmas cards. "Well, what do you know?" he said again.

"Peter Lodge?"

"Close – Carl Cortoni."

"Okay, I'll call you . . . yes, they're here now . . ." Winters came back into the room; he appeared to have recovered himself.

"Any particular enemies?" Tyler asked, leaving the window and the view of the frozen lake and sitting on the Chesterfield, which sighed beneath his weight.

"Come again?"

"You said he was bound to have made enemies. Anyone special?"

"I'll have to think about it," Winters said, chinking the ice in his glass. "Maybe you could come back when I've got over a little of the initial shock."

"Those the clothes you were wearing at the party?" Saul asked.

"These? No, no. These are my Sunday clothes. At the party?" He frowned. "Why, does it matter?"

"Where are the clothes you were wearing at the party?" Saul asked.

"At Betty's place."

"Betty's place?" Tyler queried wearily.

"Betty – that's my wife – has a florist's on the East Side,

73

close to Danny's apartment as it happens. It's got a studio behind it and we sometimes spend the night there. You know, it's handy for changing for dinner."

"I know what you mean," Saul said. "I live in Brooklyn and I keep a change of clothes in the locker-room at Homicide."

They asked Winters what time he had left the party and he told them around 2 am. There had been a group of them left 'chewing the fat.' "I guess maybe we were a little high," Winters said.

"Sniffing coke?"

"I don't touch drugs," Winters said. "This is my only drug," holding his glass up. "And I don't hit that too hard."

When they asked who had been in the group, he told them without hesitation: "Marty Padget – he and Danny were old buddies – and the two whizz-kids of the boutique business, Carl Cortoni and Peter Lodge."

Tyler said: "I assume you left first, Mr Winters."

"As a matter of fact I did," Winters said. "Did the others tell you?"

74

VII

John Remick was more than just a doctor who specialised in police work. He was a crusader. He believed implicitly that it was within the powers of law-makers and law enforcement agencies to control the spread of crime.

He didn't accept that organised crime was an integral part of American society; he did not accept that ghetto crime should be confined rather than eradicated; and he did not accept that the drug scene was here to stay. Thus in many quarters of officialdom John Remick was considered to be a big pain in the ass.

But although he preached reform such as the speeding up of the courtroom processes and the clarification of laws that favoured the criminal, he was sensible enough to confine his more positive activities to his own field. And by his own field he did not mean merely physical medicine. He believed that as a police surgeon he should explore the possibilities of crime solution and prevention through the mind.

He was, after all, a doctor concerned with the whole human condition and that, even in his specialisation, surely did not confine his attention to the flesh and bones of misdemeanour.

Ever since he had joined the New York Police Department Remick had been struck by the number of prosecutions that failed – or never got off the ground – because the memory of eye-witnesses was at fault. Flawed or totally lapsed.

He believed, *knew*, that by simple hypnosis those witnesses could all have been regressed to the moment of the crime, and would then have remembered with total recall. But try and tell the Establishment that.

True, hypnosis had won a little credibility in recent years and in 1976 the New York City police had taken on an official hypnotist. But smart lawyers still got evidence obtained under hypnosis thrown out on the unspoken grounds that it was mumbo-jumbo. They knew that many judges – and juries – still believed that hypnosis was just that, and they took advantage of such prejudice.

What Remick needed to consolidate his beliefs was a major, well-publicised crime with a credible and patently honest witness who had suffered a genuine loss of memory. Remick believed that he now knew of just such a case, the Daniel York killing. He believed it would be a *cause célèbre*.

But first he had to decide whether to double-cross a man he respected more than anyone else in the world.

*   *   *

At 5.35 am on December 28th, Remick was called out from his bachelor apartment overlooking the East River and the United Nations, to examine the body of a man who had been beaten to death in his liquor store on East Twenty-Ninth.

Sitting shivering at the wheel of his chocolate Mustang, Remick considered the case of Daniel York and what he had to do about it.

Although the investigation had only lasted four days and the media was still full of it because the protagonists inhabited a glamorous and glossy world of *in* discos and restaurants, Remick knew from his conversations in the Irish pub that it had gone cold.

Boyd Tyler and Phillip Saul were faced with three possibilities: firstly, that whoever killed York hid in the apartment until everyone else had left and then stabbed him; secondly, the killer arrived *after* the party had broken up; and thirdly, that one of the four late-stayers was the murderer.

It was the last theory that was upsetting Tyler, who was in any case edgy when he was investigating a knifing because that was the way his wife had died.

Marty Padget, Earl Winters, Peter Lodge and Carl Cortoni all readily agreed that they must have been among the last to see Daniel York alive. But they all differed on one vital fact: each claimed to have left the group first.

To try and break them down Tyler had taken four signed statements and used them to try and get each to change his story. But whatever permutation he used it always came out the same: "According to the other three guests you can't have left first." And each would reply: "Then they must be mistaken, Lieutenant."

Saul had also slipped in a few tricks such as: "Who left second?" and each time had been told: "How can I tell if I left first?" Or words to that effect. Stalemate.

They had all left first and therefore could shed no light on subsequent events. Either three of them were lying or it was a concerted attempt to confuse, a mutual protection society. But protection from what?

Remick swung the Mustang down Second Avenue. The car was beginning to warm up but outside it looked bitter. The city was awakening, lights cutting squares in the high-rise, and a few cars with smoking exhausts and drivers huddled over their wheels, were heading downtown.

Fingerprints hadn't helped; there had been too many of them around. One had been found on the block of the safety-chain with traces of blood – York's blood, according to the lab – on it, but it had been smeared beyond recognition. Only Earl Winter's prints appeared nowhere, but that was because he wore gloves: the absence of his prints had as much value as the abundance of others.

The tragedy of the investigation was the absence of the night porter at the relevant time. Saul had even tried that on the suspects. "The porter reckons you left last."

"How come? He called Danny to say he was taking some time off and was leaving the doors unlocked."

If that was the tragedy then the irony was that they actually did have an eye-witness to the murder. Or believed they did. Helen Fleming. And neither Tyler nor Saul was convinced that her amnesia was genuine.

Which was what had led to the argument in the Irish pub the night before that had cut deeper than any previous disagreement. Tyler and Saul had both looked exhausted and, observing this, Remick had finally asked them why they didn't ask Helen Fleming to undergo hypnosis.

"Here we go," Saul said.

"Maybe we will," Tyler said, "as a last resort."

"As a last resort? Why not now, for Chrissake?"

"You know why," Tyler said. "We've been through all this before."

Remick searched his pockets for a pack of cigarettes; this was the sort of occasion when you needed one; but Saul wagged his finger. "Uh-huh," he said.

Remick burst out: "You know something? I sometimes wonder if you guys want to solve a crime. Here's a girl who may have witnessed a murder. Or may not," for their benefit, "and yet you won't use a proven method of finding out. What the hell's wrong with you?"

In the past these arguments, although heated, had always contained an element of mutual respect; Remick was saddened to find that this element was now eluding them.

Tyler said: "It isn't proven and you know it. Hypno-induced testimony is riddled with flaws."

Saul waved at the green-aproned waiter and ordered three more beers.

"Coming right up, sor," the waiter said.

Remick snapped: "Surely it's worth a try."

Tyler leaned across the table. "I said I'd use it. When every other *proven* technique has been tried."

"I thought it had."

The waiter banged three glasses on the table and departed with his tip humming 'When Irish Eyes Are Smiling'.

"The case is only four days-old," Saul reminded Remick. He wiped a moustache of foam from his lip and picked up the *Daily News*. "Look, still hot." MALE MODEL MURDER read the headline. And underneath: DRAMATIC DEVELOPMENTS. "Hey, what developments?" Saul asked.

Addressing himself to Remick, Tyler said: "We're checking out statements and relationships between the victim and the suspects. We're also trying to find out where York got his junk from. There's a helluva lot of routine to get through yet, John, and don't you ever knock it because that's what catches criminals, routine."

Remick tried to control his anger because he was not just dealing with a dumb cop who toiled through an investigation until it was either shelved or the criminal strode into a precinct and gave himself up. He was dealing with Boyd Tyler, shrewd, tough and honest, who just happened to believe that the system as it stood was the best there was. Not only that but he had the citations to back his beliefs.

Remick's hand again strayed towards the pack of cigarettes he had located in his jacket pocket; but he didn't bring it out, just clenched his fist in the pocket.

"Just tell me this," he said to Tyler. "What are these flaws in hypnosis?"

"You already know."

"Tell me again."

"Prejudice in the first place," Tyler said.

"Yours?" Remick couldn't resist it.

"Judges believe that any scientific evidence should have credibility."

"And hypnosis doesn't?"

"I never heard anyone claim that evidence obtained under hypnosis is completely reliable."

"And I never heard anyone claim that evidence obtained under police interrogation was as pure as the driven snow."

"Secondly," said Tyler, and there was an edge to his voice, "there is the danger that, through suggestion, a witness may be persuaded to give false evidence."

"As I've said before, not if the hypnotist knows his job and the guy employed by the New York Police Department does."

"Then there's the danger," Tyler continued inexorably,

"that when the witness comes out of the trance he will have forgotten what he described so it can't be used in court because it's hearsay."

"Granted." Remick knew all about the pitfalls of hearsay, second-hand testimony related outside the courtroom, which defence lawyers grabbed like prospectors searching for gold nuggets. "But surely to Christ it would give you a lead."

"Which is why I will bring in a hypnotist – as a last resort."

"And in any case the witness would probably retain the memory after further inductions."

"And wouldn't defence counsellor just love that? *So when you came out of the trance the first time, Miss Fleming, you couldn't remember a damn thing. Tell me, what pressure was brought to make you remember after that? Just how many times did they have to try to make you say what they wanted you to?*"

Remick shook his head in wonderment. "Boy oh boy, Boyd, sometimes you really are something else! Do you think any judge would allow a cross-examination like that?"

"That's the message the lawyer would get across to the jury."

Saul said to the hovering waiter: "Three more beers please, Patrick." And to Remick: "I've stayed neutral in the past but this time I agree with Boyd."

"What am I supposed to do?" Remick said. "Kneel and repent? Did either of you two know that it has been argued that because a hypno-subject is actually witnessing an incident then it isn't hearsay?"

Tyler said: "I'm glad it's been argued. The fact remains that any jury would be rightly suspicious of a prosecution that had to rely on facts obtained in a trance because it couldn't put its case together any other way." He sipped his beer. "No, John, leave it alone for the time being, huh? What I'm basically saying is that I don't want my case screwed up because of premature use of a technique that's manna from heaven for a smart defence lawyer."

"Voodoo?"

"You know me better than that, John."

Saul said: "And don't forget the fifth and fourteenth

80

amendments. Those could be thrown at you on the grounds of self-incrimination."

Remick changed tack. "Why do you think the girl's lying?"

"I haven't said I did," Tyler told him. "It's a possibility, that's all. What sort of a cop accepts forgetfulness and leaves it at that?"

"They said she was suffering from amnesia at Bellevue."

"It's easy to fake, you should know that."

"And she reckons she was followed in the forest on Boxing Day."

Saul said: "We looked into it and we've given her protection. Maybe she was, maybe she wasn't. Either way it doesn't prove anything."

"It proves something to me. It proves she sought the help of the police. Does that sound like a girl who's covering up?"

Tyler shrugged.

The shrug angered Remick and he said: "Do we have to go by the book because it's another knifing?" and immediately regretted the words. "I'm sorry, Boyd, I didn't mean –"

"I know what you meant and no, it's not because it's another knifing. It's because it's a murder, because it's a crime, and I believe this is the way it should be handled. And because I'm in charge that's the way it's going to be handled."

"I'm sorry," Remick said.

"You're full of shit, John," Tyler said. And walked out of the pub with Saul, leaving Remick with a half-finished beer.

Approaching Twenty-Ninth Street in his Mustang, Remick brooded on the argument. It had contained an incongruity and he couldn't place it. His comment about the knifing had been unforgiveable and today he would apologise again. But there was something else . . .

Not, he thought miserably, that Tyler would *ever* forgive him if he went through with what he had been contemplating to do today. And that quite simply was to betray Tyler; to go over his head and obtain authority to ask Helen Fleming to submit to hypnosis.

If it wasn't Tyler who was in charge of the case, then he wouldn't have hesitated so long. With the murder exciting such attention, with a possible key witness suffering from amnesia, this was the golden opportunity to establish hypnosis as a procedure as acceptable as fingerprinting.

To blow away another of the criminal's smokescreens. To open hooded eyes. Not at the expense of justice, far from it, but at the expense of a hidebound judiciary that was as reactionary as the medical establishment. At the expense of men who throughout history had rejected progress because they felt that it threatened their values. John Remick wished fervently that Tyler wasn't on their side. What was it that had jangled during last night's argument?

He turned into Twenty-Ninth and saw the police cars, three of them with lights flashing, the two uniformed cops outside the liquor store, and the crowd who, he was convinced, would materialise at the scene of a crime if it was committed in outer space. He had a theory that they were always the same spectators, connoisseurs summoned to a felony by some agency to which they subscribed.

As he climbed out of the car carrying his bag, he heard a woman's voice: "Look, there's the doctor. Took his time, didn't he?"

He went into the liquor store. It smelled strongly of whisky. The proprietor, a fat man wearing striped flannelette pyjamas and a grey dressing-gown, was lying beside the cash register amid broken bottle-glass, spilled whisky and blood. The register had been forced; word must have got around that he didn't bother to put his takings in a safe.

There was a bluish dent on the man's temple. He had also been struck in the mouth and his broken dentures were laughing crookedly. Remick tried to make up his mind which blow had been struck first, not that it really mattered.

On the other side of the cash register, beside a cardboard display for a new aperitif which apparently eased those first few 'meeting moments' between a man and a woman, sat a boy of about fifteen.

"Who's that?" Remick asked the detective in charge.

"The dead guy's son."

"Then what the hell's he doing there?"

82

The detective said: "Apparently he followed his father down when he heard a noise here."

"I asked you what he's doing here now?"

"He won't leave," the detective said. "You know, it happened a couple of hours ago. Apparently he's been sitting there ever since. He lived alone with his old man," the detective said. And then: "Say, doc, do you ever think what a tacky life this is?"

"He shouldn't be here," Remick said. "Christ, man, that's his father."

"Can't make that much difference now," the detective said.

"I wonder why they didn't kill him as well?" Remick said savagely.

"Maybe they didn't see him."

Remick went over to the boy and asked softly: "Did you see what happened, son?"

The boy, who wore striped pyjamas too big for him, probably his father's, looked up and said: "I don't remember."

It was then that John Remick made his decision. .

*   *   *

There was a scimitar moon hanging in the cold dawn sky as Remick drove north along First Avenue, past Bellevue where he spent so much of his time. The traffic was heavy now, the speed steady; at Forty-Second, he made a turn and three minutes later parked the Mustang.

Spread out on a glass-topped table in the cramped living-room was Remick's brief on the York killing, which he had been contemplating presenting to the chief of Homicide. Had been: now nothing would stop him.

He made coffee in the kitchen in which, girl friends grumbled, there wasn't room to swing a cat; then he stripped, went into the bathroom and began to shave with the ivory-handled, cut-throat razor that had belonged to his father; it was the only razor that satisfactorily removed his thick, blue-black stubble, and he loved it as other men love a favourite pipe.

As the blade, sharpened on a leather strap hanging from the

wall, sliced through his beard, Remick rehearsed his interview with the chief, Jack Knox, who was newly appointed and reputed to be enlightened. At least I've got that going for me, Remick thought, bringing the blade along his jawbone.

First he would appeal to Knox's reported desire for reform, as yet undefined. On reaching high office other law enforcement officers had in the past voiced such views, only to have them slowly crushed by the system.

Then he would cite crime statistics, cases which might have been reduced if hypnosis had been employed as a memory aid. Then cases in which unbiased authorities had allowed hypnosis – and a conviction had resulted.

The classic case, of course, was the Californian kidnapping when armed and masked men using a white van had stopped a school bus. Under hypnosis the driver had remembered most of the numbers on the van's licence plate and the kidnappers were arrested.

What's more, Remick thought, wiping the blade on a tissue, I will appeal to Knox's fair-mindedness by pointing out that hypnosis can sometimes benefit the defence as much as the prosecution.

He turned on the shower and stepped under the hot, stinging water. At least Boyd Tyler had prepared him for some of the objections that Knox would raise. What was it that Tyler or Saul had said that had lodged in his brain like a splinter?

Frowning, Remick towelled himself briskly, put on a navy-blue robe and went into the living-room where he poured himself more coffee and ate a biscuit, hardly the sort of diet he would have prescribed to a patient.

Holding the brief he proposed to leave with Knox in one hand, THE CASE FOR HYPNOSIS IN THE DANIEL YORK INVESTIGATION, and the cup of coffee in the other, he patrolled his quarters, which were cluttered with an appalling mixture of furnishings – he knew this to be so because he had been told many times – and further confined by a wall of bookshelves, crammed with everything from *Gray's Anatomy* to the latest McBain.

So he had his reasoned argument prepared. But he had yet to

find out if there was an irrational side to Knox: whether to him a hypnotist was still a vaudeville act.

In his bedroom Remick dressed quickly in a dark suit, pale blue shirt with a dark blue neck-tie. He glanced at himself in the mirror and thought: *Svengali*.

As he drove downtown to the Homicide Bureau at 155, Leonard Street, he wondered if there was any faint chance that one day Tyler might forgive him.

He doubted it.

"So what does Lieutenant Tyler think about all this?" Knox asked.

"Not much," Remick said.

"I guessed not. Otherwise you wouldn't be here." Knox leaned back in a leather chair behind an oak desk. "Well, convince me."

He was a big man, about forty-five, hair receding at the temples, eyes very dark with a wary set to them; at some time in his life his nose had been broken and re-set and he looked, Remick thought, like an intelligent, retired prize-fighter.

He was in the process of re-arranging the office on the sixth floor like a newly-elected President stamping his personality on the Oval Office. Diplomas hung on the walls but, judging by the hooks in the blank spaces, Knox didn't own as many as his predecessor. There were two family photographs on the desk; on one side of the room stood a bookshelf, on the other a leather Chesterfield; but whatever Knox did, the room would still look impersonal.

Remick opened his briefcase, took out the brief, crossed his legs and outlined Helen Fleming's role in the Daniel York killing.

"I know all about the case," Knox said.

He might scare policemen but surgeons didn't scare that easily. They had an advantage, medicine. Everyone treated a doctor with a certain amount of respect – Tyler was the exception.

"I realise that, sir, but I figured we had to run over the facts to establish just what we're talking about. And what we're talking about is a girl who in all probability witnessed a murder, suffered congrade amnesia – total loss of recall, that is – but could be persuaded by medical means to identify the killer."

"Medical means, Mr Remick?"

"Yes, sir, medical means. In 1958 hypnosis was accepted by the Council on Mental Health of the American Medical Association."

"Ah, *mental* health."

"Of course. We're dealing with the mind." Perhaps Knox wasn't as enlightened as he was reputed to be.

Knox lit a cigarette; the smoke smelled as good to Remick as coffee and bacon and eggs at breakfast time. He watched Knox inhale with evident satisfaction and thought: "He's coating his lungs with lethal tar." He took a mint from his pocket, and slipped it into his mouth.

Knox placed his cigarette in an ashtray, deep in butts at ten in the morning, and said: "You realise, of course, how the defence would tear into the hypnosis angle, all guns blazing?"

"At the moment we don't have a prosecution let alone a defence."

"Isn't it possible that a subject in a trance would respond to certain cues provided by the hypnotist?"

"That's what it's all about," hoping that his irritation didn't show.

"What I mean is that she could be misdirected. That she would say what she thought the hypnotist wanted her to say. Rapport, I believe, is the thing."

So he knew more about hypnosis than Remick had believed. "It's possible, of course," he said, watching Knox draw on the cigarette again, "but the experienced hypnotist should be able to guard against that. There are three ways in which a hypnotist can restore memory – age regression, hyperamnesia and post-hypnotic suggestion –"

Knox held up a big hand. "Spare me," he said. "I don't want to know *how* a blood analyst tests blood, I just want to know whose blood it is. Forgive me if I'm wrong," as though he rarely was, "but isn't there a danger that after the subject comes out of the trance he – she – will forget again?"

"There is that danger, yes."

"And then that statement obtained outside the court would be inadmissable. Hearsay."

"There are exceptions," Remick said.

"I know, you're going to tell me about such statements forming part of an expert's testimony."

Remick was.

"They'd look pretty damn stupid if the witness herself couldn't remember uttering them."

"There are risks."

"And you know what the greatest of them is?"

"Prejudice," Remick said.

"Damn right. Judges and juries are still suspicious of testimony obtained by polygraphs, narcoanalysis *or hypnosis*. They believe it could be distorted."

"Just as any eye-witness testimony can be, and usually *is*, distorted. Not necessarily deliberately but because human-beings are fallible. They testify to what they thought they saw not what they did see. Sometimes they're just trying to be helpful. What we've got to understand is that a hypnotist is only trying to resurrect forgotten testimony. And what *you* have to decide, sir, is whether we're going to innovate or stagnate."

"You should have been a lawyer, not a doctor." Knox squashed his cigarette into the heap of butts.

"But this case could establish hypno-induced testimony once and for all."

"Or kill it stone dead."

"It would get incredible publicity. *Beautiful Model To Re-live Murder*, that sort of thing."

"You should have been a journalist, not a lawyer or a doctor."

"And so hypnotism and the law will have a world-wide forum."

"If she remembers."

"If you're progressive you take risks."

"Okay," Knox said, "let's take them."

"Whew!" Remick slumped back in his chair and chewed his mint.

Knox said: "But aren't you dramatising the whole thing just a little? Evidence obtained under hypnosis was admitted in a case in upstate New York in 1979."

"But not a case of any great significance," Remick said.

Knox consulted a duty roster on his desk. "Did you know that our official hypnotist, a sergeant, has flown to Dallas to help out in a case down there?"

Remick nodded. "But a hypnotherapist named Hansom has agreed to deputise in an emergency. A case like this will establish a precedent." He picked up his brief. "Do you mind if I quote from an authority?"

Knox waved his hand. "Go ahead."

"From the *Ohio State Law Journal*. 'Until very recently the impact of hypnosis upon the law of evidence was miniscule; the phenomenon was judicially ignored because it was reputed to be merely a device for ascertaining truth and detecting deception.' "

"And?"

Remick frowned. "It's self-explanatory."

Knox picked up a document from his desk; he smiled faintly. "The *Ohio State Law Journal*. The paragraph you have quoted concludes: 'Most authorities agree that a general rule of reliability of the veracity of statements elicited during hypnosis cannot be formulated.' "

Remick raised his hands. "Your round, sir."

Knox said: "One other thing bothers me."

"Tyler?"

"He's a good cop, one of the best we've got, and you've gone over his head. I believe you and he are – were – buddies?" dark eyes watching Remick.

"Were, I guess."

"Then you tell him, huh?"

Remick said he would; it was the least he could do.

VIII

"Just one more," said the willowy young photographer.

The words were printed on her mind.

"Relax the pressure of your fingers just a little. You're muscling out the ball of your thumb."

She relaxed the grip on the Waterford wine glass, half-filled with red Spanish *Rioja*.

"Okay, that's fine. Hold it. Just one more."

The studio lamps found pink and crimson lights in the crystal. She blinked her eyes; the skin felt taut on her face.

That was the trouble with modelling hands – feet for that matter – you tended to neglect other areas. This morning she should have had a facial but her hands had taken precedence.

Her great fear since she began modelling had been sustaining some sort of injury to her hands. A fracture that deformed a finger; a blow that turned a nail blue-black; a burn that scarred. Then where would I be? Helen Fleming wondered. Deprived of my means of income. A painter without a brush, a sculptor without clay.

That had been Daniel York's fear; that, without his youth, with *the smile* folded in ageing skin, he was nothing. Poor Daniel York. The nightmare returned.

"C'mon," the photographer entreated. "Like I said, relax. You look as if you're hanging onto a lifeline or something. That's better, that's much better. . ." The shutter of the Roliflex clicked. "Just one more."

Since the incident in the forest up north, since she had driven back to the city followed by Katy Tanner and her boyfriend, there had been no evidence of any further threat.

But she knew it was there, it had to be because according to the police she might have witnessed a murder; that had to be the reason for that second set of tracks in the snow, and nothing had changed. Except, perhaps, that the killer knew she couldn't remember and hoped she never would.

"You're getting uptight again," the photographer said.

How could the killer know that she couldn't remember? She had told the police that she had been followed in the forest. She wasn't sure that they had believed her but Sargeant Saul had promised her police protection. In return for that, he had suggested she should co-operate. For a while she had been puzzled by the remark. Then it had dawned on her: *They don't believe I can't remember.* If only she could, if only . . . And then she realised that, if she did, the murderer would have good cause to kill her.

"Now," said the photographer, "let's turn that ring a little so we get the light shining through the wine sparkling on the diamonds."

"What are we advertising," she asked, "diamond rings or Spanish wine?"

"That's it," he said. "That's great. That's hot. Hold it just like that, baby."

The girl who was doing PR for the Spanish wine company came into the studio without knocking and said: "There's a Mr Remick to see you, Helen," and the photographer said: "Fine, crash in any time, I'm surprised you didn't walk into the picture."

"I'm sorry," said the girl, but she didn't look it.

"What does he want?" Helen asked. "Who is he?"

"He's a dream," the girl said.

"Apart from that?"

"He's from the police."

Helen Fleming shivered.

"And now one with your wrist drooping a little," the

photographer said. "You know, *nonchalant*. Right, that's great. Hold it. Just one more."

* * *

They walked north along Park Avenue from Forty-Sixth Street. Walked because after the session with the wine glass she was tired of sitting down and she needed the exercise. But she felt a little sorry for Remick because it was still very cold and he was wearing only a suit.

"Where are we going?" he asked, hands dug deep in his trouser pockets.

"Sixtieth," she said. "I've got another photo call there."

"You work hard," he said.

"Models do. Contrary to public opinion."

"You sure you wouldn't care for a coffee?"

"Quite sure. You can ask me whatever you want now. You are a detective, I presume?"

"No, ma'am, I'm a doctor."

"A doctor?" She glanced at him. His face was pink with the cold but with his black hair, as black as a cat's, and his eager face and his greenish eyes he exuded such energy that he didn't look cold. Now that he had said it he did look like a doctor, she decided, not a detective. "A police doctor?"

He nodded. "I want your help." Remick didn't waste words, she thought.

They rounded a group of Japanese tourists with a guide, who was pointing out the Pan Am skyscraper. The sidewalk was crowded and everyone was in a hurry to get out of the cold. The sky was a bleak strip, the feel of the day decidedly post-Christmas, the snow on the Christmas trees on the traffic islands soiled.

She waited for him to continue.

"I believe Lieutenant Tyler told you he thought you might have witnessed the murder of Daniel York."

"He *thought* I might have, yes. I don't know that I agree with him."

"But there is a possibility?"

Yes, she said, there was a possibility.

"So there is also a possibility that you could identify the killer."

"Except that I can't remember anything."

"With help," Remick said urgently, "you could remember. That's why I've come to see you." He stopped, took her arm. "Would you be willing to undergo hypnosis, Miss Fleming?"

"Perhaps," she said, "I will have that coffee after all."

But she had a fresh orange juice instead and he had tea with lemon in a noisy diner filling up with the early-lunch crowd. They faced each other across a brown Formica-topped table.

"Did you know," she said, "that Park Avenue used to be one of the dirtiest and noisiest places in New York before they electrified the railroad in 1907? I majored in history," she said, watching him squeeze the teabag with his spoon.

"There would be nothing to be frightened about," he said. "It's a very simple process. It's used all the time when people have lost their memory."

"Maybe my memory will just come back of its own accord."

"And maybe by that time it will be too late."

She drank some orange juice through a straw. "Isn't it unusual for a police surgeon to be as active as this in an investigation?"

"A little. But hypnosis is a branch of medicine."

"Didn't I read somewhere that it is still treated with suspicion by some doctors?"

"Come on," Remick said, "anyone who's anyone has their own shrink these days."

They were joined at the table by an elderly couple drinking vegetable soup and eating bread-rolls. While he munched his roll the man warmed his hands on his soup bowl.

The man said: "No two ways about it, I'm taking him to court. He cut that tree down without my permission and he's gonna pay for it."

"Have you thought of the legal fees?" the woman asked. "Have you thought of those? Forget it, Harry, forget it." She sucked soup noisily from her spoon.

Helen asked: "Is this your idea?"

"It won't be the first time it's been done."

"That wasn't what I asked," she said.

"Well, yes, it is my idea." His eyes searched her face.

"Why didn't Lieutenant Tyler ask me if I would undergo hypnosis?"

The man named Harry dropped a piece of roll in his soup. "That was my tree," he said. "He had no right. In any case the lawyer only takes his cut if I win."

"But he's always been a good neighbour," the woman said. "He just had a thing about that tree . . ."

Remick said: "I'll level with you. Tyler doesn't approve. He's a good cop but –"

"Old-fashioned?"

"Not even that. He just has his way of doing things."

"Is he a successful cop?"

"One of the best."

"Then why not let him carry on doing things his way?"

"Because on this one he's way out. It's obvious, isn't it. If you saw the killing –"

The old man faltered in his condemnation of his neighbour, rheumy eyes staring at Remick.

" – Then you should be helped to remember."

"What's Tyler's argument against it?" Helen asked, seeking an argument she could use.

"He reckons hypnosis would prejudice a jury and possibly a judge."

"Maybe he's right," Helen said.

"That's not the point. They shouldn't *be* prejudiced. If we can solve a big case like this, a case that's caught the public's imagination, and if we can clinch it in court, then we've gone a long way towards ending that prejudice."

"Look," she said, "just because I was found wandering on Fifth Avenue the night Daniel York was killed doesn't mean to say I saw the killing."

"That's what we would find out," Remick said.

". . . Claims it was his tree," said the woman, looking from Remick to Helen.

93

Helen said: "I think we should give Tyler a chance to do it his way."

"You surprise me," Remick said.

"No I don't. That's what you thought I'd say."

"I thought you *might* say that. When I saw you I thought no, this girl is intelligent, this girl will want to help."

"You can cut out the bullshit," she said. "And if they ever ask *you* to go in for psychiatry, forget it."

Interest in the tree was gaining ascendancy again until Remick said: "Has it occurred to you that the murderer, whoever he was, could kill again?"

"No, but —"

"And in a way you would be an accessory to that murder?"

"That's not fair."

Remick finished his tea, picked up the slice of lemon and bit into it. "I believe that violence in this country *can* be controlled. I believe that we're all too goddam complacent about it. You know, the it-couldn't-happen-to-me syndrome. If you see a guy being beaten to death hurry past, forget it, it didn't happen."

"And that's what I'm like?"

"Not you, your sub-conscious."

"So why should I be at odds with my sub-conscious?"

"Fear," Remick told her.

"So I'm like your law-abiding citizen who sees a beating and walks past it?"

"You want me to be frank?"

"I can't imagine you any other way," she said.

"By refusing to submit to hypnotherapy you *are* ducking an issue. You're collaborating with your sub-conscious."

The old eyes of the man drinking soup lost interest again. "I wouldn't have minded if it had been just any tree. But, Jesus, a red mulberry."

"I didn't like that tree," the woman said.

"Maybe you put him up to it?"

"I'm glad it's gone."

Remick said: "Don't you understand? There could be another killing. Another —"

"Maybe you . . ." the old man's voice tailed off again.

"Knifing," Remick said.

Neither the old man nor the woman spoke.

Remick said: "Perhaps we could talk someplace else."

Helen looked at the black-and-gold quartz wristwatch which Peter Lodge had given her for her birthday. "I don't know. I have to go, I'm late already."

"Come on, let's go," Remick said.

As they left the table Helen heard the woman say: "Did you hear that, Harry? Maybe we should tell the police."

At Fifty-Seventh Helen crossed the avenue towards the Ritz Tower. Remick guided her, his hand lightly on her arm.

"How about dinner?" he asked when they reached the sidewalk. "Somewhere where we can talk about it."

She considered. Peter was in Los Angeles discussing a deal to open a Hollywood boutique. There could be no harm done, police business.

"Very well officer," she said. "When?"

"Tonight?" And when she nodded: "I'll pick you up at seven. I know where you live."

"Just one thing," she said. "Do you think he should have cut that tree down?"

Her smile lingered until she reached the photographer's studio on Sixtieth. Of course Remick was right about fear. But fear of what he didn't seem to grasp. Fear that if the killer thought she might identify him he would kill her.

* * *

The following day, a Saturday, Helen went cycling in Central Park. Cycling, she considered, was less boring, more dignified and much safer than jogging – a park freak would have to be an Olympic sprinter to catch a bike with a whole range of gears.

She tied her hair in bunches and put on a pale blue track suit. Hardly the model image. But what people tended to forget when they opened *Vogue* and saw an ice-cool blonde in a Dior gown sipping a Campari at Monte Carlo, was that the girl had to keep fit.

95

The bicycle was a Dutch import. A fold-up that fitted into the back of her car. Its paintwork was crimson and its shining chrome reflected the sky which today was blue. To the front fender was attached a penant bearing a picture of Wonder Woman which she intended to remove.

She left the car in a parking lot off the East Drive and set off on her cycle southwards towards the lake.

It really was a beautiful morning. The sky was metallic-bright and the wings of snow on the grass were glistening in the sunlight as they melted. And there was a briskness about the park that was lacking on public holidays. The voices of the children were sharp, adults walked as though in a hurry to keep appointments, kites snapped in the breeze and even the barking dogs had a purpose about them. To her left was the statue of Alice in Wonderland, ahead somewhere Hans Christian Andersen. This was how old Frederick Olmsted had intended his park to be long before the muggers and bag-snatchers moved in, and it was difficult to accept that today anything vicious might occur in this sunlit place.

As she pedalled she contemplated what had happened the previous evening.

Remick had taken her to the Ground Floor on West Fifty-Second and they had eaten by candlelight at a table on which stood a red carnation in an ebony vase. Lobster for her, gammon for him. And he hadn't told her what beautiful hands she had. Instead he had told her how healthy she looked which had pleased her. On the first glass of wine he had said there was no point in ruining the whole meal by postponing the question of hypnosis until the coffee.

That, she decided, was what she liked about him, his directness. In him it wasn't a naive quality; he struck her more as a man who had been youthfully forthright, had experimented with worldliness and rejected it; in other words he had passed through three stages of development whereas so many men she met never passed beyond stage two.

As a prelude he lectured her about crime prevention and the prevailing attitudes in the United States – in the world for that matter – in which violence was dismissed as a necessary evil. In fact, he said, crime statistics were sometimes related with faint pride. "A murder every twenty-four minutes somewhere in the States, ladies and gentlemen," adopting a tough TV cop's voice. That was what we had to rid ourselves of first, tolerance.

"And then?"

"We've got to get to the children when they're still young enough to be guided. When they still trust adults. Before we become THEM. Did you know that half of the crimes in the United States are committed by juveniles? And that the peak age for violent crime is fifteen?"

Helen said: "It's pathetic, isn't it."

"And did you know that someone once estimated that by the time a kid was fourteen he could have witnessed 11,000 murders on television?"

He paused while the waiter deposited a succulent-looking lobster in front of her and a gammon steak with pineapple in front of him.

Slicing off a corner of gammon, he said: "Our criminal laws are a mess, too. They favour the criminal. If you're a burglar, whoopee – your chances of going to jail for a robbery were 1 in 412, probably less now. There are some 94,000 felony arrests each year in New York City and yet only between 5000 and 6000 people go to jail for them."

"So what reforms are needed?" she asked.

"Basically the departments have got to be integrated. Police, prosecutors, judges, prison officers . . . Then we've got to tackle problems like premature parole, free-and-easy bail that allows criminals back onto the streets, derisive prison sentences and crazy plea bargaining. Some authorities believe that if there was more room in the jails all those problems would be solved."

"And the gun laws?" In her experience most men who fulminated about crime were evasive about firearms. "I read somewhere that there are fifty-five million handguns circulating in the States – one for every four citizens."

"That goes without saying, they've got to be reformed. And many other not-so-obvious aspects of a system that's out-grown itself. Delays in the administration of justice, for instance. Today the average lapse between time of arrest and trial is eight months."

She cracked a lobster claw with the pincers. "Isn't all this much more important than hypnosis?"

"I'm not denying that; hypnosis merely happens to be my line of country. I don't suggest we're going to be iconoclasts: I do suggest that we'll be helping to break up resistance to change."

"But hypnosis used to obtain evidence could be abused, couldn't it?"

"Of course. Just as any testimony can be. But if testimony has been obtained by a hypnotist then he would have to give evidence about his technique and the depth of trance obtained."

"Surely a subject could fake a trance?"

"It's possible. Just as an ordinary witness can lie. But, just like the conventional witness, he would be cross-examined about what he claims to have remembered."

"And the hypnotist. Couldn't he be got at?"

"Sure. So can a police officer. We'd just have to make damn sure that he was incorruptible."

"Perhaps I didn't see anything," she said.

"You saw something that put you into a state of shock. When you were found on Fifth Avenue, you weren't walking home: you were escaping."

He picked up his glass of wine. His hands, she noted, were powerful, fingers on the short side. You could be very wrong about hands; people supposed that concert pianists had long, slender fingers, the only one she had met had possessed podgy hands with dimpled knuckles.

While he sipped his wine she studied his face. Half Irish, half Italian, she decided; a physician's cool with a hint of impetuosity about the eyes. He needed a shave and he was wearing the same suit he had worn that morning.

He smiled at her: "I was called out on a case, I didn't have time to go home."

"You're a mind-reader as well as a doctor."

He put down his glass of wine. "Whoever killed Daniel York might kill again," he said.

"If he thinks I can identify him, he would kill me."

"I know what happened up north. You could have been mistaken."

"There were two sets of tracks," she said.

"Which doesn't mean anyone wanted to kill you. Nothing's happened since?"

"Maybe he knows I can't remember."

"As soon as you do," Remick said, "whoever you saw will be put under surveillance, arrested maybe."

"It would be ironic, wouldn't it," she said as the waiter refilled her glass, "if I couldn't remember but the murderer thought I could."

He rested his chin on his hands and stared at her. "Your mind," he said, "is a picture gallery. In it are the portraits of your life. Everyone you've ever known. Some of the pictures have faded with time, but they're there just the same. One portrait is covered with drapes. You, your sub-conscious mind that is, have put them there." He leaned forward, looking at her intently. "We have to remove those drapes."

The drapes moved in a breeze and she trembled and he touched her hand and said: "I'm sorry, that was a little dramatic."

"As bedside manners go," she said, "it was different."

"The reformer's zeal, I guess."

"Do you want to change history?"

"Legal history, yes. Why not? It needs it."

"So there *is* a personal motive."

He smiled at her. "I'm afraid there is."

She had capitulated over the dessert.

She left East Drive at the Loeb boathouse and cycled beside the frozen lake to Bethesda Fountain. Beside the band-stand a group of youths were strumming guitars and snapping their fingers to the beat.

"Hey," shouted one, "there goes Wonder Woman." She waved to them.

It wasn't until she was cycling down the Mall between the

99

leafless elms and the busts of the famous that she became aware of another cyclist about fifty yards behind her.

There were other cyclists around, it was true, but when she had glanced behind her before, she had seen the same man on a bicycle. At least she thought it was the same man, black and wearing a tartan windcheater.

She changed gear. The pedals stiffened, the cycle surged forward. She looked behind her. The man on the bike was still behind her, the distance between them about the same. No, she thought, not on a day like this. She pedalled faster, leg muscles aching. She burst through a knot of camera-wielding tourists who shouted at her and brandished their cameras.

The man on the bicycle did the same.

I don't believe it, she thought. I just don't believe it. She whimpered. She was panting and there was an ache in her chest.

The man was gaining on her. When she looked round again she thought for a moment that he was grinning; but no, his teeth were bared with the strain of keeping up with her.

She rounded a couple walking arm in arm, so engrossed with each other that they barely noticed her. A boy chasing a ball ran across her path; she swerved, nearly fell, cycled on.

Ahead was a group of teenagers, punching and laughing and chasing each other. She slowed down fractionally and pointed behind her: "That man's . . . trying . . . to kill me . . ."

"Wow," they shouted, "it's Wonder Woman."

"Please . . . stop . . . him." The wind snatched her words.

"Put on those pants, Wonder Woman. Come on, you gotta win. Wonder Woman never loses."

To her right lay the Sheep Meadow, far away to her left the towers of Fifth Avenue. If she could reach the end of the Mall and cycle onto the driveway again she might see a patrolling police car. Except that she couldn't pedal like this much longer.

In a way it was more terrifying than it had been in the forest. More brutal and callous here in the park among all these people. On a Saturday morning.

She looked behind her. He was still there. Pain knifed her

chest. She couldn't make the end of the Mall. She braked. The machine shuddered and slowed down; she wheeled round in an arc and cycled straight at the man on the bike.

His face was contorted with shock but he still looked big and black and lethal. He tried to avoid her but she kept at him. The bikes collided, locked, crashed to the ground together. She tried to get up to run but her leg was trapped.

The man groaned and sat up. "Holy shit," he said, chest heaving, "Wonder Woman! They should've warned me."

She struggled to get free. "The police," she said, "they're following me." Her voice broke.

"*Were* following you," he said. He produced a shield. "Detective Harcourt," he said.

When she asked him later how he had managed to find a bicycle to follow her, he told her he had stolen it.

*　　*　　*

She went to bed early that night.

She saw an old man with a wicked face wearing a floppy bow-tie, standing beside a painting covered with drapes. The picture was huge, almost floor to ceiling, and in his hand the old man held a golden rope.

There was a crowd of a hundred or so gathered there for the unveiling of the picture which was called *The Revelation*. Helen waited with pleasurable anticipation. The old man opened his mouth, which was full of broken teeth, and uttered some words to her, but she couldn't catch what he said. Suddenly, while he was still staring at her and mouthing inaudible words, he pulled the rope and she saw the picture, a portrait. She tried to scream, tried frantically . . .

The telephone on the bedside table shrilled. Still shaking, she switched on the lamp and picked up the receiver.

"Mrs Jacobson?" A man's voice.

"No," Helen said. She tried to control her breathing. "I'm not Mrs Jacobson."

"Is Mrs Jacobson there?"

"You've got the wrong number." She hung up the receiver.

101

She closed her eyes again to see if the portrait returned. But all she could see was dark red light with the shape of the bedside lamp printed on it. Probably she didn't want to see it; that's what John Remick would have said. In any case, had she recognised the subject of the portrait in the dream?

She glanced at the alarm clock. Two am. She went into the kitchen and poured herself a glass of cold milk. She drank it slowly, making it last; then she finished off some tinned pineapple, left over from supper, and poured herself another glass of milk which she took back to bed with her.

She picked up the weekend edition of the *New York Times* from beside the bed and extracted the travel section. Perhaps a holiday would help. She would ask Peter about it.

She stared at a photograph of Knossos in Crete. Why had Peter been so reluctant to give the police the names of the last guests at the party? And had he been the first of them to leave?

The questions, of course, had been lodged in her mind since Christmas Day, only she had refused to consider them. But at two in the morning her will-power was weak.

So I might as well examine *all* the questions, she thought, and then I'll be able to sleep peacefully. The police obviously considered the prime suspects to be the last guests at the party. Peter – she shut her eyes and dropped the travel section – Carl Cortoni, Marty Padget and Earl Winters.

Well, with the exception of Cortoni, whom she barely knew, she didn't think any of them were capable of stabbing a man to death.

Certainly not Peter who, despite his occasional depressions, was a gentle and considerate man. (Although he could surely have seen her home that night.) Not Marty Padget who, when he wasn't flexing his muscles, was also a kindly person. And not Earl Winters who was probably the kindest man she knew. His agency wasn't among the top six agencies such as Ford, Wilhelmina, Elite or Zoli, but in the closed circuit of Manhattan fashion he was respected – and regarded with awe because, with his old-fashioned apartment and undistinguished clothes, he didn't conform.

Not only that, but in addition to supplying models for the

studios of high fashion he also owned a wholesale business in the Garment Center that provided cloth for decidedly down-market clothing outlets.

In the eighteen months she had known him, he had succeeded in placing her in a bracket where she could earn $1000 to $1500 a day. She would never be a Christie Brinkley or an Apollonia or, for that matter, a Brooke Shields who at the age of fifteen had earned $10,000 a day, but her income was sufficiently large to be a continual source of amazement to her.

Earl Winters had been responsible for getting her that sort of money; he had also prepared her for the society into which she had moved.

"You're all using your bodies," he had told her. "You have all in some way or another been blessed. But never regard your assets as anything more than tools of your trade. That way you will stay level-headed. Remember that one day those tools will wear a little thin, so even now start preparing for that day. And as for that money I've got you – bank it!"

Peter, her discoverer, had also helped her to adapt. In business he was more obviously dynamic than Earl, but he was just as level-headed . . .

No, someone had come up to that apartment after the party. While the lobby doors were open and, so she had learned from John Remick, while the porter had been busy losing the twenty dollars she had given him.

What convinced her that neither Peter, Earl nor Padget could have killed York was that if she had witnessed the murder, she would surely have remembered their faces because she had seen them since.

Cortoni? Well, he wasn't in quite the same category, but surely there would have been some sort of association of images because she had met him only a few hours before the killing.

For one heart-stopping moment she wondered if *she* could have killed York. If, perhaps, he had attacked her and, in self-defence, she had grabbed the knife and . . .

But no, there would have been blood on her hands. And in a state of panic-induced amnesia you didn't stop and wipe your fingerprints from the handle of a knife.

She switched out the light. She felt isolated. Alone in solitary confinement on the top floor of a teeming jail-house. Under surveillance. Probably a policeman sitting in his car in the street below. Probably . . .

The telephone rang. She found it without switching on the light.

"Helen?"

"Yes," she said, "who is it?" In the background she could hear music and laughter.

"It's me, Peter, in Los Angeles. Did I wake you?"

"Yes," she said, "you woke me but it doesn't matter." Relief expanded inside her; she smiled in the darkness, then switched on the light.

"What time is it there?"

"Two-thirty but it doesn't matter, Peter. Just go on talking."

"Are you okay, honey?"

"Yes, I'm fine. How did the business go?"

"Just great." His voice faded and she heard him saying: "Hey, don't drown it, Sal," and then, louder: "Are you still there?"

"Yes," she said, "I'm still here. Where are you?"

"A party to clinch the deal. We're opening up in Hollywood, honey. Isn't that great?"

"Wonderful, Peter. I'm happy for you."

"This is a party to clinch the deal," he repeated, his voice a little slurred. "What time did you say it was there?"

"The wee small hours," she said, "but I'm so glad you called."

"I'll be back on Monday."

"Can't you make it tomorrow?"

"Tomorrow's Sunday," he said.

"So it is." What difference did that make?

"Is everything okay?"

"I'm being hypnotised," she said to jolt him.

"You're being what?"

"Hypnotised."

104

"I'm afraid I don't understand. Is this some sort of gag?"
She explained.

When he spoke again his voice sounded less slurred. "Are you sure it's a good idea?" he asked.

"If I can identify the killer, then it must be a good idea. Although I must admit I had my doubts to begin with."

"Who persuaded you?"

She could imagine his face becoming closed in, watchful.

"A police surgeon named John Remick. He took me out to dinner."

"As I understand it," he said slowly, "the big snag is that when you're being hypnotised you react to suggestions without even realising it. In other words you could identify the wrong man and it wouldn't be your fault. Nor the hypnotist's for that matter."

"You've been reading about it?" she asked.

In a softer voice he said: "No, not right now, Sal, I'm on the telephone. See this? This is a telephone." In a louder voice he said: "Sure I've been reading about it. It's always been a possiblity."

Always? But he had never mentioned it. She said: "Anyway I'm going through with it. I'll tell you all the pros and cons when you get back."

"Okay," he said, "if you're happy with the idea."

"Why didn't you want to tell the police the names of the last guests?" She surprised herself: she hadn't intended to ask him.

"I didn't catch that, honey. Speak up, huh?"

She repeated the question and he said: "This is a helluva time to be asking questions like that." A pause. "But if it's worrying you . . . I just didn't want to involve guys who couldn't possibly have had anything to do with it. Marty Padget, for God's sake, and old Earl . . ."

"And Carl Cortoni?"

"Well, not him so much."

"You were protecting me, too, weren't you?" The words kept spilling out un-prompted.

"I just didn't want them, the police that is, getting at you when you were still −"

105

"Disturbed," she said.

"Anyway," he said, "I've got to go now."

"Can't you talk a little longer?"

"Well, okay, but I've got a few ends to tie up."

"I miss you," she said.

"And I miss you. What sort of a guy was this police doctor?"

"John Remick? Intelligent, civilised."

"And very persuasive," he said.

"Are you sure you can't make it tomorrow?"

"No way. You know I would if I could. Why don't you invite Katy round? Or go and see Earl?" There was a sound as though he was drinking. "I've really got to go now, honey. Take care."

"Goodbye, Peter," she said, cradling the cream receiver.

She switched out the light again and lay back on the pillows. Surely he could have got back tomorrow; he knew about the incident in the forest, knew she was scared. He hadn't even asked her how she was; well, *Are you okay, honey?* Big deal.

She curled up the way she used to when she was a child, hands tucked against her breasts, like a squirrel, she thought. What she feared most was *remembering* while she lay here alone. Suddenly seeing what the police believed she had seen. Suddenly knowing. She closed her eyes.

A black man on a yellow motorcycle was chasing her. She was also on a motorcycle, revving the engine, bursting through the crowd listening to Abba on the bandstand in Central Park, knocking screaming children aside.

The black man was gaining on her. He was standing on the foot-rests. From his black leather jacket he drew a gun and aimed it at her.

There was an explosion and her bike veered into a group of teenagers. The bullet must have hit the tyre. She saw the terrified faces of the teenagers looming up at her . . .

The phone rang. Peter! Saying yes he could come back tomorrow.

She found the receiver. "Hallo," she said. "Peter?"

"Hallo, is that Mrs Jacobson?"

"You have the wrong number," she said. "Please, please don't call again," and replaced the receiver.

This time she slept and didn't wake until 10 am on the Sunday morning. The light slanting in through the blinds was bright and she knew the sky was blue.

She poured herself a glass of orange juice, made coffee and buttered herself a croissant. When she pulled up the blinds the sky *was* blue, but she could tell it was cold the way the pigeons were again huddled beside the air-conditioner, peering into the living-room. The street below was almost deserted. A man was sitting at the wheel of a car parked outside the next block. A policeman?

She watered the 'jungle' and polished the foliage with a liquid called *Leafer*. Then she went to the bathroom to attend to her hands.

The phone rang at three minutes past eleven.

"I thought I'd let you sleep late," Earl Winters said.

She smiled at the telephone; his voice was as good as a tranquiliser. She sat in an easy-chair to talk to him.

"Any more trouble?" he asked. "I was going to call you last night but I thought you'd probably gone to bed with a sleeping pill."

"I wish you had," she said. "Anyway, you've called now. And no, there hasn't been any more trouble." She decided not to tell him about the cycle chase; she didn't come out of it too well.

"Done your hands?"

"Just finished," she said.

"That's a good girl. As a reward I've got good news for you. I've sold your face as well as your hands this time."

She put one hand to her cheek.

Winters said: "And you're touching your face now, aren't you?"

"Who wants to use my face?"

"A gentleman of excellent taste – the guy who runs Bloomingdale's catalogue."

"Is it one of those 'before and after' ads and I'm the before?"

"You've got a striking face," he said.

107

"Like an axe," she said.

"You have a beautiful face, my dear, and don't you forget it. I guess it's my fault to a degree; you know, concentrating on your hands so much. No, this is a break-through. Face and hands. They say you have an arrogant look, did you know that?"

"How wrong can you get?"

"Well, that's what they say. Arrogant and sexy. In fact, another client went a little further."

"Really? What did he say?"

"She." A pause while, she guessed, Earl edited what the client had said. "She said it would be every man's ambition to break down that arrogance and –" Another pause.

"And make me swear like a Parisian whore?"

"Something like that," he said.

"Too bad I can't speak French."

He laughed. She imagined him sitting in his awful sitting-room wearing some moth-eaten, old dressing-gown. His wife was probably at the studio over the florist's; it was rumoured that Earl and his wife didn't get along.

He said: "What's more, Santini is your make-up man."

"Wow," she said, because Santini was one of the top men in his profession.

"And that's not all the good news."

"I can't take any more."

"You haven't had too much of it lately," he said. "But on Wednesday you can pack your bag for Rome. I mentioned it at the party. Remember?"

"You're kidding." To date she had never been asked to follow the trail of top American models to Europe. Why should anyone want to import hands?

"For the Italian *Harper's Bazaar*," he told her. "They're doing a special feature on hands and they want the best hands available."

"Rome," she said. "How beautiful. Thank you, Earl."

"Think nothing of it, the commission comes in handy."

A devastating thought struck her. "Oh God!" she exclaimed. "What day did you say?"

"Wednesday. Tuesday if you want to take a look round the Eternal City, but you'll have to pay your own expenses for the extra day."

"Can't it be some other time?"

"No it can't," an edge to his voice. "What is it, Helen?"

She told him that she had to see a hypnotist. She knew it sounded stupid.

"A shrink? What the hell for?"

She told him about Remick's idea.

"Can't it wait, for Chrissake?"

"I have to start on Monday, tomorrow. One session a day. John – Remick that is – says the approach has to be very gentle. Until I finally remember . . ."

"Do they really think you saw the murderer?"

"Well, I suppose it is just possible . . ."

"Nonsense," he said, "you'd have remembered by now. A murder, Christ! It's not like forgetting your laundry list."

"Well, that's what they think and I've promised –"

"Call them up," he snapped. "Postpone it. You're entitled to your own life, to your career."

"I could try," she said without much hope. Rome. The one city which, above all, she had always wanted to visit.

"You do that," he said, 'and call me back. Good grief, Helen, this is a wonderful opportunity. You know, maybe the Romans will go for your face, too."

She found Remick's visiting card in her purse and called him. "First," she said, "thank you for the dinner."

"And you've changed your mind?" His voice was brisk.

"No, it's not that," and she explained about Rome.

He said: "It's your choice. Which is more important? Identifying a murderer who might kill again or displaying your hands to the Italians?"

"You win," she said and hung up because John Remick didn't have the monopoly on brusqueness.

When she told Earl Winters he sounded more resigned than angry and she hoped that he understood.

But Rome . . . She looked at her hands. John Remick hadn't even noticed them.

IX

New Year's Eve. Monday.

In addition to Helen Fleming, who at 3 pm was due to meet the hypnotist, it was a day of tension and emotion for several other people connected with the York killing.

For John Remick, Lieutenant Boyd Tyler, Carlos Cortoni and the male model, Marty Padget.

Remick was excited about the outcome of Helen Fleming's first session with the hypnotist but he had been warned not to expect too much from the initial treatment; in fact, he had been told that there was no guarantee she would ever remember. He was also apprehensive about meeting Tyler.

The meeting, in Remick's apartment, was not as bitter as Remick had feared; but in a way it was worse, heavy with reproach. It was only as Tyler was preparing to leave that he voiced his feelings.

"You know, John, you didn't have to go over my head."

"And you know damn well, Boyd, that you would never have agreed to it."

"I'm not that stupid. I would have used hypnosis when I was good and ready. But I figure I could have nailed this one without resorting to it. Now the use of a shrink will swing the trial against us. And supposing the girl is lying?"

"That's what we'll find out."

Tyler shook his head. "No, she'll go on lying." He opened

110

the door of the apartment. "And next time you cheat, John, let me know well in advance. If there is a next time," he added as he closed the door.

For a while Remick prowled the apartment brooding on the conversation. So Tyler would have called in a hypnotist. Or would he? Of course he would, eventually. Now you're deceiving yourself, John Remick. Whatever else he might be, Boyd Tyler isn't dumb. But he hadn't in that rape case; although that had been different – Tyler had tried for a conviction without forcing the girl to recall any more of the horror she had witnessed because he thought she had remembered enough.

For the first time Remick doubted his beliefs. Perhaps the York killing could be solved without hypnosis. But doubt was the cross he would have to bear.

He wanted a cigarette. Instead he took a peppermint from a bowl on the table and slipped it into his mouth.

So Tyler still wasn't convinced that Helen Fleming had lost her memory. Somehow this tied up with the inconsistency that had surfaced in their previous conversation; surfaced but submerged again before it could be identified.

Remick frowned. Then he had it. Saul had mentioned the fourth and fifteenth amendments. But those, as he had said, referred to self-incrimination. Tyler and Saul believed that Helen Fleming might have killed York!

The peppermint snapped between his teeth.

*   *   *

At 11.05 that morning a ruggedly handsome detective named Edmund Sheehan left the Homicide Bureau on the pretext of buying a particular brand of cigars. He bought the stogies, just in case, then went to a call box and telephoned Miguel Cortoni at his office on Maiden Lane in the Financial District.

Cortoni's personal secretary said Mr Cortoni was taking a day off and when Sheehan asked if that meant he was at his Manhattan penthouse or his home on Long Island, she said guardedly that she really couldn't say as though the existence

111

of the two addresses was a classified secret.

"Who shall I say called?"

Sheehan hung up, consulted his black notebook in which he had entered Cortoni's name in code and called his Manhattan number.

Cortoni answered.

"It's Brady, Mr Cortoni," Sheehan said.

"Hold it." A pause, followed by a click as Cortoni took the call in another part of the penthouse. "What have you got, Brady?"

"Something I thought you should know about the York killing."

Sheehan could hear Cortoni's breathing. "Yeah? What makes you think I'm so interested in the York murder?"

"Because your son was at the party, right?"

"So were a helluva lot of other people."

"Do you want to know or don't you?" asked Sheehan who sometimes got disgusted with himself. "You were keen enough when I told you that the Fleming girl was supposed to have seen the killing."

"Okay, okay, give."

"This is two hundred and fifty bucks' worth."

"I'll decide how much it's worth."

"No more, no less," Sheehan said wearily. "Is it a deal?"

"It's a deal."

"It's about the Fleming broad."

"I thought you said she'd lost her memory."

"Sure she lost it. But they're going to try and get it back for her. She's going to a hypnotist, Mr Cortoni."
found department."

"How do you want the money?"

"The usual way," Sheehan said.

Five minutes later Cortoni took a cab to the boutique on Lexington where his son was working that morning. He found him supervising a display of suede and leather in the window. They adjourned to the office behind the shop where Cortoni told him about the hypnotist.

Staring hard at his son, Cortoni asked: "Does that worry you, Carlos?"

112

"No," Carlos Cortoni said, "why should it?"

*   *   *

It was Earl Winters who told Marty Padget about the hypnotist. They were sitting in Winters' office on Madison discussing a new contract. It was early in the morning.

On the walls of the office hung photographs and advertisements of beautiful girls and handsome men. Winters' desk, covered with gold-embossed red leather, was neatly piled with magazines and brochures. The room should have looked smart but Winters' rumpled presence spoiled it.

"So," Winters said, "it looks like we finally weaned you off swim-suits. Not before time; they're strictly short-term."

"You mean I'm beginning to bulge?"

"We're none of us getting any younger," Winters said, gloved hands picking up the new contract for a company in Chicago manufacturing male cosmetics.

Padget combed at his thick moustache with his fingers and said: "Would Danny have got that contract if –"

"He might have," Winters said. "And then again he might not."

"I don't like stepping into a dead man's shoes."

"And another thing," Winters said, "you'll have to shave off that moustache."

"I don't think I can take the cosmetic dodge. I was very fond of Danny."

"Was there anything between you?" asked Winters who knew the life styles of all his models.

"A long time ago I had a thing about him. Crazy. You know, he was square."

"Nothing recent?"

"Not like Christmas Eve if that's what you're thinking."

Winters tossed the contract in front of Marty Padget. "There, sign next to the pencilled crosses."

"I don't think I can," Marty Padget said.

"Jesus," Earl Winters said, "another *prima donna*. Yesterday it was Helen Fleming turning down offers."

Padget looked up, interested. "Peter Lodge told me she might have witnessed the killing but couldn't remember it. Is that true, for Chrissake?"

Earl Winters nodded.

"What did she turn down? Washing-up liquid?"

"She turned down a trip to Rome, would you believe?"

"I find it difficult to. Why?"

Winters told him about the hypnotist.

Padget's fingers went to his moustache again. "Someone's sweating somewhere, aren't they."

"Aren't they just," Winters said. He reached for his jacket. "Are you going to sign or aren't you? Because if you aren't I'm going to call Garry DaSilva. He hasn't even got a moustache."

"I'll sign, I'll sign," Marty Padget said.

X

His name was Hansom and it suited him, Helen Fleming thought.

Dependable without any of the mystique you associated with hypnotism. And there was certainly nothing mystical about his appearance. He was on the short side with thinning brown hair and brown eyes, and he wore a brown suit and shoes to match. His handshake was warm and dry, his voice quiet and unremarkable.

His consulting rooms were on the third floor of a block near Bellevue. Although they weren't luxurious, far from it, you were enveloped in an atmosphere of tranquility as soon as you entered reception. The floor had been carpeted, the pictures hanging on the walls were gentle pastoral scenes and the middle-aged woman at the desk wore a tweedy suit instead of starched white.

The inner sanctum was also carpeted, in fawn, and the lighting was indirect and subdued. On one side of the room was Hansom's desk, on the other a couch; that Helen *had* expected. She and Remick sat in deep, comfortable chairs opposite Hansom, who sat behind a sensible sort of desk flanked by two bookcases closely packed with thick volumes.

Hansom stood up, leaned against a corner of the desk and smiled at them. A nice brown smile, Helen thought. "You see," he said, "I haven't even got staring eyes. I'm afraid Franz

Anton Mesmer has a lot to answer for." And he explained about the Austrian doctor (1733–1815) who had "started it all – at least in the last half of this millenium." Mesmer had believed that human beings discharged a magnetic field which, in illness, flowed imperfectly. He also believed that he was one of the few blessed with the gift to redirect that flow. "Hence mesmerism," Hansom said.

"Did his ideas work?" Helen asked.

"Most certainly in some cases. But not for the reasons poor old Franz Anton supposed. He practised in Paris but refused to submit to an inquiry by a government commission which, as it happens, included the United States Ambassador to France, Benjamin Franklin. He was denounced as a fraud. You know," he said abruptly, "I think this is going to work."

She looked at him in surprise.

"You see, one of the qualities common to those who are susceptible to hypnosis is curiosity. And, thank God, you have an inquisitive nature, Miss Fleming."

Hansom's no-nonsense approach was impressive; because, she supposed, it was so contrary to what she had expected. He reminded her of the family doctor who had treated her for measles and chicken-pox and middle-ear disease; a stethoscope had perpetually hung from Dr Miller's neck and once when she was delirious it had become a microphone into which he had crooned a lullaby.

Hansom picked up a silver cigarette box. "Do you smoke, Miss Fleming?"

She shook her head and was surprised to see Remick's hand stretching forward. He looked guilty, like a boy caught stealing cookies, and placed his hand inside his jacket. "I'm in the process of giving it up," he said. "It's not easy."

Hansom replaced the box and sat down on his swivel chair, gently and noiselessly moving from side to side, fingertips together.

"So what we have to do today," he said, giving the impression that there would be many more days, "is to rid you of Franz Anton Mesmer's legacy of eyewash and the claptrap that still lingers from the days of the old vaudeville hypnotists."

116

*   *   *

While Hansom was trying to define hypnosis the man wearing the hearing aid was placing a telephone call to the lobby of the apartment block where Helen Fleming lived.

Speaking from a diner two blocks away, he told the porter to expect an engineer in ten minutes to check out the elevators.

"But we had a check–out a couple of months back," the porter said, waving at a friendly girl from 203 as she marched across the lobby, high–heels tapping. He was swarthily handsome in his blue uniform and believed that many of the women living in the block were secretly attracted to him.

"Yeah, and we found a little wear and tear. You know, nothing serious. Maybe nothing would happen for a year or so. But prevention is better than cure, am I right?"

"Sure you are," said the porter, imagining the elevator plummeting from the top floor to the basement. "What's the name of the guy who's coming to fix it?"

"Kramer, give him ten minutes, maybe a quarter of an hour, okay?"

Outside the diner the man considered his light-sensitive spectacles. He had bought them because when someone who had seen you outside thought he could identify you he might change his mind when he saw you indoors, when the lenses had lost their tint. But today he needed really dark shades *indoors* just in case the porter was ever asked to identify him.

He stopped at a drugstore and selected a pair of wrap-around shades on a stand next to a display of get-well-soon cards. The coloured girl at the desk said: "You going on vacation? Some people have all –" but when she saw the expression in his eyes, just before he put on the shades, she stopped herself because she didn't want to have anything to do with this man.

He walked out of the store, swinging a metal box in one hand, peak of his blue cap well down over his forehead, grey woollen scarf wrapped round his neck above his grease-stained boiler suit.

"Kramer," he said to the porter. "You're expecting me."

117

The laundry was just arriving in neat packages at the same time as a delivery boy was waving a bouquet of pink and red carnations, and the porter was a little flustered. "Kramer, right, you want the top?" And when he nodded: "Okay, take the elevator up to the twenty-third, then walk up five steps. I guess you can find your way."

On the twenty-third floor he stepped out of the elevator and removed the shades which were pinching the bridge of his nose. The five steps led up to the right a few feet from the yellow door of Helen Fleming's apartment. It really was too fucking easy; no wonder the crime rate was what it was.

He pushed open the metal door which swung easily on its hinges. Ahead of him lay ponderously moving machinery, oily clean, cables thick with grease. Elsewhere, outside the cage surrounding the machinery, the dust was thick. He opened a door in the cage and peered down the well of one of the elevators; far below him he saw the top of an elevator ascending; he stepped back feeling dizzy.

With sweating hands he opened the tool box and took out the .38 Cobra. Then he jammed the door with the tool-case so that he could see down the five steps to her door; the top floor was, thank Christ, a kind of tower and there were only two other apartments there.

Then he sat down to wait, wondering why suddenly there had been such a panic. After he had lost her that time up north, when the old fart had chosen *that moment* to loose off his shotgun, the contract had been cooled.

Then at 2 pm this frantic fucking phone call with the man bawling him out for being unavailable – which was true because since Saturday night he had been at Coney Island – and saying that even now it might be too late. Now just what had he meant by that? The sonofabitch should've counted himself lucky that he had worked the elevator trick before when he had hit another mark living on a top floor, and that he could get it together again fast.

Anyway this time he would really make it last to pay her back for that time in the forest. Risky but that would make it better. This time he would rip off those classy clothes and really hurt her. Before he killed her.

With the fingers of one hand he explored the acne scars on his face, a habit of his.

*   *   *

Hypnosis, Dr Hansom said, was almost impossible to define. Particularly as even the leading authorities disagreed about it. But inarguably there was a phenomenon stemming from the mind that had a therepeutic potential as yet largely untapped, which could make some patients impervious to pain to the extent that operations could be performed on them without discomfort; it could undoubtedly be employed to treat certain kinds of nervous disorders.

Here Hansom smiled at Helen and said: "Promise me one thing? Promise me you'll never refer to me as 'my pet shrink.' "

"I promise," she said.

And certainly, Hansom said, hypnosis had been misused by showmen to persuade human beings to make fools of themselves. "To put them in the circus ring."

Of its many other uses, regression – escorting patients back through time – was probably the best known. And the most spectacular. It had even been suggested that a subject could be regressed to another period of history with the implication that he was the reincarnation of another being. Dr Hansom was sceptical about such claims. And angry about any frauds who claimed to work miracles.

He pushed a button on the intercom. "I'd like a cup of tea," he said. "How about you two?"

Helen said she'd have one, but Remick said: "No, it makes me want to smoke."

Hansom said: "Two teas, please, Dorothy." He stood up and walked round the room, pausing in front of the window and stared out at the grey day. She had expected a darkened room with a swinging orb on which she would have to concentrate; but he hadn't even asked her to lie on the couch. "So now," he said, "let's try for that definition, but it isn't easy."

The woman in the tweedy suit, Dorothy, came in with a tray bearing a china teapot, cups and saucers, milk and lemon. Helen wondered if the teapot contained teabags; she doubted it. She took her tea with lemon while Remick fidgeted in one of his pockets, the one containing cigarettes.

Hansom sat down, sipped his tea appreciatively and said: "In our ignorance, the nearest we can get to a definition of hypnosis is a change in the state of mind so that it is more receptive than normal to suggestion. Not very good, is it?"

"Two questions have always bothered me," Helen said.

"Can you be persuaded to do something you believe to be morally wrong? And can you be hypnotised against your will?" Hansom asked.

Deflated, Helen nibbled her slice of lemon, nodding her head.

"The answer to the first is probably not unless it's something you've sub-consciously always wanted to do. But you can be tricked into such an act." He put down his cup which chinked melodiously against the saucer. "I'm not doing myself any favours, am I? I'm supposed to be establishing trust and here I am holding forth about trickery."

"You're being very frank," Helen said. "That helps." *And the voice, a little monotonous, and the brown suit and the cup of tea.* "What's the trick?"

"Well," said Hansom, reaching behind him and placing a leather volume with vellum pages on his desk, "if I could persuade you that this book rightfully belonged to you then I might be able to persuade you to steal it."

"And the second question?"

"No, you can't be hypnotised against your will. But there wouldn't be much point in consulting a hypnotist, would there, if you didn't want to be?"

"Unless you'd been persuaded against your better judgement to go to consult the hypnotist."

Hansom frowned. "But I understood –"

"So did I," Remick said.

"Don't worry," Helen said, finishing her tea, "I'm willing."

*   *   *

120

He wanted a cigarette but if someone getting out of the elevator saw smoke drifting down the steps . . . Instead he chewed a strip of strawberry-flavoured gum.

He glanced at his wristwatch. Three-fifty. Hopefully she'd be back before five. That's what the man had reckoned. *If it wasn't too late already.* What the hell did that mean?

If she made him wait any longer then he'd make it last even longer. Make her go down on him first. And she modelled hands, didn't she? Maybe he would break a few fingers in those beautiful, cared-for hands.

From the tool-box he took a tiny electrician's screw-driver and began to gouge the dirt from under his fingernails.

*   *   *

"You see," Hansom said, glancing at his watch as though the session was nearly over – and he hadn't really done anything! – "what you have to remember is that hypnotism is far more natural than medicine. Everyone is susceptible to stimuli, that's natural. What the hypnotherapist and the psychiatrist do is to increase that susceptibility."

"I think I'm pretty susceptible," Helen said. "I fell asleep driving a car once."

"Daydreaming," Hansom said, "that's a mild form of hypnosis. Bible-thumpers, they're using hypnosis. You're hypnotised to an extent by ads on television, by their repetition."

He looked at his watch again. A Longines Admiral. A glint of gold caught her eye; she stared at it, her attention riveted. She blinked. She was susceptible all right, no doubt about it.

Tomorrow, Hansom said, he would test her susceptibility. Relax her at the same time. He felt that they had already established rapport. Hearing the note of finality in his voice, Remick and Helen stood up.

Before they left Hansom handed her a booklet on hypnotism by Kenneth S. Hansom, PhD, and suggested that, although it was New Year's Eve, she find time to peruse it before tomorrow's consultation at the same time.

121

Outside Remick asked her if he could see her that evening to discuss the hypnosis and what procedures they would have to follow if Hansom succeeded in regressing her.

Surprised, she asked him how he normally spent New Year's Eve. With a couple of buddies, he told her, but tonight that wasn't possible.

"One of them's Tyler?"

He nodded. "Tyler."

"I'm sorry," she said, "but Peter – Peter Lodge that is – is due back today. Peter and I . . . you know. Maybe I should call to see if he's left any message before I go back to the apartment."

They were standing next to a couple of booths. She went in one of them and called the answering service.

"Miss Fleming? Only one call, Miss Fleming." The woman's voice was flat and impersonal. "From a Mr Lodge in Los Angeles. He said to tell you he'd been held up and wouldn't be in New York till Tuesday."

She held the receiver away from her and stared at it. On top of everything else no Peter. Self-pity swept through her and her eyes smarted. She could hear the woman still talking on the phone. She hung up the receiver and stepped out of the booth.

"So where shall we go?" she said.

*　　*　　*

Four-forty pm. Where was the bitch?

He had missed lunch and his stomach whined with hunger; he spat out the gum in disgust, then retrieved it because you never knew, maybe they could get a print of your teeth from it.

Behind him the machinery whirred and the great cables snaked up and down ceaselessly as the elevators climbed up and down the shafts.

He imagined the lights flicking up and down the indicator in the lobby. Perhaps even now she was stepping into the elevator. He ran his tongue round his dry lips.

The elevator stopped directly below him with a thick clunk

122

and there was a gentle hiss as the doors opened. He grabbed the gun and peered through the opening in the door and saw the swarthy porter bounding up the stairs.

Confused, he stepped back as the porter swung open the door, smiling cheerfully, and said: "Hey, how's it goin?" and when he saw the gun: "What the fuck —"

With one hand behind him, the man with the hearing-aid opened the door of the metal cage at the head of the lift-shaft. "Shut that door behind you," he said nodding towards the door leading to the steps and prodding the air with the Cobra.

"Are you crazy?" The porter closed the door. "Haven't you fixed —"

"Shut the fuck up. Move over there."

"Now take it easy," the porter said, circling warily, moving a little nearer. A hero.

As the porter lunged he jumped back and stuck out one leg and watched, gun ready, as the porter teetered on the brink of the shaft before pitching forward screaming.

He gazed down the shaft. The porter was clinging to one of the greased cables two floors below. The cable shuddered as the elevator began its ascent and the porter lost his grip and fell down, down, until his body met the upcoming lift.

Again he felt dizzy. He stepped back and closed the door of the cage, wiping the handle with an oily rag. He packed the gun in the tool-box and closed it, took a last look behind him, then shut the door leading to the steps behind him, pausing to wipe that handle with the rag.

He began to run down the stairs because the elevators had stopped. Half way down he remembered the shades and stopped, panting, to put them on. It seemed to take forever to reach the lobby.

When he got there people were standing around in shock while others shouted orders. He shouldered his way through them. As he walked out of the electronically-controlled glass doors, a girl walked in. The girl on the photograph in the pocket of his boiler suit. Helen Fleming.

He ducked his head down and walked into the street where, as the first police car arrived, siren wailing, he soon lost himself in the early evening crowds.

*　　*　　*

When Remick arrived to pick her up she told him about the accident. It had been so close to her apartment and, although she hadn't inquired about the details, it sickened her.

He mixed her a drink, a Scotch on the rocks, told her to pack an overnight bag, called the St Regis and booked her into a room. They had dinner in the King Cole bar of the hotel and at midnight he wished her a happy New Year.

"This year's got to be better," she said, "surely."

Then he took her to her room and left her at the door. It was the quietest New Year's Eve she could remember.

XI

Lieutenant Boyd Tyler dreaded New Year's Day.

His wife, May, had been murdered on New Year's Day four years ago. Every policeman's nightmare – the criminal's revenge on his family.

He and Phillip Saul had arrested the boss of a crime syndicate named Nicky Bruschi for the killing of a club owner on Bleecker Street who had refused to pay protection. He had been beaten up and died in the process.

Bruschi's elder brother had threatened Tyler, hardly an uncommon occurrence, and indirectly his family; his wife and unborn child. Tyler had requested police protection for May and got it. But for how long could you maintain such protection? Forever, if all such threats were taken seriously.

Six months later, after the protection had been lifted, May had been stabbed while out shopping near their small house in Flatbush, Brooklyn and her purse had been snatched; by the time the ambulance reached the hospital she was dead; they tried but failed to save the unborn child, a boy.

Tyler had tried to implicate Bruschi's brother, but at the time he had been in Montreal, and in any case Tyler wasn't allowed to handle the case.

The killer was never caught and there were those in the police department who suspected that the murder was a run-of-the-mill crime of violence. Tyler knew differently and blamed himself for not extending the protection and employing his own guard.

Every New Year's Day May sat in the car beside him with the baby inside her.

Today as he drove his tan Chev Caprice along Flatbush Avenue towards Manhattan Bridge he tried to ignore her, to concentrate on the York killing.

At least Remick could have consulted him before going to Knox. Surely such decencies still existed. Remick of all people. There had been understanding between them, or so he had believed.

Remick should have realised that ultimately he would have taken the girl to the hypnotist. It was so obvious, too obvious. Hypnotism was riddled with dangers. Supposing Helen Fleming had killed York . . . gone back to his apartment for her purse and knifed him as he tried to have sex with her . . .

She could have faked the amnesia: she could just as easily fake a trance and name an innocent man. Then again the amnesia might be genuine and so might the subsequent trance; but even so she might sub-consciously defend herself, or protect the killer.

No, first it had to be done the proven way.

"Do it your way," May said beside him, "like the song. Don't let the guys who knock routine ever bother you. Routine is like a cliché: it's only become what it is because it's good. And you've got the brains to give that little extra shine to routine. To lift it. To *create*," she said.

May had been like him. Sensible. People knocked that too. They never dreamed of the wonders within sensible people because it was they who were ordinary. Sometimes May had been inspired, especially when they made love. His son would have been sensible too. And inspired.

Concentrate!

The trouble with this case was the routine was running out and he had *created* nothing. None of the clothes the suspects had worn at the party – or claimed they had worn – had revealed any traces of blood and those that had been to the cleaners had been all-too-thoroughly cleaned.

They had run a routine check on all the cleaners in the city. Eleven had received blood-stained clothing on Christmas Eve but none could be connected with the murder.

In any case, Tyler was no longer sure that there would have been so much blood on the murderer's clothes. According to the medical evidence the knife had been plunged into York's back while he faced his killer, possibly locked in a struggle; so York's own body would have protected his assailant from any spurts of blood. *And it would be easy enough to wipe clean the sleeve of a mink jacket.* He pressed his foot on the gas-pedal and the Caprice surged forward past a muddy white Cadillac.

"Not so fast, my love," May said, "we aren't driving to your funeral."

He slowed down, and considered the four principal male suspects (five if you included the night porter). What was lacking with all of them was apparent motive – although both Helen Fleming and Peter Lodge had said they had seen Cortoni and York quarreling.

But Tyler was a stranger to the fashion world – he felt a little clumsy in it – and within its rarefied atmosphere there possibly existed motives which would not have occurred to him.

Their professional lives had all touched each other; God knows what jealousies could have been spawned before the party.

And any one of them could have been supplying York with his drugs. Deprived of his fix, a junkie would pick up a knife almost as a reflex movement.

But surely if it had been Lodge or Winters whom she knew better than anyone else in New York, Helen Fleming would have remembered? Winters with those black gloves – wouldn't they have jogged her memory? (The gloves, of course, would explain the absence of fingerprints on the knife and door; but, no, they had been wiped clean, a precaution that wouldn't have been necessary for a gloved killer.)

And Lodge? Well, she slept with him. You might conceivably forget the face of a stranger, of an acquaintance, but surely not your lover.

You would have thought, too, that she would have remembered Padget whom she knew reasonably well, had modelled with him, and Cortoni because she had met him and talked with him for some time on the night of the murder.

Tyler would have liked to question Helen Fleming more closely, to have gained her confidence; but now she was under Remick's wing and when he had called at her apartment following the death of the porter – who could conceivably have disturbed a killer – Remick had already taken her away.

Perhaps today or tomorrow she would *remember*. Whatever she was cued to remember. Or whatever, consciously or subconsciously, she *wanted* to remember. Become an honest or dishonest liar.

"Now, now, my love, don't get mad," said May.

He was over the East River and there were shoals of silver lights on the water below, ripples of hope on this first day of the new year, but Tyler paid little attention to them, or to the clouds gusting over the high-rise.

Two motives for the killing appealed to him. Blackmail (by York) or drugs.

In pursuit of the latter theory Tyler and Saul had spent a lot of time at the Narcotics Bureau in the Financial District which was where he was going now.

According to an experienced narcotics officer named Levine, York had been a confirmed addict, poised for the classic physical and mental decline.

"Using shit for maybe five years," Levine had said looking at the corpse in the morgue. "He must have been earning a lot of bread because when a guy's hooked like that it can cost a fortune."

Levine, a lieutenant, was a big, bleak-faced cop, who spoke cynically about the dead and slow-dying human beings he encountered every day and spent most evenings working at a rehabilitation centre for teenagers on the Lower East Side.

York, he reckoned, confirming what Remick had earlier surmised, had probably taken a shot of heroin some time on the day of the party. But he was probably getting scared that night, anticipating what he would go through if he didn't get a fix.

"I don't have to tell you," Levine had said. "Spasms, pains in the gut, sweat and all the time the need that can make you steal or kill to cop some dope."

Tyler had asked him if there was any hope of tracing the pusher who had supplied York; Levine had shrugged. "A model living at a classy address like that? Christ knows." He rubbed his beaky nose. "The only models I ever met were snorting coke and they didn't keep that up too long, either, because they realised what it was doing to their pay-checks, their looks and their bodies."

"Who supplied the cocaine?"

"A whole pack of pushers. But we can check 'em out for you. As you know, we can't touch the assholes without possession. Sometimes I figure the law was drawn up to protect scumbags like them."

"I know what you mean," Tyler said.

"But I don't figure a guy like York would cop from some small-time pusher selling ten-dollar pops cut with lactose. Not in the circles in which he moved. No, a junkie with that kind of life-style would get his shit from someone higher up the pyramid. Someone between the receiver and the two-bit pusher. Someone with a touch of class himself. But someone who would get as tough as a hit-man if he didn't get paid. Did York have cash?"

"When he was working," Tyler said. "When he was killed he owed six months rent. They were going to toss him into the street if he didn't find the dough."

"There you go," Levine said. "Maybe you got something. I'll get some of my guys to ask around their stoolies. Of course," Levine added thoughtfully, "the guy supplying the shit could have been a guest at that party, couldn't he?"

"Couldn't he just," Tyler said.

But Levine hadn't come up with anything. Nor had Tyler and Saul when they questioned the guests whom Lodge and Winters had seen sniffing cocaine. (Helen Fleming couldn't remember any names and Cortoni hadn't seen *anyone* sniffing.) The guests themselves had simply denied taking the drug.

129

As Tyler parked the Chev outside the First Precinct, where the Narcotics Bureau was housed, he said to May: "You wait here, I'll only be a couple of minutes," but when he turned to her the seat beside him was empty.

Narcotics was situated on the third and fourth floors of the ancient precinct on the Old Slip, between Water Street and the river. Built in graystone, the precinct was a poor place compared with the edifices of Wall Street nearby.

Saul was already in Levine's shabby, green-painted office when Tyler arrived. "Hi," he said, "happy New Year," and before Tyler could reply: "And maybe it's going to be, because we just got lucky."

Tyler looked inquiringly at Saul – and Levine who was sitting at his wooden desk.

Saul explained. An anonymous informant, a man, had called Homicide and laid information against – "Guess who?"

"No games," Tyler said. "Who?"

"Carlos Cortoni."

Tyler sat down. His hands inside the pockets of his grey topcoat were tightly clenched. "What kind of information?"

Levine put down a plastic cup of coffee and said: "Drugs. Now don't you think it's kind of funny that this guy calls Homicide instead of Narcotics?"

Saul said: "Not if he knows that Cortoni's a murder suspect. Not if he knows York was a junkie."

Levine shrugged. "Go ahead," he said, "tell the Lieutenant what you told me."

The phone message had been brief, they usually were. According to the caller Cortoni's business interests weren't confined to boutiques: he also pushed drugs. Not in the usual sleazy locations but in the fashionable districts. And his clients had included Daniel York.

"With his money?" Tyler said. "He must be crazy."

"Not *his* money," Saul reminded him. "Papa's money. Maybe the old man was tight with it."

When the detective who took the message had asked where Cortoni stored the heroin, the informant, his voice muffled as

130

though he was speaking through a handkerchief, said he didn't know. And when the detective had suggested a meeting, promising anonymity, the caller had broken the connection.

There was silence for a few moments after Saul had stopped speaking, his angular frame tense.

Then Tyler said: "We do know that York and Cortoni were quarrelling that night. Maybe York wanted a fix but Cortoni wasn't giving him one till he got paid."

Levine took a pipe from an ashtray on his desk and lit it. "My drug," he said. And: "So now your investigation moves right into my territory. I'm not just helping any more, *we* are collaborating, right?"

Tyler nodded.

"Like I told you, we have to bust him with possession. Presuming, that is, that this stoolie was genuine."

"No stoolie," Saul said, "he didn't want paying."

"Maybe he'll get around to that. So what we have to do is to apply to the Supreme Court to put a tap on Cortoni's phone and set up 24-hour surveillance on Cortoni himself and hope that one or the other leads us to the shit. And then, if we get real lucky, hope that we find it on premises that he owns, or better still on him. If he's only a pusher he probably won't have a helluva lot. A kilo perhaps, fifteen thousand bucks worth on today's market. You know, the price varies according to the supply. If a delivery of opium is stopped en route from Turkey or Thailand or wherever, or the refined heroin – as you know, it's an opium derivative – is seized on its way from say Marseilles or Corsica, then up goes the price and up goes the crime rate. Sometimes I wonder . . ." But Levine didn't say what he wondered.

Tyler said: "You know the implications of this?"

"Cortoni's old man?"

"If he gets to know we've put a wire-tap on his little boy . . ." Saul said.

"That as well," Tyler said. "I was wondering whether old man Cortoni's in it too. He's got the right connections. Just supposing," Tyler went on, "that we found the junk at Miguel Cortoni's place out on Long Island."

"Oh boy," said Levine, "then we're in business." He puffed at his pipe; it had gone out. "My protection from nicotine poisoning," he said, waving the pipe. "It never stays alight longer than five seconds."

Tyler stood up and said: "Okay, so you fix the wire-tap, we'll look after surveillance."

"So who makes the collar?" Levine asked.

Tyler said: "I'm investigating a murder. Doesn't that give me precedence?"

"Here," Levine said, "we investigate mass murder."

* * *

Half an hour later Tyler returned to Helen Fleming's block, where he had arranged to meet detectives from the local precinct investigating the apparent suicide of the porter.

The snag with this obvious theory was that, according to his colleagues, the porter had possessed a zest for living with a busy sex-life that, real or imagined, had stirred up considerable envy among them. However, it wouldn't be the first suicide that Tyler had encountered where the dead man had ostensibly been living the life of Riley.

But why had he chosen such a messy way of killing himself? Again, suicides didn't necessarily take the easy way (drugs) to kill themselves and Tyler had known worse – self-mutilation and subsequent death from haemorrhage among them.

Accident? Unlikely: the door to the cage surrounding the elevator shaft opened outwards.

The only other answer was that the porter had disturbed someone, possibly waiting for Helen Fleming to return home. He asked the detectives from the precinct to continue their enquiries: tried and trusted techniques might still prevail.

* * *

By eleven that morning Saul had staked out the boutique on Lexington, in the Forties, which Cortoni apparently used as his headquarters.

132

Round the corner he had parked a souped-up Buick, which was all right in the city but out in the country no match for Cortoni who owned a silver Porsche Turbo Carrera, capable of 150 mph; no match, come to that, on any fast highway where the Porsche's acceleration would quickly put a lot of traffic between the two cars.

But there was nothing Saul could do about that: the New York Police Department didn't run to Porsche Turbo Carreras. With luck Cortoni would stay in the city travelling between his boutiques, his apartment and his father's penthouse.

Luckily there was a cafe opposite the boutique from which Saul could keep observation. From time to time he saw Cortoni's shiny fair hair above the curtain at the back of the window. Business seemed to be good: a succession of men of varying ages, some of them surprisingly old, entered the shop, some of them leaving with packages.

At 1.10 pm Cortoni, wearing a fawn raincoat, emerged from the shop and stood on the sidewalk for a few moments, apparently undecided which way to go. Saul left the cafe and crossed Lexington. Every tail's dilemma: whether to follow on foot or by car. If you followed on foot the suspect suddenly leaped into a cab and disappeared; get behind the wheel of a car and he bolted down a one-way street. Thank God for his blond hair.

Cortoni lived in the Sixties, not far from Helen Fleming – or Daniel York for that matter – which was a long way for a busy young man like Carl Cortoni to walk, so Saul opted for the Buick. And congratulated himself because Cortoni hailed a cab. Saul followed the cab down Lexington, onto Forty-Second and up Third. Cortoni was going home.

*   *   *

By midday permission to instal the wire-tap had been granted and the telephone company had cut off Cortoni's phone to enable the Criminal Intelligence Bureau, on receipt of Cortoni's complaint that his phone was out of order, to call at his

133

apartment and plant the bug.

At five minutes past two Cortoni called to report the fault and later expressed pleasure at the alacrity with which the telephone company had responded.

By 4 pm a detective was installed in a plant, a listening post in the basement of an adjoining block.

One call made by Cortoni particularly excited the detective. Cortoni said to a man named Alan: "Okay, I'll pick up the stuff at the warehouse at six o'clock." Nothing else except a discussion about the prospects of a horse named Brewster's Boy at the Aqueduct the following day.

The detective called Narcotics who passed the message on to Homicide: Tyler called Saul on the radio and said: "This could be it, don't lose him."

Nothing about sending a relief, Saul noted. But on the whole the day could have been worse, considering the way Tyler usually was on January 1st.

XII

"Now," Dr Hansom said, "I want you to relax."

She relaxed.

"This is much more like it, isn't it?" he said, smiling down at her on the couch. "Did you read my little book?"

She had, and had found it more comforting than instructive. Much of it had been repetition of what he'd already told her; that hypnosis was merely a reaction to suggestion and that some subjects were more susceptible to it than others.

But she did learn that between eighty and ninety per cent of the population was susceptible to hypnotism; of those only a quarter could be induced into the ultimate hypnotic state, somnalism. Those who were not susceptible were consciously or sub-consciously resisting the hypnotist's suggestions. There were many variations of this resistance but the most common was pig-headedness – the no-one-can-master-me syndrome.

The pamphlet also dispelled two popular myths. It was *not* true that the more simple-minded you were the more suscept-ible you were – in fact the opposite was true. It was *not* true that women were more susceptible than men.

The hardest person to hypnotise? A hypnotist, in Dr Han-som's view. "As you've gathered from the booklet," Hansom said, his voice soft but firm, "we hypnotists know far less than we would like about our subject. But we do know that our ally is suggestion."

Suggestion. Such a lovely, lingering word.

"By reading my little thesis," he said, "you have helped to establish trust between us. I now know that you are serious."

"I wouldn't be here if I wasn't," she said.

"That doesn't always follow." He paused. "And now I want to test this mutual feeling of ours, this trust, this . . . respect, that's a better word." He held out his hand. "I want you to get off the couch and then I want you to stand quite still. Will you do that?"

She took his hand and stood beside the couch in her navy skirt and twinset – sensible, for Dorothy's benefit – and stockinged feet.

"That's fine," he said. "Just fine. I'm sure that we're going to work well together. New Year's Day – a good augury."

She stood beside the couch, waiting.

He asked her to place her feet together so that her heels were pressed hard against each other and explained that he was going to show her how *his* suggestion could affect *her* mind. Then he told her to close her eyes and try to think about nothing. "You will find that it's almost impossible but don't worry. Don't try too hard; just relax completely and don't think about anything."

She felt very relaxed, happy with it.

"Now," he said, "you will find that you cannot stand perfectly still. You cannot stand perfectly still," he repeated. "You cannot stand perfectly still because you are starting to sway from one side to the other."

Of course I shan't, she thought as she began to sway.

"And now," he said, "you will begin to sway backwards and forwards. Very gently you will begin to sway backwards and forwards."

Of course I shall, she thought. Very gently, backwards and forwards.

"And now you will stop swaying and you will be standing perfectly still. Wonderful," he told her as she stood still. "The perfect subject."

She was delighted.

He pointed to his own chair behind his desk: "Please sit

down there. We have discovered that you are amenable to suggestion. Now I want to show you just how normal suggestion is. I am going to show you that you are amenable to suggestion from yourself."

She sat down and looked at him expectantly.

"I see you don't wear rings," he said.

She rubbed the fingers of her left hand. "Sometimes," she told him, "but they leave a mark when you take them off."

"Of course, I forgot. Your profession. Then we shall have to use mine." He slid a plain gold wedding band from his finger and she thought: *He's going to ask me to stare at it.* Instead he tied a length of black thread to it and attached the other end to a yellow pencil. "Now a little experiment, one of the oldest in the business."

From a drawer in the desk he took a foolscap sheet of paper and with a felt-tip pen drew a line down it. Then he handed the pencil with the ring hanging from it to her. "Now," he said, "I want you to hold the pencil at the end farthest from the ring between your thumb and forefinger, so that the ring is suspended an inch or so above the line. Concentrate on the line and you will find that the ring will start to swing backwards and forwards along the line like a pendulum. Don't try to make it do that, don't try to stop it: it will just happen."

She stared at the line. The ring stayed motionless.

She looked up at Dr Hansom who said: "Concentrate on the line."

The ring began to swing above the line. Slowly at first, then more quickly.

"You see," he said, and turned the paper round so that the line ran in the opposite direction. "Continue to concentrate."

The ring on the end of the thread changed direction to follow the line once more.

He took the pencil from her. "You see, suggestion is such a normal phenomenon that unconsciously you make suggestions to yourself and carry them out. We owe that experiment," slipping the gold band back onto his finger, "to a gentleman named Chevreul who did a great deal to expose the hocus-pocus of hypnotism that was prevalent in his day. You

137

see the ring was made to swing by the slightest movement in the muscles of your hands, so slight that they are barely visible."

"Will you be able to make me remember?" she asked.

"I'll try."

"At first I didn't want to remember . . ."

"I can understand that. But *we* have to try, don't we?"

She nodded.

"And you mustn't be frightened because whatever you saw – if you saw anything – is all over. And now I'm going to give you a little rest, I always find that's best." He consulted his diary. "Shall we say in three days? That's Friday."

"That will be fine," she said. "Do you think I witnessed the murder?"

"Do you?"

"Yes," she said.

* * *

When Peter arrived at her apartment he looked tired and his limp was more pronounced than usual, but he made love with abandon.

It was the first time, she reflected as she undressed, since the murder. It was wild and wonderful and she heard herself crying out as he thrust into her; and for her, part of the pleasure was to see Peter, normally so contained, discarding his inhibitions.

Afterwards, as she lay naked under the sheet, he put on a robe that he kept at the apartment, opened a bottle of champagne, poured two brimming glasses and said: "Happy New Year."

"Happy New Year," she replied sipping her champagne.

The quarrel began when Peter brought up the topic of the hypnosis by asking: "So how's the shrink?"

"I promised not to call him that," she said.

"So it's like that, huh?"

"It's not like anything," she said, surprised. "It was just that he made me promise never to call him my pet shrink."

138

"Two sessions," he said, "and you're promising him things." He poured more champagne into their glasses. "So, have you started to remember?"

"That's the next session," she said. "In three days' time."

"Two sessions and you haven't even started?"

"It has to be gentle," she said.

"I'll bet."

"You should see him, Peter, you really should. He's not a bit like . . . like I imagine you think he is. He's on the small side, unassuming . . . But I thought you wanted me to go ahead with it."

"And you really haven't remembered anything?"

"You seem very concerned."

"Of course. Everyone is."

"You seem more interested to find out whether I haven't remembered than whether I have."

"In my book," Peter said, pacing the bedroom, "that amounts to the same thing."

"Not quite." She put her glass on the bedside table; she couldn't quite believe that this quarrel had developed after making love. "Are you hoping I won't remember, Peter?"

"Perhaps. For your sake. Or hadn't you thought of that?"

"If I'm prepared to go through with it, you should support me."

"You will be witnessing a murder. Or –"

"Or?"

"It doesn't matter," he said, but his tone said it did. "I wonder what York and Cortoni were quarrelling about that night."

"I remember you saying something about a lovers' tiff."

"I must have been drunk. York wasn't gay. And I'm damn sure Cortoni isn't. Maybe York was after some sort of job. Did you know York was a junkie?" he asked suddenly.

"The police told me."

"Perhaps he was asking Cortoni for money to buy a fix."

"Perhaps they were discussing baseball," Helen said with spirit.

"Or hang-gliding," he said.

139

The bitterness began to ebb from the conversation.

Peter sat on the edge of the bed. "We've got to face the fact," he said, "that there are four principal suspects. Me, Winters, Padget and Cortoni."

She took his hand. "Or the night porter or anyone, just anyone, who got up to the apartment – after all the porter had left the street doors open – or any one of the guests who returned. If it had been any of you four," she said, squeezing his hand, "I would have remembered."

"Why Cortoni?" Peter asked. "You'd only just met him."

"That's why I would have remembered him."

"Perhaps . . . Then there's the question of motive." He paused, hand responding to her pressure. "I suppose you could say I had a motive."

She gripped his hand tighter.

"You see," Peter said, "York was a blackmailer. If you're into that sort of thing there's plenty of opportunity in the fashion world."

She waited.

"He was putting the bite on me. Nothing very serious – a few tax irregularities. But if he had blown them, it would have finished me."

She considered this. "But why didn't you tell me before?"

"I figured you had enough worries."

"Have you told the police?" she asked, knowing the answer.

"It wouldn't help them, would it?"

Helen wasn't sure.

"Incidentally I didn't kill him," Peter said.

"I think it was a total stranger," Helen said. "Perhaps I'll know in three days' time."

Peter took off his robe and slipped back beneath the sheet; half an hour later they made love again. But this time it wasn't quite the same.

*   *   *

The following morning she called on Earl Winters at his Madison Avenue office. Marty Padget was just leaving.

"Guess what," Padget said in the outside office, "I'm into after-shave," gently slapping his cheeks with the tips of his fingers. "Poor Danny's after-shave, I guess," dropping his hand.

"I was into Rome," she said.

"I heard, poor baby. How's it going with the shrink?"

"Does everyone know?"

"Everyone in fashion. Have you begun your journey back through time yet?" He looked at her intently.

"On Friday. He's going to –"

"Regress you. I was into psychology once." He winked at her. "Safe journey," and was gone.

Earl Winters had forgiven her. "I shouldn't have gotten mad with you. Of course you've got to help the police. You know, I was just thinking about your future. It was such an opportunity."

"Hands *and* face," she said, sitting down. "Who got the job?"

"Some girl in London with the second most beautiful pair of hands in the world." He leaned back in his chair, the light from a wall-lamp gleaming on the baldness above his fringe. "So how are the sessions progressing?"

"At least you didn't say it."

"Didn't say what?"

"At least you didn't say shrink."

"Ah."

"And they're going very well. He's so . . . sensible."

"Does he think it's going to work?"

"He doesn't know."

"At least he's honest."

"But he thinks there's a chance."

"Scared?"

She nodded and told him about the apparent suicide of the porter at her block. "It just seems kind of strange that it should have happened so close to my apartment."

"If you're going to throw yourself down the well of an elevator, then I guess you go to the top."

"And the time in the forest," she said.

141

"That could have been anyone. But not imagination," he added.

She smiled at him. "Thank you."

"When's your next session?"

"In a couple of days' time."

"That's great," he said, "because I've got a date for you tomorrow. At the Metropolitan Museum. Diamonds. How about that?"

Later it occurred to her that now three of the 'suspects' knew that her day of reckoning was Friday.

The fourth was Carl Cortoni.

*   *   *

At 09.03 that morning Detective Edmund Sheehan had again called Miguel Cortoni at his penthouse and Cortoni in his turn had called his son at his apartment.

The message from Cortoni senior had been brief: "The girl hasn't remembered anything but she's got another session in a couple of days' time." And his son had replied: "Okay, thanks, but you needn't have bothered," and the connection had been cut.

The detective in the plant in the basement next door to Carl Cortoni's block, duly recorded the exchange and passed it to Narcotics who relayed it to Homicide.

142

XIII

On January 2nd the police made several discoveries, which they viewed with mixed feelings, because when you had a good, hard lead like the Cortoni-drug connection you didn't necessarily welcome diversions.

The first discovery was that Marty Padget had at one time tried to force his attentions on Daniel York, a highly speculative approach because, judging by his correspondence, York had been indisputably heterosexual.

This revelation followed the second perusal of letters that York had kept in a wall-safe; Padget's letter, two years-old, had lodged inside an envelope containing another letter from a distraught woman in New Mexico.

The second discovery was that a few days before the killing York had quarrelled bitterly with Earl Winters because Winters wasn't getting him enough work, the sort of work, that was, that his vanity allowed. Source of this information: a phone call from Marty Padget.

"As motives they both stink," Saul said.

Tyler said: "When a guy needs a fix that bad, anything'll trigger him off."

The third discovery was that Peter Lodge had been less than honest with the tax authorities. Source: the tax authorities, who were about to instigate an investigation into the profits earned by the Lodge boutiques and their own surprisingly small share of them. It had come to their notice through the newspapers, they said, that Peter Lodge had been at York's party; they hoped that their information, which would of course be treated in the strictest of confidence, might be of some help.

"I still reckon that Cortoni's hot," Saul said.

The previous evening he had followed Carlos Cortoni to a warehouse behind the waterfront in Brooklyn and summoned help from Homicide and Narcotics; but all Cortoni had done was to dump two packages in his Porsche; they were badly packed and contained leather jackets or coats.

Perhaps there was heroin inside the packages, but neither Saul nor the narcos was prepared to find out because the risk was too great. If the packages were clean they would merely have alerted Cortoni.

Better to maintain the surveillance. Patience – a virtue of which Tyler possessed an abundance, Saul rather less. Although on this case Tyler wasn't quite as patient as usual and Saul sensed that, despite Tyler's instincts and training, he wanted to crack this one before Helen Fleming remembered under hypnosis.

The monitored call from Cortoni senior to his son had helped. Why should he think that his son would be interested in whether Helen Fleming remembered or not? Although his reply to his father: "Okay, thanks, but you needn't have bothered," wasn't strong and could be used to advantage by his attorney.

"Christ," Saul thought, "we've got the sonofabitch in court already!"

He was sitting in Tyler's office in Homicide. Even more bleak than most police offices – table and two chairs, green metal filing cabinet, bookcase containing books with a never-been-opened look about them. The only homely touch was the picture of a woman on the desk and this, Saul knew, was the bleakest item in the room.

Saul had been up most of the night. He had managed to grab three hours sleep and now, before staking out Cortoni again, he wanted some coffee. And a little praise.

144

He got the coffee. As he drank it, thinking that as usual it tasted of mud, Tyler told him that he had consulted Levine and he was going to see a judge to obtain a search warrant for the warehouse. "Meanwhile you stake out Cortoni again."

"What are you going to do about Padget, Lodge and Winters?"

Tyler shrugged, Red Indian features taut with fatigue. "So one had sex problems, one tax problems and one employment problems. We'll check it all out. Who knows, maybe blackmail was the motive."

But Saul knew that Tyler hoped it was drugs.

* * *

Detective Sheehan heard about the search warrant at the same time he heard about the surveillance. Sheehan had been wounded in a gun battle in Spanish Harlem three years earlier and had been given a desk job. Feeling sorry for him other detectives kept him up to date with their cases, believing that he enjoyed participating from a distance.

They were right: he enjoyed the vicarious excitement. But it wasn't enough to compensate for the old days. So he found another excitement, gambling. He currently owed $21,586.

Sometimes when he questioned officers in the field closely about their investigations, he felt that they regarded him curiously. One day their curiosity would sharpen into accusation. In a way he longed for that day.

He heard about the search warrant in good time, but with the surveillance he was late.

Just after midday he yawned, stretched and said to the policewoman sitting at the desk next to him: "Guess I'll just go across the street and get me some cigars."

She wrinkled her nose in disgust. "Why can't you smoke cigarettes, Ed?"

"A cigar's a man's smoke," he said.

"But it's almost time for lunch."

"Maybe I'll take an early lunch. How about swopping?"

"Okay," said the girl, who thought Sheehan handsome.

When he had bought his stogies, Sheehan tried to reach Miguel Cortoni at his penthouse and his downtown office but he wasn't available and no-one knew where he was.

When he called Cortoni's Long Island home a woman's voice said: "Mr Cortoni is in Manhattan. Can I take a message?" Sheehan hung up.

For lunch he ordered a beer and a sandwich in a bar. He drank the beer, left the sandwich. Before returning to Homicide he tried Cortoni's numbers again with the same result.

Imagining Cortoni's reaction when he learned that his son had been under surveillance since some time yesterday and that he hadn't been tipped off about it, Sheehan made another call and bet $100 on a horse in the third race at Belmont.

It lost.

* * *

Saul took over the Cortoni stake-out in a brown van with battered fenders bearing the scarcely visible legend in once-gold letters BARNEY'S BOOT CENTER.

"What kept you?" asked the bored young detective at the wheel.

"I went to your parents' marriage," said Saul. "Now move over, asshole."

The van was parked across the street from another of Cortoni's boutiques in Greenwich Village on West Fourth, between Sixth and Seventh. A little down-market, Saul noted, compared with the shop on Lexington.

He glanced at his wrist-watch. Midday. Bohemia was abroad on the sidewalks. A group of Indians wandered past snapping away with their cameras. But not, Saul hoped, at police vehicles disguised as vans. He looked for the Porsche. No sign of it. If Cortoni went anywhere perhaps he would get a cab, please God.

Through the window of the shop Saul could see Cortoni talking to another man, the manager probably. He wondered if they were discussing male fashions or dope. Cortoni could stash the heroin almost anywhere; if, that was, the anonymous

146

informant had been telling the truth.

Of all the criminals he had encountered, Saul loathed the drug suppliers – receivers, wholesalers, pushers – the most. Maybe he should become a narco but no, he couldn't take it; he knew of several narcotics detectives who had committed suidice. Who wouldn't, he thought, if they saw a fourteen year-old kid being fed candy, not because he was a kid who liked candy but because the candy temporarily relieved the screaming need, the nausea, the convulsions of drug addiction.

If he caught Cortoni with the dope he wouldn't feel too contrite if he happened to shoot him. But that was the trouble with narcotics: it got to you.

Cortoni emerged from the shop. It was 12.28.

Saul picked up the radio handset. "Subject leaving premises on West Fourth. Proceeding on foot. I'm following on wheels."

"Ten-four."

Saul replaced the handset. Cortoni was walking briskly through the crowds, his fair hair a beacon. Saul kept fifty yards behind him. And there was the silver Porsche.

Cortoni got behind the wheel and took off. Heading south. With luck towards Manhattan or Brooklyn Bridge and the warehouse in Brooklyn. Saul wondered if Tyler had got the search warrant and was already inside the warehouse.

He got through on the radio. "Still heading south. Probably for *the* warehouse. Repeat *the* warehouse. Inform Lieutenant Levine of Narcotics as well as Lieutenant Tyler."

"Okay. Ten-four."

It would be interesting, Saul thought as he drove across Manhattan Bridge, if Cortoni arrived at the warehouse to find Tyler and other detectives inside with a search warrant.

It would also be interesting when old man Cortoni heard about it, because he would bring in the best lawyers in New York City and if they weren't good enough, the best in the States.

Ideally they had to catch Cortoni in possession. But if Cortoni found Tyler inside the warehouse they could kiss that one off. And wait for the lawyers.

If only they could catch Cortoni cutting the shit someplace. Saul's hands tightened on the steering wheel of the van, and he had to remind himself that he was a homicide cop not a narco.

Leaving the bridge, the Porsche headed in the general direction of the warehouse at a leisurely pace. Cortoni was a sensible guy: you don't run the risk of being busted for a traffic violation when your business is drugs. Or murder.

Cortoni was taking an exit off the Gowanus Expressway when the message came over the radio that Tyler and a detective from Narcotics *were* inside the warehouse.

Cortoni parked the Porsche in a yard outside the warehouse, a gaunt building with a flat roof in a side street one block from the Upper New York Bay waterfront. Light rain was blowing in from the river as Cortoni, collar of his fawn raincoat turned up, climbed out of the car and made for a side-door.

He didn't appear to be in a hurry, didn't even look behind him as he rang the bell. Why should he? The door was opened by a guard, a paunchy, broad-shouldered man in his fifties.

Saul hoped that the guard was acting, hoped that Tyler had briefed him. Saul took his gun from his holster, laid it on the passenger seat, and, as the rain spattered against the windshield, waited.

*   *   *

Tyler and the Narcotics detective, a younger version of Levine named Kohl, entered the warehouse, accompanied by a wolfhound trained to sniff out drugs, half an hour before Saul and Cortoni arrived.

In the cramped office heated by a butane-gas fire, Tyler showed the guard his shield and the warrant and asked him who owned the warehouse and who was expected to call that day.

A company named Schulman's Storage owned the warehouse, the guard said, warily eyeing the dog held on a short lead by Kohl. It was leased out in sections.

He consulted a pencil-written list on the wall. He was expecting two more collections that day, marble table-tops and cane chairs, and one delivery of carpets.

But that didn't mean there wouldn't be casual callers, he said, hitching his trousers high up his belly. "Anyway, what are you guys looking for?"

Tyler said: "Any callers, you act normal. You never saw us, right?"

As the wolfhound bared its teeth the guard said it was all right.

"You got the keys to every section?" Kohl asked.

"Sure, in case of fire."

Kohl held out his hand. The keys were on one ring, each bearing a name inked on a coloured tab. "You stay here," Kohl told the guard.

Each section inside the warehouse was self-contained, walled-in with its own door. Cortoni's section was in a corner. Kohl opened it up with a key on a red tab.

Inside were half a dozen portable racks, the sort you saw being wheeled around the Garment Center; hanging on them were hundreds of suits and jackets.

Behind the racks, on broad shelves, stood bulky packages obviously containing clothes.

While Tyler kept observation from the window overlooking the yard, Kohl released his dog and said: "Okay, boy, go."

The wolfhound stood still for a moment, tail sweeping from side to side. "It's difficult for him," Kohl said, "if the shit's packed. But Clyde's the best dog we've got."

Tyler didn't think the wolfhound looked like a Clyde.

The dog began to whine. "Go on, boy," Kohl said.

The fur on the dog's back rose. It loped behind the racks and with its teeth pulled at a parcel wrapped in brown paper. Behind the parcel was another smaller package. The dog, whining louder, pushed at it with its muzzle.

"There's your junk," Kohl said. "Good boy," he said and gave the wolfhound a biscuit.

"Are you sure?" Tyler asked.

"Gotta be."

"Better be," Tyler said, "because here comes Cortoni," as the Porsche drew up outside.

149

While Kohl snapped the lead on the dog's collar, Tyler replaced the two parcels the way they had been.

Kohl shut the door behind them. The nameplate on the door of the next section read JAMIESON & RADNORS, HOSPITAL SUPPLIES.

Kohl found the key on a blue tab. Inside, the dog began to growl and wag its tail. "Hey," said Kohl, "I figure we've stumbled on a whole heap of junk here," looking at the packing cases piled up to the ceiling.

Tyler said: "For Chrissake keep that dog quiet."

Kohl put his hand round the dog's jaws and whispered in its ear. The dog stopped whining, and when Kohl removed his hand sat wagging its tail and laughed at him.

Tyler stopped the door closing. Through the slit he watched Cortoni walk down the concrete-floored space between the sections. He was carrying a black leather brief-case. Then he heard a key slide snugly into the lock in the section next to them.

A few minutes later they heard the door shut. Tyler gave it a couple of seconds, drew his gun and stepped out. "Hold it," he shouted at Cortoni's retreating back. "Police."

Cortoni stopped. His right shoulder moved. "Forget the gun," Tyler shouted. "Drop the case, turn around."

Cortoni turned round firing with a small black automatic. The first bullet hit the dog which howled as it spun round, pulling Kohl to the ground; the lead whipped round Tyler's legs taking him down as the second bullet hit the wall at the level where his head had been.

Then Cortoni was gone. Through the door leading into the office, out into the yard.

Tyler leaped to his feet and ran. Kohl didn't follow.

Cortoni gunned the silver Porsche. Tyres screaming, it headed towards the exit from the yard. Went into a wild, swerving turn as Saul blocked the exit with the brown van.

From the doorway of the office Tyler took aim with his .38 Special and shot out one of the rear tyres of the Porsche. Trapped, the Porsche circled the yard again, smoke streaming from the wrecked tyre.

From the blocked exit Saul took aim. Another rear tyre. The rims of the wheels grated on the concrete as the Porsche circled again, slower this time, lurching from side to side.

Tyler shot out a front tyre. The Porsche rolled past Saul as he shot out the last tyre. The car hit the brick wall ponderously. The nearside door fell off. Smoke and steam rose from the bonnet.

Saul wrenched open the door on the driver's side and, gun in hand, said: "Out, hands behind your head. Try anything, no fucking head."

When Tyler reached them, Saul said: "Fairground stuff, we must try that again," as he pushed Cortoni against the wall to search him.

They found Kohl kneeling beside his dog. "I think he's going to be okay," he said, and there were tears in his eyes.

The heroin, fifty glassine bags of it, was in the briefcase and later that day Cortoni was booked on a drugs charge and, for good measure, illegal possession of a firearm.

Within half an hour of the charges being lodged, an attorney named Adler, by general consent the best criminal lawyer in New York, was preparing an application to get Cortoni released on bail.

Tyler consulted Knox in his office. "Do you reckon he'll swing it?"

Knox said bitterly: "He can swing most things."

"How about a murder rap?"

"That," Knox said, looking questioningly at Tyler, "would be a little more difficult to him. Do you have enough?"

"I don't know," Tyler said. He counted on his fingers. "We've got him cold on drugs – and York was a junkie. We know they quarrelled on the night of the killing. I figure I can prove that Cortoni was the last to leave the party – lean on the other three a little. I've got a warrant to search Cortoni's apartment. Saul's round there now. We might dig up something there like a list of his junkies . . ." Tyler's voice trailed away.

Knox leaned across his desk. "Boyd," he said, "don't try

151

and kid yourself and don't try and kid me. We both know that, barring Saul striking gold at Cortoni's place, you don't have a case to take before a Grand Jury. You know what I reckon?"

Tyler shook his head.

"I reckon your only chance is Helen Fleming."

XIV

When she left her apartment – and Peter in bed – at 6.30 on the morning of Thursday, January 3rd, to go to the Metropolitan Museum, she found a uniformed policeman on duty outside her door. He was fair-haired with a slow smile and a small moustache; he called her 'Miss' and said his name was Niedherhoffer without volunteering a first name.

She guessed that he had been posted there at Remick's request. He escorted her down in the elevator and across the lobby, leaving her in the cab she had called because her Honda was being serviced. It was spitting with rain.

As instructed, she told the driver to wait to enable her police escort to get in position. Today the escort, she had been told, would be driving a blue Fairmont; to avoid confusion they had given her the license plate number.

The police had also promised to call every day and give her a description of the escort to avoid a re-occurrence of the incident in Central Park. But today no-one had called because, she supposed, they assumed she would still be asleep.

Nor had she called last night to give them her schedule for today because, absorbed with the stories in the late editions of the newspapers about Cortoni's arrest, she had forgotten.

The papers stated that Cortoni had been booked on a drug charge and reminded readers, without making any direct implications, that he had been at the party on the night York died. But the inference was there, especially if you knew more than the average reader. York had been a junkie . . . Cortoni was into drugs, presumably pushing them . . . pusher and junkie had quarrelled during the party . . . pusher had returned after the party and there had been a fight . . .

A sense of relief had at first swept through Helen. Until she had realised that, if Cortoni *was* the killer, it was now even more imperative for him to have her killed. His father would organise that for him, probably had done so already. Hadn't a witness disappeared during Miguel Cortoni's own trial?

The Fairmont pulled up twenty-five yards behind the cab. She checked the licence plate, correct.

"The Metropolitan," she told the driver.

"Opera, Club or Museum?"

"Museum," she said, sinking back in the seat. She wore jeans, boots, old cony jacket and beneath it a shapeless black sweater. From the other girls she had learned not to waste time dressing up for work; besides, it was pleasant to be shabby instead of chic.

The location at the museum was the brainchild of *Vogue* magazine. An issue containing a long feature on the theme that being an intellectual didn't preclude you from being a fashion-plate knock-out. To help prove the point the magazine had hired the Medieval Sculpture Hall for three hours before the museum opened at 10 am.

The summons to model there was an honour because it implied that you looked as though you possessed brains as well as beauty. (According to Earl Winters they would be photographing her profile as well as her hands; although she suspected that, because the notice had been so short, she was second choice for the diamonds.)

As the taxi pulled up outside the museum, she paid the driver and ran quickly through the drizzle into the main entrance. Glancing behind her, she saw the blue Fairmont pull up behind the departing cab.

Inside she was directed to the Romanesque chapel which was being used as one of the changing-rooms. Some of the models were changing beside the collection of *Virgins*

Enthroned; at least, one of the girls commented, the organiser had a sense of humour.

A silver-haired woman from Cartiers was waiting for Helen. She showed her an engagement ring and earrings set with Wesselton diamonds sparkling in a jewel box in a nest of purple satin.

A black model with small, perfect breasts pointed at them. "For real?"

The woman from Cartiers said: "As real as you want them to be."

Katy Tanner arrived breathlessly, late as usual, red hair in disarray. She grinned happily when she saw Helen and, as she began to undress, said: "Have they got the guy who followed you in the forest yet?"

"So you believed me."

"Sure I believed you."

"Your boyfriend didn't."

"Oh him!"

"Another one bitten the dust?"

"Great mouthfuls of it," Katy Tanner said. "But you haven't answered my question."

"No, no-one's been caught." She told Katy about the death of the porter. "But I've got a personal bodyguard now, a cop."

"I think I saw him in the hall outside, on the steps beside the postcard shop. At least I saw his back. And I thought, 'He's a cop.' I tell a lie," Katy said, putting on a robe, "I didn't think any such thing until you told you."

They sat beside each other while the make-up men tended their faces. Opposite them, hair in rollers, sat a famous teenage model with her personal make-up man.

Helen told Katy about Rome.

"Rome at this time of the year? It's worse than New York, honey."

"I think I would have loved it," Helen said.

"Who wouldn't?"

"Did you read they've arrested Carl Cortoni?"

"I saw it on television last night."

Helen told Katy about the hypnotism; how she was scared

155

about what might happen to her between now and the crucial session tomorrow.

The teenage model looked at her with new interest.

"Then you must move in with me tonight," Katy said.

"If I don't remember tomorrow it could be an extended visit."

"Stay for the rest of the year," Katy said.

"I'd love to," Helen said without hesitation.

The make-up man, a Philippino, applied a blusher stick to Helen's cheeks and she examined his handiwork in the mirror. Her face was softer; the Philippino was a worker of miracles.

While Katy carefully rolled sheer stockings up her gorgeous legs – *her* pay-check – Helen put on an autumn-toned costume and a ranch mink. The woman from Cartiers fixed the earrings, Helen slid the ring onto the fourth finger of her left hand.

She said to the woman: "This is for an autumn number of the magazine?"

The woman touched one of the earrings lovingly. "October," she said.

"Then if I were the sort of woman who wore diamonds and ranch mink, I'd wear gloves."

Katy, stepping into a green skirt, said: "Are you trying to talk yourself out of a job?"

The woman from Cartiers said: "Maybe you dropped your glove to attract the attention of an elegant young gentleman."

"Wearing an engagement ring?"

"You're an unfaithful hussy," the woman said. "Now get out there."

In the gallery of tapestries leading to the Medieval Sculpture Hall, she noticed a man wearing a black raincoat examining a series depicting the *Sacrament*. My bodyguard, she thought. He was wearing a hearing-aid – unusual, surely, for a police-man – and for a moment his face seemed vaguely familiar.

But as she entered the crowded hall she forgot him.

* * *

156

He had spotted the cop immediately. Sitting behind the wheel of a Fairmont parked opposite her block.

He parked a block away in the white Pinto hired with stolen papers. If a passing patrolman asked what he was doing there at six in the morning he was waiting to drive his boss downtown. If the patrolman's partner decided to check out his papers on the phone then he would take off, dump the Pinto, postpone the killing. Again.

"Fuck up this time," the man had said, "and I hire another guy and his first contract is you."

Now that they had positioned a uniformed cop outside her door, it would have to be away from the apartment. No sex first. But this time, although he still carried the Cobra, he would use a knife, watch the expression on her face as the blade pierced her clothes, slid through her ribs.

She left the block at 6.30. From where he was sitting she didn't look as classy as usual; but under those tacky clothes her body was class, no doubt about it.

As she climbed into the cab, the Fairmont moved up behind. He gave them a couple of seconds, then took off, wipers switching on the windshield.

He left the Pinto a hundred yards from the main entrance to the museum and sauntered along Fifth. When the detective had followed her into the museum he opened the kerbside door of the Fairmont – thank Christ cops, like hit-men, had to be ready for a quick getaway – and released the catch on the bonnet.

"Need any help?" asked a man holding an umbrella as he gazed at the engine.

He shook his head. Raindrops sizzled on the hot metal. "No thanks, it's a garage job." When the man had moved away he disconnected the battery with a small wrench, shut the bonnet and made his way to the museum entrance. Whatever happened, the cop wouldn't be able to chase the Pinto.

A mini-bus was disgorging a team of lighting technicians outside the museum. He joined them and walked inside.

He lingered in the echoing Great Hall looking for the detective. No sign. He followed a couple of model girls dressed as shabbily as the bitch, up some steps. At the end was a room like a chapel; part of it had been screened off and from behind the screens he heard women's voices, laughter.

Ahead, in a big room hung with tapestries, he saw the cop, big and balding with what looked like a knife scar down one cheek. He retreated down the steps.

Behind the screens he could still hear the models. Some of them were naked, he guessed. He licked his lips with the tip of his tongue, gripped the handle of the flick-knife in his raincoat pocket.

After a few minutes he decided to wait in the toilets because she wasn't going anyplace. He gave it half an hour then returned to the steps and peered into the room hung with tapestries. The detective had disappeared. He walked into the room and, just in time, saw the detective standing on the other side of the entrance leading to the hall where all the action was taking place. He turned quickly and studied a tapestry – as Helen Fleming walked past, glancing briefly at him.

First there were some promotion shots for the benefit of the media because it was an event to find a bevy of New York's top models assembled in the setting where, in 1963, the *Mona Lisa* had been on display.

The girls posed in one corner of the hall beneath the wrought-iron choir screen that reached almost to the ceiling. The arc lights bore down on them. Managers and agents hopped around, making sure that their properties weren't demeaned or exploited. Television cameras whirred, still-cameras clicked.

Finally an executive from *Vogue* said: "Okay, ladies and gentlemen, that's it."

Katy Tanner, wearing a red fox over a green jersey dress, said: "Wait for it," and cupped one hand to her ear as photographers chanted: "Just one more."

When they had gone a Japanese fashion photographer hung with cameras guided Helen past the sculptures and bas-reliefs to the French masterpiece, *Virgin with Child*, fashioned in painted wood.

"Exquisite, isn't it," said the Japanese photographer, attaching a Hasslebad to a tripod. "Fourteenth century, I believe."

"Thirteenth," Helen said.

"Your hand. Point towards the exhibit. Good, good, a beautiful ring. Those diamonds. Your head a little higher. A trace of a smile. That's it, that's just beautiful," he said, as he clicked away.

He took off the black raincoat because it was conspicuous and slipped the flick-knife into the pocket of his blue windcheater. A technician had left a portable floodlight in the tapestry room and he knelt down beside it.

He was examining the filament when the detective left the Medieval Hall and walked briskly past him. Going to take a leak, he guessed, convinced that the girl was safe in there. He considered his options. It would be possible to use the knife if she became isolated. In and out, and he would be away before anyone had realised what had happened. Possible, but hardly practical. He really needed to use the knife in a crowded street where he could vanish immediately.

But supposing she went from here to some place where he couldn't reach her: the bitch was born lucky. Supposing at the end of the day his only option was a gun in a darkened street as she climbed out of a cab. Supposing he only wounded her.

Fuck up this time and I hire another guy . . .

He draped the raincoat over one arm and wheeled the floodlight into the hall.

Blinding lights . . . stink of perfume and powder . . . arrogant, snotty cunt everywhere . . . noise . . .

She was standing beside some sort of exhibit, pointing at it with one finger with a ring glittering on it. There was ice on her ears, too.

Pushing the floodlight with his body, he took the flick-knife out of the pocket of his windcheater and, holding it with his right hand, slipped it under the raincoat on his left arm.

He pressed the button. Felt the blade shoot out. Touched the blade with one finger. In, out. In through the ribs, up into the heart. Beautiful . . . But I've got to be quick, he thought,

159

before the cop gets back. Luckily the girl and the Jap photographer were on their own. He pushed the floodlight towards the tripod supporting the camera.

"Hey, what the –" shouted the Jap as the floodlight sent the Hasslebad crashing to the floor.

This detective was bright, Helen thought, as she saw him walking towards her. He had found himself a floodlight and was blending with the scene. But a hearing-aid? She frowned. A picture was surfacing. Her head ached.

She braked sharply as a Jeep Cherokee loomed up in front of her; without realising it she had changed lanes. Horn blaring, an old grey Thunderbird overtook her in her original lane. Behind her, but slowing down, was a black car. She noticed that the driver was wearing tinted glasses and a hearing aid.

She saw the knife as the floodlight cannoned into the tripod. He was holding it beneath the raincoat but the blade gleamed in the bright light.

"You stupid prick," the Japanese photographer screamed as the man with the hearing-aid pushed aside the floodlight and came at her.

And then she was running, screaming, past the cameos of fashion groups around the sculptures. She saw the black model . . . Katy Tanner . . . the teenage model . . . faces staring at her in astonishment . . .

She tripped over a wire. Sparks fizzed. A floodlight died. She looked behind her. He was coming after her, knife in hand. Someone tripped him. He sprawled. Then he was on his feet again as, sobbing, she ran into the Medieval Treasury. Where was the detective? Dear God, where was he?

The fall had displaced the hearing-aid. He could only faintly hear her screams and the clatter of her footsteps. The partial loss of hearing seemed to have affected his other senses: the handle of the knife was thick in his hand and he seemed to be running in slow motion.

There was still a faint chance. They were only just giving chase behind him. If he caught her he could still sink the knife

160

in and get away. If the museum security operation wasn't put into motion, that was. Oddly, what he could hear loudest was the thumping of his heart.

She ran past the *Entombment of Christ*. Past glass cases filled with religious treasures. Into the Italian Galleries. An old-fashioned bedroom, a study . . . Which way? She ran to the right. She was in a long chamber filled with suits of armour, swords and ancient guns. A horseman wearing a helmet with two horns spouting from it peered down at her. A woman cleaner stared at her. History was her thing and she was going to die immersed in it.

The detective was behind him now; the rest had dropped behind. Just the three of them.

He was still carrying his raincoat over his arm and he threw it aside. He transferred the knife from his right to his left hand; from the holster under his windcheater he took the Cobra. His heart was thumping out pain. As he ran he half-turned, pointed the pistol behind him and squeezed the trigger.

The explosion cannoned around the armour; the detective spun round clutching one arm. His gun clattered to the floor.

The woman cleaner screamed.

But turning and shooting had slowed him up. The girl was escaping. He would have to use the gun on her. He tried to take aim but, running, it was difficult. He fired again as she rounded a corner and disappeared, and the bullet hit a suit of armour. The suit of armour swayed, then righted itself.

Ahead of her was an elevator; to her right a flight of stairs. She plunged down the stairs. She imagined herself framed between the walls of the staircase. A perfect target. Then she was in the auditorium, running towards some sort of office. Perhaps the door was open . . . a key on the inside.

She fell, breaking the heel of one shoe. She kicked off the shoes, struggled to her feet. But he was right behind her, close enough to use the knife; instinctively she knew that it was the knife he wanted to use, not the gun.

She reached the office as, dropping the gun, he transferred the knife to his right hand.

The door opened. OPENED! As he lunged at her.

But she was inside. Turning, she slammed the door. The door trapped his hand at the knuckles. She heard the knife fall on the other side and she heard him scream.

She pulled the door hard towards her, felt the bones in the hand crack. Pulled again and watched the fingers convulse. It was a terrible hand. Fingers dirty and uncared-for. Nails broken, with grease embedded beneath them. A really shocking hand; it would take a manicurist at least a month to do anything with a hand like that. And what was that seeping down the fingers?

As she slid unconscious to the floor she felt that she was peering into a pit filled with memories.

XV

His name was Frank Bruton; he was twenty-eight years-old and he had previous convictions for armed robbery, assault and rape. He was also reputed to be a hit man, but the police had never been able to make any homicide charge stick.

Bruton had been born in Buffalo and, Tyler thought savagely, it looked as though he might die in New York City because, with his hand trapped in the door in the museum, he had suffered a heart attack.

He was in intensive care in Bellevue and there was no way, the doctor in charge said, that he could be questioned. Tyler had summoned Remick to the hospital for a second opinion because, if he could obtain a statement from Bruton naming Cortoni as the man who had paid him to kill Helen Fleming, he would have enough to charge Cortoni with murder.

So far the assistant district attorney handling the case had successfully opposed motions by Adler to get Cortoni released on bail. But he had told Knox and Tyler that he couldn't hold out much longer. Unless Tyler could come up with enough evidence to book Cortoni for murder.

Remick, wearing a green surgical gown, joined Tyler in the corridor outside Intensive Care.

Tyler said coldly: "Go in there and see what you can do. I've got to see him."

"I can't let you endanger a man's life, you know that."

"In your opinion he might be well enough to be questioned."

"Interrogated?"

"Just two questions," Tyler said. " 'Did Carl Cortoni give you the contract to kill Helen Fleming?' And if the answer's negative: 'Was it Miguel Cortoni?' "

"Leading questions, Boyd."

"We're not in court," Tyler snapped.

"Because you want to nail Cortoni before Helen Fleming names him?"

"Because I want to catch a killer," Tyler said.

"But if Bruton names him then you figure you've got a case without resorting to hypnosis?"

"With a statement from Bruton," Tyler said tightly, "we would have enough evidence to take before a Grand Jury."

"And you would have proved that you can still catch killers the good old-fashioned way?"

Tyler shook his head wearily. "It was luck, the girl had guts. In any case she's still going to be hypnotised, so what the hell?"

Remick turned to go into Intensive Care. "Tell me one thing," he said, "why are you so uptight about Bruton?"

"Think about it," Tyler said.

It wasn't that difficult, he shouldn't have asked. Bruton carried a knife: Tyler's wife had been killed with a knife.

"Okay," Remick said, re-emerging through the swing doors, "you can see him for a couple of minutes."

"Is he going to pull through?"

"He's out of intensive care," Remick said.

Bruton was in a single ward. Beside the bed an electrocardiogram bleeped his heartbeat; a drip-feed was taped to one arm; his ruined hand, lying on a rest, was covered with gauze.

Remick said: "You realise Adler will rip a statement obtained under these circumstances to pieces?"

"Let's leave that to the Grand Jury," Tyler said. He turned to the nurse standing beside the electrocardiogram. "I'd like you to listen."

She took a step forward, exuding disapproval.

Tyler sat down. Bruton stared at him, eyes almost black in his waxen, pitted face.

"We're police officers," Tyler said, including Remick. "Do you understand that?"

With his good hand Bruton slowly tapped one ear.

Remick said: "I understand he was wearing a hearing-aid."

"Then where is it for Chrissake?"

The nurse shrugged. "I guess it was removed in Emergency."

Tyler leaned forward, speaking louder. "Can you hear me, Bruton?"

Bruton whispered: "I hear you."

"I want to know who put the contract out on Helen Fleming."

A pause. Then a whisper: "I don't hear you any more, Lieutenant."

Remick said: "He can hear you."

Tyler leaned closer: "Tell us who gave you the contract and —" He stopped himself: if he offered to reduce the charge the nurse would repeat his words on the stand. "Who was it, Bruton?"

"I don't hear you . . ."

The expression on his face changed — fear — his eyes closed and his body jerked once. The blip on the electrocardiogram lost its rhythm.

The nurse shouted: "He's gone into arrest," and Remick said to Tyler: "Just get the hell out of here," as he turned to Bruton.

Tyler learned later that Bruton had been pronounced clinically dead half an hour after he left the ward. So now there was only Helen Fleming.

*   *   *

Helen had been driven to Katy Tanner's apartment on East Forty-Fourth and that was where John Remick went after Bruton died. She was lying on a sofa; when Remick entered the room a doctor was taking her pulse.

Remick stood back, smiled at the red-haired girl who had opened the door and studied the living-room with approval. If you were suffering from shock it was the sort of room to be in, far better than a hospital ward. Warm colours, russets and oranges, and soft wall-to-wall carpets, comfortable furniture, blinds patterned with gold and silver leaves.

When the doctor had finished taking Helen's pulse the red-haired girl introduced them: "Dr Remick, Dr Bowen – and I'm Katy Tanner." And to Bowen: "How is she?"

"She's recovered remarkably well," Bowen said, smiling at Helen.

"The police called again," Katy said. "They want to take a statement."

"They'll have to wait," Bowen said, looking towards Remick for confirmation.

"I agree," Remick said, reflecting that his attitude to Helen Fleming was wildly different from that towards Bruton. But he had sensed that Bruton was going to die so there had been nothing to lose, everything to gain.

Bowen, plumply prosperous, stood in front of the window, thumbs in the pockets of his vest, and said: "So, what are the police going to do? She can't take much more of this."

"Well, as you know, the man who attacked her is in police custody." He didn't elaborate: strictly speaking Helen had killed him.

"Which doesn't mean to say there won't be others."

"Police protection is being stepped up."

"It didn't do much good today."

Helen said: "How's the policeman who got shot?" She was very calm; Remick saw from her eyes that she was under sedation.

He told her: "He's fine. A flesh wound in the arm."

Bowen said: "I don't imagine his future on the police force is so fine."

Remick shrugged.

Katy said: "Coffee everyone?"

"Not for Helen," Bowen said. "But I'd like one."

"Black," Remick said. "And strong."

Katy disappeared into the kitchen.

Bowen lit a cigarette and Remick looked at him enviously: it really was extraordinary what a bad example doctors set.

Helen waved one hand at Remick. "Will-power," she said.

Remick wondered what drug Bowen had administered: she was bearing up surprisingly well after what she had been through. Remick wished that he was Helen's doctor; that he could prescribe for her. And comfort her.

Katy brought in the coffee on a tray. Steaming mugs of it and a plate of ginger cookies.

Bowen squashed his cigarette in an ashtray half-smoked. Waste! He said: "I don't think there's any doubt that we should postpone this appointment with the hypnotherapist tomorrow."

Remick bit into his cookie.

"If she remembers," Bowen said, "there's bound to be more shock. We can't subject her to that."

Katy Tanner said: "Surely that goes without saying," sitting on the edge of the sofa beside Helen. "How much more does she have to go through?" She and Bowen both looked at Remick.

But before he could reply, Helen said: "Of course I've got to go through with it. Don't you understand? This . . . this nightmare . . . will go on until I have remembered. It's the not-knowing that scares me most, the knowledge that I might suddenly remember." Her voice was soft and deliberate. "That I might suddenly see the killer standing in front of me."

Katy said: "But surely you should give it a little time, honey. You know, after what happened today."

Helen shook her head. "I've got to know. And, okay, even after I've remembered, *if* I remember, then whoever's trying to kill me might go on doing so to stop me testifying against him. But at the moment he's desperate to stop Dr Hansom having an opportunity to regress me to the night of the killing. To identify him. When I've done that, when I've made a statement, then maybe he'll realise that he's lost out and leave me alone."

Bowen finished his cookie and said to Remick: "Do the

police figure Cortoni killed York?"

Very politely Remick said: "I have no idea, I'm only a police surgeon."

"But you must —"

"No idea at all," Remick said. "And I think Miss Fleming has a point about seeing Hansom as soon as possible."

"As her physician I must advise against it. Good God, Remick, have you any conception of what she's been through today?"

Katy said: "I don't know any more but would anyone like some more coffee?"

No, they said.

"Anyway," Helen said brightly, "you can all stop worrying about it because I am going to see Hansom."

"Well," Bowen said, a touch of petulance in his voice, "I've told you what I think. Don't blame me if it has an adverse effect on you."

"I might blame you," Helen said, "if I got killed."

"Well, I must be going," Bowen said. "Take another tablet in six hours. I'll call again this evening. And no statements to the police yet," wagging one finger at her.

Remick wondered if that included police surgeons.

When Bowen had gone, still shaking his head reproachfully at the door, Katy said: "You're very cool, Mr Remick."

"Cold is what you mean to say," Remick told her. "Cold-blooded. But you're wrong. I just happen to think it's best for Helen."

"And best for whoever decided that Helen should be hypnotised?"

"Best for everyone," Remick said, reaching for his coat.

Over steaming bowls of tomato soup and crusty rolls, Katy said: "He's a good-looking guy."

"Rugged," said Helen, blowing on a spoonful of soup.

"Doctor *and* cop. An odd combination. Compassion and ruthlessness."

The telephone shrilled: soup spilled from Helen's spoon.
"It's Cartiers," Katy said. "They want to know how you are."

"Well, tell them I'm fine."

"And . . ."

Helen looked up questioningly.

". . . Can they please have their diamonds back."

XVI

The story broke in the morning papers.

MODEL GIRL IN TRANCE MAY NAME YORK KILLER ... AMNESIA VICTIM TO BE HYPNOTISED BACK TO DEATH SCENE ...

Beneath the headlines the reports speculated on the danger in which Helen was placing herself. *"She is virtually challenging the killer to get to her before the hypnotist,"* wrote one journalist.

The stories all highlighted the chase in the Metropolitan and anticipated the security operation that would be mounted.

Their anticipation was accurate: all offices and apartments overlooking Katy Tanner's home were checked out and marksmen were positioned around the block as, at 8.30 am, Remick led Helen from the block to his chocolate Mustang.

"Who told the Press?" Helen asked Remick as he drove away.

Remick shrugged. "They have their sources. I'm surprised it wasn't leaked before. At least they don't seem to know where you're staying."

"They'll follow us back from Hansom's consulting rooms," Helen said.

"We're not going to Hansom's consulting rooms," Remick replied and, as they turned into Third Avenue: "Are you sure you want to go ahead with this right now?"

"I'm sure," she said. "Where are we going?"

"To another hypnotherapist's place near Cornell Medical Center. He's a friend of Hansom."

She unfolded the copy of the *New York Times* he had bought. "I see they've named Cortoni again without implicating him."

"He could be free tonight," Remick said. "He's got a smart lawyer. On bail," he explained.

"I'm scared," she said.

He squeezed her white-gloved hand.

She asked: "Did Peter ask you where we were going?"

Remick nodded.

"Did you tell him?"

Remick shook his head.

"Why?"

Remick said: "We're here," as police closed in around the Mustang.

*   *   *

The consulting room was similar to Hansom's. Fawn wall-to-wall carpeting, indirect lighting, couch, desk and bookshelves. A second door led to a room where Hansom's colleague kept his records; it was shut. Behind the door sat Tyler and Saul. On one of the green filing cabinets stood a tape-recorder.

Hansom had told them that police in the consulting room would distract Helen, so Tyler had planted microphones where he and Helen would be sitting.

Beside Tyler and Saul sat a stenotype operator, a fat man wearing a check jacket too small for him.

"Why the Q and A man?" Remick asked as he came into the room. "No statement taken under hypnosis is admissable in court – it's hearsay."

"I like to be thorough, you know that," Tyler said, grey eyes staring at Remick. "And we've got to have a record. If the tape gets screwed up what have we got?"

"I believe," Remick said, "that you want to hear what Helen's got to say under hypnosis even more than me."

171

Tyler said coldly: "I always said we'd use it as a last resort. Bruton's dead, Phillip didn't find anything in Cortoni's apartment, so this is the last resort – before Adler springs Cortoni."

Hansom came in wearing a brown suit, cream shirt, brown tie. "I hope you know exactly what we're going to do to this girl today," he said.

"Regress her," Remick said.

"And you know what that entails?"

"Jogging her memory," Saul said.

Hansom turned to Saul. "Much more than that, my friend. We are going to try and effect a catharsis, to purge Miss Fleming of a traumatic experience. To cure her. But when we regress a patient she actually relives an experience. In this case murder."

"Good morning, Helen," Hansom said brightly. "Another ordeal yesterday, I gather."

She nodded. She was wearing the same twinset she had worn last time – for Dorothy, but Dorothy wasn't here.

"Well," he said, sitting on the edge of the desk, "I want you to *try* and put all that out of your head. Not easy, I know, but try. I know you will because we work so well together."

She nodded again without speaking. She had been trembling but already she felt more composed. She sat down opposite him as he motioned her to a chair.

"And now, Helen, I want to tell you what we're going to do. I always believe in that. You see," he said, massaging his hands together, "there are three types of amnesia. What we call retrograde, which means loss of memory of events *before* an incident. Anterograde, loss of memory *after* an occurrence. And congrade, failure to remember the event itself. And I don't have to tell you that you are suffering from the latter."

She watched his hands moving. The chair was very comfortable. The room warm. Somewhere a clock was ticking.

"So what we have to do," Hansom said, leaning forward, "is take you back to that incident. And you mustn't be afraid, because it happened ten days ago and can never happen again."

172

He smiled at her and she trusted him. "But first, of course, I have to hypnotise you and we both know that you are susceptible to my suggestions; in other words we have rapport, you and I."

Hansom stood up, came round the desk and pulled up a chair opposite her. She had intended to ask him why she couldn't lie on the couch, but the words wouldn't come.

"This is much better than the couch," he said as though he had heard her thoughts. He turned down the desk lamp. "Now," he said, looking into her eyes, "I want you to concentrate on what I'm saying. You're feeling very warm, very relaxed . . . concentrate, that's it . . . it's so comfortable in that chair . . . so comfortable that you want to relax completely, to close your eyes and just listen to me . . . to close your eyes."

But I don't want to close my eyes, she thought. I am in this consulting room looking at Dr Hansom and it's not going to work. She closed her eyes.

"And now you are so relaxed . . . so relaxed . . . your body and your arms and your legs are relaxed . . . you are not thinking about *anything* . . . nothing . . . your arms, your legs, are heavy . . . and you are thinking of nothing, just concentrating on my voice . . . sleep is coming but you can still hear my voice and you are concentrating, concentrating on what I am telling you . . ."

She didn't think she would sleep; but she *did* feel drowsy.

"And you feel a little numbness in your arms and legs . . . but this is not an unpleasant feeling, it is all part of falling asleep, of falling deeper and deeper into the darkness . . ."

And there was darkness, with billowing, gossamer shapes in it. And it wasn't that her arms and legs were heavy, it was merely that she didn't want to lift them. His voice, the warm brown voice, reached her and the darkness was brown . . . a brown study she thought . . . She smiled.

"You are relaxing, relaxing . . . deeper, deeper . . . and as you sink down into this deep, comfortable darkness your breathing will get slower, deeper . . ."

Her breathing slowed. His voice came to her from far away. Compelling.

"And now you are in a deep, deep sleep . . . sinking deeper as you relax even more. You are sleepier, sleepier . . . so tired, so tired . . . sinking into the deep, soft pillows of sleep . . ."

He paused, looking at her intently. She swayed slightly. Her breathing was still slow and deep. On her wrist he saw the flutter of her pulse, steady and rhythmic.

"Listen to me," he said, "and concentrate . . . Today is Wednesday . . . or Thurday . . . and it's late in the afternoon . . ."

Saul scribbled on a piece of paper: *He doesn't even know what day or time it is*! and handed it to Remick who had sat down between him and Tyler.

Remick scribbled back: *Time confusion, part of the technique.*
Saul pulled a face.

Remick spread his hands, shrugged. He wasn't an authority on hypnosis but he knew that Hansom was using one of three recognised treatments for amnesia.

You could employ post-hypnotic suggestion to persuade a subject to re-enact whatever he had forgotten; you could try hyperamnesia when a patient merely explored the attics of his memories without reliving them. Hansom was using the third method, regression, putting Helen into a deep trance and then disorientating her about time. From the ensuing confusion she should develop a chronic need to have an incident in time stabilised.

It was a common practice to regress patients back to childhood to discover some forgotten trauma that had affected their adult behaviour. Even their voices and handwriting became child-like. But were they children once more? Hardly, when a five year-old in a trance might answer a question about physiology, plainly knowing the meaning of the word.

Hypnosis was still a young science. But, particularly since the successful treatment of Vietnam neuroses, its acceptance was becoming more widespread. And I intend to establish it in the law of the land, Remick thought as Hansom, having created his confusion in time, began to lead Helen towards the party.

174

"It is just before Christmas . . . the night before Christmas Eve and we are going to a party . . . I know you don't particularly want to go but it will be fun . . ."

"I'll go if you want to go, Peter," she said.

"And now we're at the party and saying hallo to our host . . ."

Her eyes moved rapidly behind closed lids. "I don't see him," she said.

"But here he is . . . you must relax more . . . deeper, deeper into that deep, dark sleep . . . and this is our host."

"A glass of Chablis, thank you," she said.

"And it *is* a good party, isn't it . . . you *are* enjoying it . . . meeting lots of new faces . . ."

"Carl Cortoni . . . *Are you a model, Miss Fleming?*"

"Hands . . . anything that goes on hands I model it. Anything from nail lacquer to soap powder."

"It's a much better party than you thought it was going to be, isn't it?"

"It's the Chablis."

"And you know more people than you expected."

She said to Marty Padget: "But swim-suits at Christmas?"

"*Don't tell me. You get frozen assets.*"

And there was Earl Winters.

"*I don't know how the agency survived before I met her . . . How are you, Helen? Happy Christmas.*"

Now she was eating, dancing . . .

" . . . *No deal,*" said Cortoni.

"*More time . . .*" York.

"And now you want to leave," Hansom said.

"They're sniffing cocaine over there . . ."

"It's getting late and you've called a cab and the cab's waiting outside . . . you're going home . . . going home . . . going home . . ."

The knuckles of Tyler's hands showed white and shiny. Remick searched for his cigarettes. Saul closed his eyes, buried his faced in his hands. The tape on the recorder whirred gently as the soft fingertips of the stenotype operator fluttered over the keyboard of his machine.

175

"This is it, lady," said the bearded cab-driver.

"I'm sorry, I've left my purse behind."

"You mean you haven't got the fare?" eyes glaring through the screen.

"I mean you'll have to take me back. Then you'll get paid."

"This was going to be my last trip."

"Do you want to get paid?"

The cab jerked forward.

She settled back in the seat. The cab smelled of stale cigar smoke. Snowflakes flew past the window. Like moths, she thought. You would have thought Peter would have driven her home. Business? He had no intention of selling out to Cortoni! Perhaps, she debated, he was still there and perhaps his business talk was finished and perhaps he would drive her home and then perhaps . . .

The cab turned into York's street and pulled up outside his block.

"I won't be a minute," she shouted as she ran across the slippery white sidewalk.

Hunched over the wheel, pulling at his Fidel beard, the driver didn't reply.

She pushed one of the swing doors. To her surprise it opened. There was no sign of the porter. Perhaps he'd already found somewhere to blow the twenty dollars.

Brushing the snowflakes from her mink jacket, she walked across the deserted lobby to the elevator. She pressed the button and the lights on the indicator began to flicker downwards. Maybe I'll give the cab driver a handsome tip, she thought. Perhaps he had a sick wife and two starving kids. It *is* Christmas.

The elevator settled, the doors opened. She pressed the button for the tenth floor. The elevator began its ascent. She wondered what Peter had bought her for Christmas. The elevator stopped and she was in the corridor walking towards York's apartment at the far end.

176

The door was ajar, held by the chain on the inside. She peered through the gap.

The scream took Hansom by surprise.

As she rose from her chair he pressed his hands gently but firmly on her shoulders. "There's nothing to worry about . . . you have returned to the apartment and through the gap in the door you can see . . ."

"What?" Saul whispered.

Remick said: "He's torturing her," but he didn't move.

Tyler didn't speak.

The stenotype operator's fingers stayed poised above the keyboard.

She stared through the gap between the door and the wall and saw . . . In the consulting room she sobbed and said: "He's killing him."

"Killing him?"

"Carlos Cortoni . . . he's stabbing Daniel York."

Gently Hansom began to take her through the dehypnosis procedure.

*   *   *

Later that morning the distinguished lawyer Thornton Adler, sixty-two, with luxuriant silver hair – rinsed according to his enemies, of whom there were more than a few – and a somewhat theatrical manner, appeared confidently before Judge Erskine Peters to apply for Carlos Cortoni's release on bail.

But, having read about the proposed hypnosis of Helen Fleming in the morning newspapers, his confidence ebbed a little when he observed the equally assured air of Robert Flores from the District Attorney's office, a lawyer whom he respected.

Before Adler could speak Flores, swarthy and sardonic, said: "May it please Your Honour, I propose on all our behalves to curtail these proceedings. At 11.28 this morning a formal complaint was issued charging Carlos Cortoni with the murder of Daniel York. In view of the nature of the charge

I suggest that the motion brought before you by Mr Adler becomes superfluous."

Judge Peters, lean and acerbic, asked: "Have you got anything to say to that, Mr Adler?"

"Only that if it's got anything to do with this hypnotic farce it will be laughed out of court," Adler snapped.

"That will be quite enough, Mr Adler," Judge Peters said. "Motion refused."

Outside the court room Adler said to Flores: "Am I to assume you're claiming that this girl remembered what happened under hypnosis?"

"You can assume that, yes," Flores told him.

And it was only later during the day that Flores learned that, although Helen Fleming *had* remembered, she had forgotten when she came out of the trance.

XVII

"I don't believe it," Flores said prowling Knox's office. "I just don't believe it."

Knox, Tyler and Remick watched him warily because he was a dangerous-looking man. Of Mexican extraction, flat-featured with wings of grey in his black hair, he had been chosen for the People v. Cortoni for two reasons. First, he had a court room style which matched Adler's; it wasn't as flamboyant but it had a feline intensity that Adler's lacked. The brooding pauses in his questioning dramatised the answers he elicited, and in cross-examination he was brief, incisive, deadly. If he had a fault it was an air of ruthlessness that could alienate a jury.

Secondly, like Remick he was a crusader. If anyone should prosecute in a case leaning heavily on evidence recalled under hypnosis, then it should be Robert Flores.

But not, Flores was saying furiously, when the vital witness could no longer remember a damn thing. "You mean to tell me that the police report handed to me before I signed the complaint charging Cortoni with murder was rigged?" he demanded.

Knox, battered face sombre, said, "Nothing was rigged. The girl named Cortoni. That's all the report said."

"But then she forgot again, and in my book," Flores said, stabbing his finger at Knox, "that's dishonesty by omission.

179

It's improper and that's the understatement of the year."

"The doctor has a persuasive line of reasoning," said Knox, pointing at Remick who was sitting next to Tyler.

"Then let's hear it for Chrissake." Flores leaned against the wall and waited.

Remick said: "It's not so crazy. Helen Fleming did remember. The hypnotherapist heard her, I heard her, Lieutenant Tyler and Sergeant Saul heard her. What's more it's all on tape and stenotype –"

"None of which matters a goddam. Everyone in this room knows that's hearsay, ie evidence of words uttered outside court, not uttered under oath, not subject to cross-examination and therefore inadmissable as evidence."

"There are exceptions," Remick said.

"Sure there are, but this isn't one of them. Please continue, Dr Remick."

"The point," Remick said, feeling as though he were testifying on the stand, "is that Helen Fleming did remember and she will remember again. Under further hypnosis she will retain that memory. We – Mr Knox that is, and Lieutenant Tyler – had to act quickly before Adler got Cortoni out of jail. By the time we go into court we'll have a statement signed naturally, not under hypnotic suggestion that is, and she'll be able to testify naturally to what she saw."

"Oh boy," said Flores, leaning against the wall and staring at Remick, "will Adler have a field-day." He pulled at the lobe of one ear. "Tell me, doctor, how did you get involved in the case?"

"Because I believe in progress," Remick said.

"Wow!"

"I believe that hypnosis should be a legitimate part of the judicial process. It's an accepted part of therapeutic procedure. Why shouldn't it be as acceptable in the courts as any other medical evidence?"

"An ego trip, doctor?"

"Maybe," because there was no point in lying to this man. "Surely most men or women in history trying to effect change, however small, have been egoists. I wonder if anything would ever have been achieved if it hadn't have been for an element of self-conceit. You should know about that, Mr Flores."

Flores, accustomed in court to insults under pressure, turned his attention to Tyler. "And you, Lieutenant, you're in charge of this case I believe. Apart from the doctor, that is," inclining his head towards Remick. "I was told you always played it by the book. Straight that is. But you knew, all of you knew, that this girl, Helen Fleming, had remembered – and forgotten! How do you justify such a deliberate falsehood?"

"If we hadn't come up with something," Tyler said, "then Cortoni would probably be sunning himself on some palm-fringed beach in the Bahamas by now."

"And that's justification?"

Tyler thought about it, then said: "Criminal investigation is by definition a devious procedure. I believe in a framework of honesty. But, when you're dealing with crooks, then that framework has to be adorned with subterfuge. If we didn't use subterfuge, Mr Flores, then our jails would be empty."

"So you're distinguishing between subterfuge and down-right dishonesty?"

"Sure I am. Subterfuge is a means to an honest solution."

"The legal profession doesn't know what it's missing," Flores said. "So you agree with this particular . . . subter-fuge?"

"If it helps to convict a guy we know to be a killer then sure I do."

"*Know* to be? Sometimes I figure an honest cop is far more suspect than a corrupt one."

Knox said: "Knock it off, Flores. We're here to tie up an investigation, not hold a forum on police morals."

"To tie up an investigation," Flores said, "I need to know the ethics of my police officers." He swung round – from judge to jury, Remick thought – and said: "I'm still interested in your ethics, doctor."

Remick said: "You interest me, too, counsellor."

Flores raised his eyebrows.

"I read a report of a speech of yours the other day. In it you

181

advocated far-sweeping reforms in our criminal laws."

Flores pulled at his ear. "You read right."

"Including reforms in laws that allow hardened criminals to be released on bail to commit more crimes."

"Please continue, doctor."

"And laws that permit criminals to make a monkey of the law by appealing forever against a verdict. One appeal is enough, I believe you said."

Flores pushed himself away from the wall, a faint smile on his brooding features. "I also said that deterrence, not punishment, should be the cornerstone of our system. In fact, I was repeating what the Chief Justice of the Supreme Court said in an address to the American Bar Association in Houston."

"I'm glad to hear it," Remick said. "I was beginning to think we'd gotten the wrong Flores."

"And what's that supposed to mean?"

"I understood the Flores who was going to prosecute in this case possessed a touch of the reforming zeal. That he was the sort of guy who would consider this case to be one of considerable moment in the history of the United States legal system."

"I do," Flores said. "Going to a Grand Jury with a witness who can't remember what she saw is all of that."

"But wasn't the essence of what you were saying in your speech that, as the law stands, the criminal takes precedence over the victim?"

"That's about it," Flores agreed. "But that doesn't mean to say I advocate a position where the rights of an accused person should be abused."

"Nevertheless," Remick accused, "you do believe that the prosecution should have the same advantages as the defence, and that sure as hell includes obtaining crucial evidence from a witness suffering from amnesia as a result of the actions of the accused."

Flores turned to Knox. "Is everyone in this room a goddam lawyer?"

Relentlessly Remick went on: "And in some circumstances the only way to do that is by hypnosis which is why, because

182

this case is going to attract maximum publicity, we are in a position once and for all to get hypnosis written into our legal system in indelible ink."

"But what if we lose?" Flores asked.

* * *

Faced with a fellow zealot like Remick, Robert Flores dropped his objections to the prosecution, "with considerable misgivings."

And before he left the office he reminded Knox, Tyler and Remick that only two weeks remained before the Grand Jury hearing. Two weeks in which to persuade Helen Fleming to retain her memory; two weeks in which to amass as much supplementary evidence against Cortoni as possible; two weeks in which to resist the succession of motions that would be hauled before the judge by Thornton Adler, spurred on by the fury of Cortoni's father.

At 2 pm that afternoon Carlos Cortoni appeared before Judge Erskine Peters for arraignment. He pleaded not guilty.

* * *

At dusk that evening Tyler received a visit at his home in Flatbush from Miguel Cortoni. When he rang the front-door bell he was alone. But in the twilight Tyler could see a bulkily-built man with his coat-collar turned up, waiting on the sidewalk outside the small grey and white house with its handkerchief of winter-pale lawn.

Tyler's immediate reaction on seeing Cortoni was to wonder how he had discovered his address. An informant at Homicide? Whoever killed May had discovered the address, followed her from the house and stabbed her in the shopping precinct.

"Come in," Tyler said, "but don't make yourself at home."

Tyler was aware that his house was humble but it didn't worry him: although shabbier, it was as it had been when May and the unborn boy had been alive. The living-room suite was

183

ordinary, imitation velvet wearing thin; the carpet was ordinary, plain blue and threadbare at the doorway; the imitation logfire was ordinary and the black and white television went out with the ark.

Tyler pointed to a chair and said: "Sit down, Cortoni, what the fuck do you want?" and heard a voice: "*Play it cool, my love.*"

"Nice place you have here," Cortoni said, settling himself in the chair, smoothing back his sleek, centre-parted hair. He wore a camel-coat and he looked, Tyler thought, like an actor playing a hood. A very good actor.

Tyler said: "It's a dump and you know it so what do you want?"

"Any coffee?"

Tyler shook his head.

"Then maybe we could have a little heat," pointing at the imitation log fire. Tyler flicked the switch: the bars glowed, a light began to rotate inside the plastic coals.

"You're not wired or anything?" Cortoni asked in his Spanish-accented voice.

"Why the hell should I be? I wasn't expecting you."

"This hypnosis," Cortoni said, "it stinks."

"It stinks for your son."

"Correction. It just stinks."

Tyler sat down opposite Cortoni. "So what do you want?"

"We have a situation where everyone in the States knows that the prosecution's star witness couldn't remember a goddam thing, right?"

"But now she can."

"Sure, she's had it fed to her. It's been suggested to her and she's agreed that she saw my son commit a murder. Did you know, Lieutenant, that people in a trance lie just like everyone else?"

"Why should Helen Fleming lie?"

"Because she's been told to by the cops, is why. Because the cops think that because a Cortoni's involved then he's got to be the killer, and even if he isn't then he's the fall guy."

"I reckon," Tyler said evenly, "that you Cortonis take

184

yourselves too seriously."

Cortoni warmed his hands in front of the glowing bars of the fire. "Isn't this supposed to be your case?"

"The People's case," Tyler said.

"I mean the investigation. You're in charge, right?"

"Up to a point."

"From what I hear you've got a doctor in charge."

"You hear wrong."

"Who brought in the shrink?"

"The New York Police Department has employed a hypnotist for some time."

"Sure they have. In LA there are cops trained in hypnosis and you know what they're called? The Svengali Squad! You know as well as I do, Lieutenant, that evidence obtained under hypnosis isn't worth a can of beans if it's impeached by a smart lawyer – and a smart lawyer is what I've got."

"And you know as well as I do, Cortoni, that the identification under hypnosis is only part of the prosecution's case."

"A part of nothing. I figure that girl's all you've got, Lieutenant. The last excuse to bust my son for murder before Adler sprang him. The last excuse to haul him before a Grand Jury."

"That's in two weeks," Tyler said. "Maybe they'll toss the case out."

"No chance. We both know that. You don't have to prove guilt before a Grand Jury, just give them enough to prove there is 'probable cause' to believe the suspect committed the crime. And so my son stays in jail for maybe six months awaiting trial on a case that will be laughed out of court. Justice, Lieutenant?"

"You know your law," Tyler said. "It's your logic that's way out."

"I know my cops," Cortoni said.

Tyler said: "Murder apart, there's no way even Adler can get your son acquitted on the narcotics charge."

"Narcotics?" Cortoni gestured with one hand, the Spanish way. Forget it, the hand said. "So he was pushing a little skag. Strictly small time. Why the hell he did it I don't know."

185

Tyler, who believed him, said: "He was pushing in the right circles, making a lot of dough. Okay, so he had a chain of boutiques. But bought with your money Señor Cortoni. And mortgaged up to the hilt, they tell me. So what did Carlos do for pocket money?"

Cortoni brooded. Then he took his hands away from the fire and plunged them into the pockets of his coat. "You can guess why I called," he said.

"You tell me."

Cortoni took a roll of crisp new bills from one of the pockets and tossed it on the coffee table between them. Each bill was a one hundred dollar denomination; or at least the top and bottom bills were, thought Tyler, ever cautious.

Tyler said: "Ten grand?"

"It's yours."

"For what? Your son's been charged. I can't change that."

"Your case depends on one witness, right?"

"Our case depends on a whole lot of evidence."

"What I propose," Cortoni said, picking up the roll with one plump hand and rifling the bills with the other, "is that you persuade this Fleming girl to forget what she's remembered."

If only you knew, Tyler thought as he picked up the roll of bills, stuffed it into the pocket of Cortoni's coat, grabbed him by the lapels and bundled him out of the house.

*   *   *

Police had suggested moving her to a safe house on Long Island, but when Katy Tanner said she could stay with her as long as she liked she accepted. Wherever she went word would get around: secrets didn't collect dust in the Manhattan fashion world.

When Tyler told her that afternoon, after Cortoni's arraignment, that she was still in danger, she replied: "Don't think I haven't figured that one out for myself, Lieutenant."

No-one had told her what she had said under hypnosis. But almost immediately after the session Cortoni had been

186

charged with murder, so it didn't require any great deductive ability to conclude that it was he she had named.

And so, having failed to stop her from remembering, it was equally apparent that the Cortoni camp might now try and prevent her from giving evidence. What better way than killing her?

Her fear was not now so acute – the enemy had been identified – but it was compounded by a new anxiety stemming from the fact that a murder charge had been based on her memory *when I haven't remembered*. What if she never did?

As she understood it from Remick, hypnosis was legally acceptable as an investigatory technique and statements made as a result of that technique were admissible in court. Fine. But not if you had forgotten what you had remembered because then your hypno-induced statement was hearsay.

The police had instructed her not tell anyone that, without assistance, her memory was still a blank. But she had insisted on telling Katy Tanner – she had to share the suspense with someone when Remick wasn't around – and reluctantly they had agreed.

She wasn't sure that she approved of what was happening – charging a suspect on forgotten evidence – but when Remick called at the apartment that evening he reassured her. "What happened to you is fairly common. If something scared you once it stands to reason that it will scare you a second time and your minds says: 'Not again.' But pretty soon your mind will get used to the idea and you won't forget. Then the case against Cortoni will be sewn up."

He smiled at her and accepted a gin-and-tonic from Katy. "You'll be purged," he said.

"How soon is pretty soon?" Helen asked. She poured herself some more Chablis and drank it quickly as the anxiety returned. In a way it was worse than the fear: it didn't stab her – it slithered into her consciousness. And it contained a quality of unease that she couldn't quite place . . .

"Tomorrow," Remick said. "The next day . . ."

"Sometime never," Helen said.

"Dinner?" Katy asked.

187

Remick shook his head, and stood up. "I was going to ask Helen out for a meal but I think she should get a good night's sleep."

"Why didn't he ask me?" Katy said as the door closed behind him.

* * *

There were three more visitors to the apartment that evening. The first two were Earl Winters and Marty Padget who arrived together. They had, they said, read all about the trance and the murder charge in the papers.

"Poor baby," Marty Padget said, flopping into an orange easy chair. "So you finally remembered, huh?"

"What can I get you to drink?" Katy asked. Helen decided she was giving her time to compose an answer.

Winters said he would have a beer, Marty Padget a screwdriver.

"Fantastic, wasn't it," Helen said.

"I never liked the guy," Padget said. "Daddy's boy."

Unseen by Padget, Winters pulled a face at Helen. "Maybe he'll get off with manslaughter," Winters said. He sat down on the Chesterfield. "You know, Danny, desperate for a fix, attacked him and Cortoni grabbed the nearest weapon, the carving knife . . . I'm sorry," he said to Helen.

Katy handed out the drinks. She sat down opposite Padget. It was all very cosy, Helen thought, but all very strained.

Padget said: "Just tell me one thing, Helen, baby. How come you saw it? I mean was Danny's door open?"

Katy said firmly: "Knock it off, Marty. You know what she's been through."

"Sorry," he said, stirring his screwdriver with a cocktail stick.

Winters wiped some foam from his lip. "So you let me know when you want to start work again. I've got plenty lined up. You and Marty here."

"Danny's specialities," Padget said. "Poor Danny."

Poor Danny, they agreed. Earl Winters then said it was time

188

to leave and Marty Padget, pulling at his moustache, followed eagerly behind him.

The third visitor was Peter. He was very sweet and, over a Scotch, suggested that she take a week's vacation in Florida.

No, she told him, she had to see the hypnotist again. He looked surprised – "I thought that was all over. You remembered, didn't you?"

Katy said: "Who'd like an omelette?"

Yes, Helen said after a pause, she had remembered.

"Then why go back to the shr . . . to the hypnotist?"

Katy said louder: "I asked, 'Who'd like an omelette?' "

"Please," Helen said and Peter raised his hand.

"I mean," Peter said, sitting down and rubbing his bad leg, "what's the point?"

"He said something about post-hypnotic therapy."

"And what's that supposed to be?"

"A sort of soothing thing, I suppose."

"I figure a week in the sun would be more soothing." Peter shrugged, dismissing his good intentions. "So it was Cortoni after all."

Without answering, Helen picked up a copy of the *New York Post*. "All over the front page," she said.

Over their Spanish omelettes Peter told them that business was looking up. He had clinched the deal in Los Angeles and was opening another boutique on Long Island at Sag Harbour.

After they had finished eating Peter kissed Helen, told her to get a good night's sleep and departed. As he walked towards the door, Helen noticed that his limp was less pronounced than usual.

*   *   *

This time I will remember, she decided as she sat in the deep, comfortable chair the following day, listening to Hansom's quiet voice and trusting him. This time there will be no fear because I know now what happened and it was a long time ago.

"You are so tired and you are relaxing and you are sinking

189

back into deep, soft pillows . . . the deep, soft pillows of time . . ."

This time she knew where to go: to the taxi waiting outside her apartment in the snow.

This time the journey back to Daniel York's block was quicker; there was a blizzard and the snowflakes streamed past the windows. Across the sidewalk, across the echoing lobby. Anxious to get there. Lights above the elevator twinkling, doors sliding apart. As she walked down the corridor, a voice reached her from outside her vision:

"What you see will have no fear for you . . . and . . ." the voice boomed and echoed and for a moment she lost it . . . "when you awake you will remember. . . the fear will be gone and you will remember."

She saw the bright blond hair, Cortoni, and she saw the knife in his hand, and she saw the knife plunge in, in, and she saw the spurt of blood, and she saw York's face suddenly old, so old, and she thought: *That's what he feared, age.*

Hansom said softly, firmly: "In just a moment you will awake . . . I am going to awake you . . . and when you awake you will feel good, full of life . . . and when I touch the handkerchief in my breast pocket you will remember what you saw because the fear will be gone . . . you are coming out of that sleep . . . it is becoming lighter all the time . . . and when you are awake I will touch the handkerchief in my breast pocket and you will remember . . .

"And now I am going to start counting like this . . . ten, nine, eight . . . and with each digit your sleep will become lighter until you are awake, really awake . . . seven, six . . ."

On "one" she opened her eyes and smiled at him. He nodded at her, smiled back.

"Well?" he said.

In the adjoining room Tyler, Remick, Saul and the stenotype operator waited. They looked at each other, looked away. A wrist-watch ticked loudly . . . a foot tapped . . . the tape whirred . . .

Hansom touched the tip of the fawn handkerchief tucked into the breast pocket of his jacket.

190

"Well?" he said again.

"I saw Carl Cortoni pick up the knife and stab Daniel York in the back . . ."

No fear now. Just relief.

Just relief as, later, she signed the detailed statement she had made in the presence of Lieutenant Tyler and Sergeant Saul.

* * *

Thirteen days later a Grand Jury handed down the indictment Flores had been seeking against Carlos Cortoni and the case was sent for trial.

* * *

The two crusaders sat together at the bar in the Irish pub on East Forty-Fifth Street. John Remick drank a gin-and-tonic, Robert Flores a bourbon-on-the-rocks. It was the evening after the Grand Jury hearing.

The barman who had larded hair and a blotchy face regarded them respectfully, wondering whether to give them a drink on the house: Remick was a policeman of some sort and for all he knew the other man might be the Attorney General, even if he did look like a chicano.

"So," said Flores, twisting his glass between his fingers, "we've got something like four months until the trial, four months in which to tie it up. Tell me, is there any chance this Fleming girl will forget again?"

"Every chance," Remick said, "according to Hansom. He got her to remember by post-hypnotic suggestion. By telling her there would be no fear when she came out of the trance and that she would remember everything when he touched his handkerchief."

"Holy shit," said Flores. He swallowed his drink and pushed the empty glass towards the barman.

"There have been cases when a subject has had total recall aided by post-hypnotic suggestion and total amnesia again twenty minutes later."

"Are you telling me we're lucky she managed to retain the memory right up until the Grand Jury hearing?"

"We're lucky she remembered at all," Remick said.

The door leading to the street opened. Remick looked towards it. He hoped Tyler would come in. A panhandler walked in and was promptly ejected. Tyler hadn't been in the pub since Remick first went to Knox.

Flores said: "I heard about you and Tyler."

Remick said: "But Hansom reckons that she should retain her memory. It's been a couple of weeks now and it's still good."

"Unless," Flores remarked, chinking the ice in his bourbon, "someone gets to her and scares her so badly that she forgets again."

"Or kills her," Remick said, pushing his glass towards the barman.

"She's a brave girl," Flores said, dark eyes on Remick. "I admire your choice." And before Remick could answer: "Let's just say she does forget on the stand. Can we get Hansom to sit at the front of the spectators and finger that handkerchief of his?"

As Remick spun round, Flores grinned slyly: "Forget I said that. But you tell me what I do in court when Miss Helen Fleming looks me straight in the eye, shakes her beautiful head and says: 'To tell you the truth, sir, I don't remember a goddam thing.' "

Remick rasped his hand over his chin. "I was going to save this," he said.

"Now he wants to spare my feelings."

"But we're both progressive, aren't we?"

Flores looked at him warily without replying.

"So I'll tell you what you do. You have her hypnotised *in* court."

In the silence that followed the barman made up his mind, leaned across the bar and said: "How's about the next one on the house, gentlemen?" and replenished their glasses because the silence remained unbroken.

Part Two

XVIII

The Trance Trial, as it had been dubbed, opened on June 6th, a gentle day poised between spring and the long sweat of summer.

Because the murder had been committed in Manhattan in New York County, the trial was to have been held in the County Courthouse in Downtown Manhattan.

But fresh evidence had been discovered suggesting that Cortoni had conspired in Brooklyn (Kings County) to kill Daniel York. A charred list found in the warehouse incinerator naming twenty-eight drug addicts – a cross beside York's name; the remains of a letter to an unknown person stating that York would be 'fixed' . . .

This enabled the lawyers to apply for permission for the trial to be heard in Brooklyn in the Kings County Courthouse at Adams Street, where delays were then shorter than in Manhattan.

Outside the grey building, eleven storeys high, the grass in the park area containing a statue of Christopher Columbus was still salad green, and the shadows of soft, white clouds slid across the East River to the sea. But none of this serenity reached the ninth floor of the building. Not with what *People v. Cortoni* had to offer. A fashion parade in court, a beautiful model who had allegedly recalled a killing under hypnosis, Miguel Cortoni's son charged with second degree murder and

195

facing a maximum sentence of life imprisonment . . .

The corridor was crowded with reporters and disappointed spectators, the benches inside packed. The regulars were there, grey and knowing, but today they were far outnumbered by elegant men and women who, having strayed from familiar haunts, sat uneasily absorbing their surroundings – wood-panelled walls, counsels' tables, bench, witness-stand – and smiling at each other's nervous jokes.

When Cortoni entered the court room and sat at the counsel table there was a murmur as though a breeze had passed through them.

Cortoni, wearing blue blazer, grey trousers, black-buckled shoes, blue silk shirt and a striped tie, smiled hesitantly as his father gave a thumbs-up sign and sat down. Although pale, he was still looking fit, blond hair shiny under the indirect fluorescent lighting.

He talked for a while with Thornton Adler, who had acquired a tan that accentuated the silver of his hair; Adler was very conscious of his hair and from time to time he rifled his fingers through it.

At the prosecuting attorney's table to Adler's left sat Flores, still and taut, reading a statement, lips moving slightly.

Then Judge Raymond Garvey, brisk and bespectacled, noted for his wit and outspoken support for judicial reform – he had gone on record as suggesting that TV cameras in court could keep judges on their toes – entered the court room, and the selection of the jury began. It dragged on for two days so that it wasn't until June 8th, when a jury consisting of six men and six women had been empanelled, that Robert Flores rose to make his opening statement:

"Your Honour, Mr Adler, ladies and gentlemen of the jury: It is our intention to prove during this trial that with premedi-tation and deliberation Carlos Cortoni murdered Daniel York by stabbing him in the back with a knife. It will come as no surprise to you to know that, in part, the evidence for the prosecution depends on a witness whose memory has been refreshed by hypnosis."

Flores stood in front of his table, arms crossed, and gazed

levelly at the jury; he paused, pulling at the lobe of one ear.

"I don't really have to tell you in this day and age, ladies and gentlemen, that hypnosis is a scientifically accepted phenomenon and, as such, has its rightful place not only in medical but also in legal practice. In other words, as an investigatory device to produce evidence for you, with guidance from the court," nodding towards Judge Garvey, "to dissemble."

"I don't really have to tell you . . . then why am I? Because it is my belief that attempts will be made to disparage evidence initially recalled by hypnosis by regenerating ancient prejudices against hypnotism. I want you to remember that when the witness in question takes the stand, the presentation of her testimony will differ very little from the presentation of testimony being given in a dozen different court rooms in this building at this very moment. All that has happened is that her memory has been jogged just as the memories of witnesses who have not been hypnotised are jogged by interrogation, persuasion and association. And, just like those witnesses, she will be exposed to the usual scrutinies and safeguards of court room practice written into our judicature in the interests of justice."

Flores returned to his table. He stood for a moment, hands deep in the pockets of his trousers, staring at the floor. When he looked up again at the jury he gave a slight smile. "In other words she will be no different on the stand to you or me. I just thought we should get the record straight." He sat down.

The judge said: "That was refreshingly brief, Mr Flores," looking inquiringly at Adler who, thumbs in the pockets of his vest, rose and said in ringing tones: "Your Honour, Mr Flores, ladies and gentlemen," and, less audibly: "*Ancient prejudices?* Do you know, I almost thought he was going to say mumbo-jumbo."

Judge Garvey said: "Speak up, Mr Adler."

Adler turned towards the jury as though about to embark on a long speech and said: "I shall be even briefer than Mr Flores. In fact, I had intended to waive my right to make an opening statement because in my view it serves little purpose – the evidence speaks for itself."

Adler swept one hand through his hair.

"However, as Mr Flores has thought fit to warn you about *ancient prejudices* it is only fair to point out to you that those prejudices still exist. And it is for you to decide whether they should be dismissed so derisively merely because they are *ancient*. Wisdom is ancient, is it not? But I would ask you this, ladies and gentlemen, don't you think that the gentleman on my left doth protest too much?"

Adler sat down abruptly.

*   *   *

Flores' first witness was the Puerto Rican maid who had found York's body. She wore a worn, mustard-coloured coat and a little hat with artificial flowers on it; she was eighteen years-old and, as she testified, she shivered and began to cry.

When she had finished her direct evidence Adler said he had only one question. He turned to the maid: "I'm not going to bite you, although you're a pretty girl and I wouldn't mind." When she managed to smile he asked her: "What was the state of the door that terrible morning?"

She stared at him uncomprehendingly.

The judge said: "Was it open or shut?"

"It was shut. But it wasn't locked. That was the first thing I noticed. The first thing wrong . . ." She began to cry again.

After the maid had been led sobbing from the court room, Flores called the two policemen who had answered the emergency call from York's block. Both said that a party appeared to have been held in the apartment.

Flores' fourth witness was Chamberlain, the finger-print expert, plump and important, who immediately clashed with the judge.

"Sure there were scores of latent prints in the room. That was only to be expected, wasn't it?"

The judge said: "That may be so, Mr Chamberlain. But could you please spare us the benefit of observations outside your specialisation and just answer the questions."

"Yes, Your Honour, there were scores of latent prints," Chamberlain said.

"Among them the defendant's?" Flores asked.

"Yes, sir."

"And in the kitchen, were there a lot of prints there?"

"Sure there were. You see in a kitchen there's a lot of grease –"

The judge snapped: "Mr Chamberlain, you have given testimony on hundreds of occasions?"

"Yes, Your Honour."

"Have other judges asked you to keep your answers pertinent to the questions?"

"They have, Your Honour," Chamberlain said sadly.

"Then please do so in my court.'

Flores asked: "Were the defendant's prints among those in the kitchen?"

Adler said crisply: "Objection. He's leading."

"Okay," Flores said to Chamberlain, "then tell us whose prints you found in the kitchen."

Among the prints listed by Chamberlain were Cortoni's.

"Whereabouts in the kitchen did you find Cortoni's prints, Mr Chamberlain?"

"On a table near the cutlery drawer."

"You mean knives and forks –"

"And spoons, Mr Flores," the judge said, "that's cutlery."

"Were there any knives there?"

"No, sir, not that I could see. The cutlery was distributed all over the apartment with the plates and things."

"Now let's move to the area immediately around the body. Did you find any prints there?"

"No, sir. Only smears."

"On the knife?"

"Another smear. In my opinion . . ." He looked up at the judge and stopped.

"Why do you figure there were no prints, just a smear, on the knife-handle?"

"I guess someone had wiped it clean."

"And the door-handle. Was that clean?"

"It was."

199

"A pretty thorough clean–up, huh, Mr Chamberlain?"

"It was effective, I guess."

Adler rose and stood near the stand to cross-examine. "You could say almost everyone who went to that party left their prints somewhere in the apartment, Mr Chamberlain?"

"There were a lot of prints, yes."

"Among them Mr Cortoni's?"

"That's right."

"And there were a lot of prints in the kitchen?"

"Yes."

"Among them Mr Cortoni's?"

"That's right," Chamberlain said. "I just testified to that."

Adler said silkily: "Please leave the conduct of this cross-examination to me – and to Mr Flores and His Honour the judge." He twirled a bloodstone fob on the gold watch-chain looped across his vest. "You testified that you found prints on the table where the cutlery was found. Did you happen to notice if the carvers were kept there, too?"

"I did, sir. And they weren't," Chamberlain said carefully.

"Where were they kept?"

"There were slots for three carving knives in a wooden board. The board was on the other side of the kitchen. There were only two knives in the slots. The third –"

Adler said: "We know where the third was, Mr Chamberlain. Were there any prints near the wooden board containing those knives?"

"Only the deceased's."

"Thank you, Mr Chamberlain," Adler said, glancing at the jury, "and now, to conclude, let us return to the body. Mr Flores has asked you and I am going to ask you again: Did you find any of Mr Cortoni's fingerprints in the immediate vicinity of the body?"

Chamberlain shook his head. "No, sir."

"Thank you, Mr Chamberlain. Thank you very much."

In redirect examination Flores asked Chamberlain if it was common for an accused person's fingerprints to be absent from the immediate scene of a crime.

"Only too common," Chamberlain said.

200

"In fact, in only a tiny percentage of such cases, say five per cent, do you find a defendant's prints in close proximity to the crime?"

"That's true, I'm afraid."

"But there was a smeared print on the knife-handle?"

"There was."

"Thank you, Mr Chamberlain."

For a moment Chamberlain hesitated as though he wanted to address the jury; then he stepped down.

He was the last witness on the third day of the trial.

*　　*　　*

Tyler liked Chinese food.

Over a bowl of Tan Mein with side dishes, a bowl of fried rice and a long glass of lager, he reviewed developments in the York case in the five months that had elapsed since the Grand Jury hearing.

The restaurant in Chinatown, not too far from his office, was near the corner of Dovers Street and Pell Street, known in the days of Tong warfare as Bloody Corner. Appropriate, he thought, for my deliberations.

He lifted a shrimp from the noodle soup and chewed it; it was delicious. He drank some lager.

Since January one unassailable fact had emerged about Daniel York: he had been a blackmailer.

In a false drawer in a desk in York's apartment Phillip Saul had found a small, Yale-type key. This had led him to a safe-deposit box in a bank in Newark. In the box he had discovered a list of names typed in a code so elementary (a simple Caesar cipher using a displaced alphabet) that detectives had cracked it without recourse to the FBI.

The list was intriguing, the names included a prominent Broadway producer, a Society hostess, a Middle East delegate to the United Nations and a Congressman. Whether or not they had all submitted to blackmail wasn't clear; probably not, because York had been broke when he died.

The grounds for extortion, ranging from sexual perversion

201

to corruption, were equally intriguing. Obviously a lot of dirt collected under the skirts of Manhattan fashion, Tyler reflected, picking up a button mushroom on a china spoon: it was worth bearing in mind in the future.

He had passed all the names to police headquarters to be computer-filed. Only three had any obvious connection with the killing because they had been at the party.

One of them was Marty Padget. Padget was gay, hardly ammunition for the extortionist in this day and age. Unless he was directing his attentions towards juveniles and this, Tyler inferred from the evidence in the safe-deposit box, was precisely what Padget had been doing.

A case for future investigation by vice officers? Tyler stared through the window at a young Chinese telephoning from a callbox with a pagoda roof. The Chinese caught his stare and turned his back. Tyler didn't like using information obtained by a blackmailer; on the other hand, Padget hadn't sought police protection and therefore hadn't been given any promises.

The second name relevant to the killing was Earl Winters. But there was no reference to anything incriminating beside his coded identification. Just a question mark.

To try and find out what York had been questioning, Tyler and Saul had investigated Winters' model agency, his wholesale outlet in the Garment Center and his social life. But apart from the fact that his wife was unfaithful and his marriage was on the rocks, they hadn't come up with anything.

An old Chinese waiter stood beside him with the menu, staring into the evening sunshine. Tyler ordered Honey Apples and coffee. Wordlessly the waiter disappeared into the kitchens. Tyler apart, there were only four diners in the lantern-hung restaurant. Tyler remembered days long ago when, with his beautiful young bride, he had eaten here. He wasn't sure but he thought they had been served by the same waiter who didn't seem to have aged since.

The third relevant name had been Peter Lodge. Grounds for extortion: tax evasion. Which wasn't news to Tyler and Saul. Without revealing that they knew the answer, they had asked

202

Lodge why he thought his name was on York's list. He had reacted incredulously.

Tyler, a lifelong observer of incredulity, had nodded understandingly and said: "Okay, Mr Lodge, thanks for your time. If anything comes up we'll give you a call."

Subsequently Winters, Lodge and Padget had all made Q and A statements but they hadn't in any way advanced the investigation.

The waiter placed a dish of apple rings, dipped in honey and batter, deep fried and served with icing sugar, in front of Tyler. Tyler thanked him and the waiter inclined his head, still peering through the dusty sunshine into the future, or the past. As Tyler bit into an apple ring his mouth watered.

Disappointingly one name had been missing from the list. Carlos, or Carl, Cortoni. Which didn't mean that York hadn't enough material to put the bite on Cortoni; patently he had known that Cortoni was pushing drugs. But by blackmailing Cortoni, York would have been endangering his own supplies. Nevertheless, desperate for a fix, he might have threatened Cortoni with exposure.

Lying sleepless in bed, brooding about the case, Tyler sometimes 'eavesdropped' on the quarrel between York and Cortoni at the party:

York: Carl, give me a fix, look I'm pleading with you, grovelling, for Chrissake have pity . . .

Cortoni: Can you pay for it?

York: I'll find the bread.

Cortoni: No bread, no shit.

York: Look, I need a fix, *need* it . . .

Cortoni: Give me a call when you can pay.

York: If you don't give me a fix now then I swear to God I'll tell the narcos.

Cortoni: And cut off your supplies?

York: I'm telling you, Cortoni, if you don't come over then I'm going to make that call . . .

Cortoni: Okay, Danny, I'll call back later.

And Cortoni had called back later and to end the hassle from a junkie who couldn't pay, a junkie who into the bargain was threatening extortion, had provoked York into a brawl, picked up the carving knife and stabbed him.

In saner moments Tyler admitted to himself that neither Cortoni nor York would have referred to drugs within earshot of guests; the wording would have been muted; but his private version of the argument encouraged him and helped him to sleep.

In fact, there was no evidence about the reason for the quarrel, but Flores reckoned they had enough without it. Provided Helen Fleming came across.

That was what they all dreaded: their star witness forgetting again.

Tyler finished his Honey Apples. A pretty Chinese girl had entered the call box; her boyfriend waited outside mouthing kisses; the girl placed kisses on the palm of her hand and blew them to him. The girl noticed Tyler, smiled, and blew him a kiss. Tyler felt better.

Since the Grand Jury hearing the Narcotics Bureau, working closely with Homicide, had been trying to establish Cortoni's rating in his drug pyramid. He certainly wasn't at the base, occupied by street-corner pop pushers; on the other hand he was nowhere near the apex.

But the standing of his customers was such that Levine hoped he might be close to the next level of the pyramid occupied by the wholesaler. From the wholesaler, if you still believed in miracles, it might be possible to trace the receiver.

So far Levine had failed. But by now Flores should have received a list of witnesses subpoenaed by Adler so detectives could now interview them. Who knows, some of them might lead the narcos to the top of the pyramid.

If they didn't, they would be useful to Flores if their testimony in court differed from what they had told those detectives. At worst they might refuse to make a statement. "Why?" Flores would ask, "if you were so ready to make a statement on behalf of the defendant did you refuse to co-operate with the police?"

Tyler glanced at his wristwatch. 6.20. At 6.30 he was meeting Knox and Flores in the Chief of Homicide's office. He paid his bill and over-tipped the waiter who inclined his head a little lower.

Outside the girl in the callbox blew him another kiss. The boy waiting outside looked sulky. Which was a compliment of sorts.

*   *   *

Flores, Tyler thought, never stopped prosecuting.

Now he paced Knox's office, speaking quietly but intensely, swarthy, flat-featured face taut.

Tyler wasn't sure about Flores. He admired his dedication but questioned the derring-do of his approach to the case. Or am I biased because he's in league with Remick? Tyler wondered.

Knox leaned back in his swivel chair listening and watching, the wily pugilist biding his time. Knox was an innovator, too, and I'm the odd man out here, Tyler thought. Too rigid. So rigid that I've got the best record of arrests and convictions in Homicide, that's how rigid I am!

He crossed his legs, and tried to relax.

Flores was running through the list of witnesses subpoenaed by Adler. "At this stage I don't know what they're going to testify about. That's for you to find out," pointing at Tyler, "but I can guess. Three guests at the party – they'll state categorically that they didn't hear any quarrel between Cortoni and York there. I like witnesses who testify categorically," Flores said, pulling at the lobe of his ear.

"And this lady," he went on, stabbing at a name on the list, "I'll take a bet that she's going to testify that she was safely tucked up in bed with Cortoni at the estimated time of the killing. She might even coyly admit that they were balling. *Do you always make a note of the time when you're making love, Miss Sawicki?*"

Flores picked out another name. "The porter at Cortoni's block. He'll testify to the time Cortoni got back. An educated guess says his evidence cost a thousand bucks, maybe a little more with inflation."

Flores handed the list to Tyler. "There you are, Lieutenant, they're all yours."

Knox said: "How has it gone so far?"

"Predictably." Flores sat down. "I think I won out with the jury selection. You know, Adler was looking for solid citizens who still think a hypnotist is a magician and I was looking for, well, more enlightened members of the public. I don't think our jury – well, perhaps just a few of them – will expect Hansom to materialise on the stand in a cloud of smoke. We're lucky with Judge Garvey, too. Enlightened," glancing at Tyler.

"What did you think of Chamberlain's testimony?" Tyler asked.

"Tell me, Lieutenant, is he always like that?"

"He's a lecturer."

"You can say that again. Can't he confine his lectures to college?"

"He's the best fingerprint man in New York City," Tyler said.

"But not on the stand," Knox said. He began to straighten out a paper-clip on his desk.

Flores said: "Anyway Adler made the point that Cortoni's prints were nowhere near the part of the kitchen where the carvers were kept. Who reckoned the carvers were kept with the rest of the cutlery?" looking at Tyler.

Tyler shrugged. He didn't know.

"Then, of course, he got mileage out of the fact that there were none of Cortoni's prints near the body, but I made the point that this was so in the majority of murder cases. I also made a lot of the fact that the knife had been wiped clean. An act of deliberation and it's a short trip from deliberation to premeditation."

Knox tried to straighten out the last bend in the paper-clip. "All set for tomorrow, Lieutenant?"

Tyler who was taking the stand next day said he was.

Flores said: "I've decided not to attempt to introduce the statement Helen Fleming made to you after she had retained her memory outside a trance. Adler will only go to town on

206

the circumstances under which it was obtained. We'll let him have his moment when – hopefully – Miss Fleming gives the same testimony on the stand. By the way," he said, "has she been threatened in any way recently?"

Shaking his head, Tyler told him that, despite her protests, she had been moved to a safe house on Staten Island.

"How safe, Lieutenant?"

"As safe as we can make it. Too many people got to know where she was staying in Manhattan."

Flores said thoughtfully: "The attempts on her life stopped after she had *remembered*." He paused.

Knox abandoned the still-bent paper-clip. "So?"

"Presuming that it was the Cortonis, father and son, who wanted her out of the way, doesn't it strike you as odd that they don't any more?"

"Maybe they figured that if she'd remembered there wasn't any point," Knox suggested doubtfully, adding: "No, I guess that doesn't make sense."

"Of course it doesn't. If they'd got to her before she remembered fine, just fine. The case against Carlos Cortoni would have been sunk before it was even launched. But now she has remembered, now the case has been launched, they should be trying to stop her from testifying. It wouldn't be the first time the star prosecution witness has disappeared from a case involving a Cortoni. Do you know what I think, gentlemen?"

The two-man jury shook their heads.

"I think the defence regards Miss Fleming as *their* star witness."

XIX

And now I'm a prisoner, she thought.

The house, on the fringe of St George, was neat, medium-sized, with a red roof and white clapboard walls. The furniture was practical, uninspired; the rooms smelled of fresh paint and distemper, but in the open-plan living-room the air was fumed by the winter's log-fires; it wasn't an unpleasant smell.

The house was called Bay View but you couldn't see the bay. Unless you stood on the chimney.

The great advantage of Bay View was its position. It was one of a row of houses but, unlike the others, it was set in relatively spacious grounds; and not only were they spacious, but they weren't planted with trees or shrubs which could provide cover for an assassin. The lawns were green and shaved, the flowerbed, filled with Petunias and Antirrhinums, were well tended.

Katy Tanner moved in with Helen, and round-the-clock police surveillance was mounted. Even when Helen went to court a policeman was left watching the empty house in case someone broke in and lay in wait for her.

In other circumstances Helen would have enjoyed staying at the house; it was rather like taking a working vacation in another city, especially if, instead of using the Verrazano-Narrows Bridge, you took the ferry from Downtown Manhattan, feeling the salt spray in your face as you skirted the Statue of Liberty.

The police tried to insist that she and her escort should always travel on the bridge because, they reasoned, it was quicker and therefore safer. But when she pointed out that it was doubtful if a hit-man would try and kill on board ship because, short of diving into Upper New York Bay, he wouldn't be able to escape, they sanctioned the occasional journey by ferry.

For the first two days of the trial Peter accompanied her and her police escort in Remick's chocolate Mustang, once across the bridge and once on the ferry; and stayed one night.

The police suggested that she should keep her new address, her fortress, a total secret but again she overruled them. They now knew who had been trying to kill her, the least they could do was to allow a few friends to visit her.

On the ferry on the second day, Peter and Helen wandered away from Remick and stood leaning against the deck-rail. The water was June-calm, the sky evening blue; behind them the clustered towers of Manhattan were searching for the stars; to their right stood the Statue of Liberty.

"Odd to think it was built by a Frenchman," she said.

"History again?"

"Not *everybody* knows. His name was Frederic-Auguste Bartholdi and he used his mother as a model. And Gustave Eiffel, more famous for his tower, designed the framework. But we did build the pedestal."

Peter slipped his arm round her waist. "I love you," he said.

She kissed him, half closing her eyes so that the evening sunlight on the water was a golden blur. "Someone doesn't," she said after a moment.

"It will soon be over."

"But it will leave scars," she said.

"Us?"

"Why didn't you tell the truth when Tyler and Saul first questioned you, Peter?"

"About Nurse Bulmer? I didn't want them to know you were under medical supervision; I didn't want them to find out that you'd had this black-out. It seemed to make sense at the time . . ."

"Because you thought I might have killed York?"

"There was always that possibility," Peter said carefully, "however remote."

"I'm grateful," she said. "You were protecting me."

In front of them a fish, silver bright in the sunlight, leapt in the air and fell back into the water with a splash.

She said: "But why did you tell the police you didn't know the names of the last guests to leave the party? Because that's what you told them, wasn't it Peter? Until they came round to the apartment on Boxing Day."

"I guess I was trying to protect them," Peter said. "Marty, Earl – I explained all that when I called you that time from Los Angeles."

"Cortoni?"

"Not him so much," Peter said. "And I think I've been interrogated enough by the cops, don't you?"

"I'm sorry," she said, "but there's still a lot I don't understand. You didn't do a deal with Cortoni, did you, Peter?"

"Are you kidding?"

"I still can't understand why you stayed on at the party talking business with him when you'd told me earlier that you would never sell out to him."

"And this," Peter said, "is where I say, 'Don't you worry your little head about it.' " But if the words were jocular, the tone of his voice wasn't.

And later as she and Peter prepared dinner in the kitchen while Katy and Remick chatted in front of the empty, autumn-smelling grate, his voice still had an edge to it.

"Well," she said, tossing a green salad as the steaks sizzled on the grill, "I might just get it all off my chest here and now."

He stirred the dressing for the salad adding a little mustard. "Go ahead," he said tightly.

"Why didn't you tell the police you were being blackmailed? You never really explained . . ."

"Because I'm not that dumb."

"But they would probably have granted you immunity against prosecution."

"Would the tax authorities?"

"Do the police know York was blackmailing you?"

Peter considered. Finally he said:"They know my name was on a list in York's possession, that's all."

"Then they must have their suspicions."

"Why should they? Unless you've told them."

She stared at him. "You think I would do that?"

"No," he said, "I don't and I'm sorry."

He poured the dressing onto the salad and took it into the living-room. Helen followed him.

Remick finished his drink and said to Helen: "Okay, same time tomorrow morning?"

"Do you have to go?" Helen asked. "I've grilled four steaks."

"Give the guy a break," Peter said. "He probably wants to do the town," and he limped to the door to let Remick out.

* * *

At the end of the third day of the trial Helen returned to the house in a police car. Remick had been called out on another case; Peter, not expected to testify – about the quarrel between York and Cortoni – until much later had been granted permission to drive to Sag Harbour to consult an architect about his new boutique.

Helen experienced the usual surge of relief when she arrived on the island as though the water separated her from danger. I have developed an insular mentality, she thought. The street was comforting, too. Sprinklers on the lawns, cars in the driveways, children on roller-skates on the sidewalk. Here people enjoyed their homes.

Katy was waiting for her, red hair falling glossily down to her shoulders, dressed for a date.

"With Bally Shoes," she said. "Their PR guy. Is that okay, Helen? I won't be late and you've got two husky patrolmen in the grounds."

Helen said that of course it was okay. The trial was going to continue for God knows how long – about fifty witnesses – and Katy couldn't be expected to stay at home every night.

At dusk she peered down the street. It had emptied and the sprinklers had all been turned off. In a couple of windows she could see the coloured flicker of television sets. Down the road stood the police car. Even in summer there was a touch of cruelty to this pre-dark time. She bolted the door and fixed the chain.

In the kitchen she toasted herself a cheese and tomato sandwich and poured herself a Coke. She never drank wine on her own; she didn't know why. She switched on the television. A police series. She switched channels. An old movie about the Plaza Hotel in which Walter Matthau played three different roles. She had seen it before, but it was worth seeing again.

What would I do, she wondered as Walter Matthau began to set up a seduction, if I wanted to break into this house? Set up a diversion to entice the police away?

She started as the telephone rang. She took the call in the hallway at the foot of the stairs beside an empty fish tank.

"Hi," Earl Winters said, "I thought you might be lonely. I heard Peter was on Long Island and I know Katy's doing a deal with Bally."

His voice warmed her. "Can you come over, Earl?"

"Not tonight, honey. Tonight I'm hustling for us all. Let's face it, this trial might not be such a bad deal after all. Every day you've been on television, in the papers. Paris, Rome, London, here we come. When do you testify?"

"In a couple of days, I think."

"Mmmmmm. And you'll be on the stand a long time. Me? I guess I'm a half-day job, even though I knew Danny better than most."

She heard a click on the line. "Earl, are you still there?"

"Sure I'm still here, but I've got to go . . ."

Perhaps the line was bugged. Perhaps? No, of course it was.

". . . See you in court, Helen. I just figured a friendly voice on the phone might help pass the evening. Take care." Click.

She returned to the movie. Matthau was now a Jewish father whose daughter was refusing to go to her own wedding.

And how would I cause a diversion? Stage some sort of disturbance nearby; no cop would be able to resist that. And then . . . The phone rang again.

"How you doing, doll?" Helen stared at the receiver. Why should Marty Padget call her? "Just a friendly call. Earl said you were all alone."

"That's nice of you," Helen said.

"We witnesses have got to stick together."

"Why are the prosecution calling you, Marty?" she asked.

She heard him sigh. "You might as well know, the whole wide world will know pretty soon. I've got a skeleton in my cupboard – my bedroom cupboard – and poor dear Danny knew about it."

"Blackmail?"

"He was going to put the squeeze on," Padget said. "This guy Flores wants to prove that Danny wasn't all he was cracked up to be. That he was the sort of guy who might threaten Cortoni and get a knife in his back for his pains."

"I know," Helen said, "Peter told me," wishing immediately that she hadn't said it because Peter had not said anything about testifying that he was being blackmailed.

"He did, did he?" A pause. "I wonder . . . Ah, to hell with it. Not to put too fine a point on it, our Danny headed a lot of people's shit lists. You want to know why he was going to put the bite on me?"

"No," she said, "keep it for the jury." Another click.

"See you in the morning, doll." The line went dead.

In the living-room Matthau was pleading with his daughter through a closed door.

Toss a brick through a shop window, set off a fire-alarm, that would shift the police.

She parted the curtains. Saw the silhouette of a patrolman on the lawn. A cigarette glowed in his cupped hand.

The phone rang again. It seemed louder each time. She picked up the receiver. Had the fish in the tank died?

"Hallo," she said. She heard someone breathing. "Hallo, who is it . . . ? Is that you, Peter?"

The breathing quickened. "Hallo . . ." The breathing steadied, continued. "Please . . ."

Click as the line went dead. Slowly she replaced the receiver.

Her body began to shake. She went back to the living-room, switched off Matthau.

If only Remick were here. Or Peter. She tried to control the shaking. Poured herself a glass of wine.

She remembered a story she had once heard about a woman waiting for her husband in a mansion in the forest. The telephone had rung and she had heard breathing. She had rung the exchange to ask if they could trace the call. A few minutes later the operator had called back. Yes, they had traced the call. It had come from another telephone *inside* the mansion. She gulped down the wine and poured herself another glass. Well, at least the call couldn't have come from inside this house.

Faintly she heard the sound of breaking glass and a bell ringing followed by running footsteps. The stem of the wine-glass broke in her hand and blood flowed from the ball of her thumb. She went to the bathroom, washed her hand and stuck a plaster over the wound.

A car drew up in the street outside.

In the living-room she parted the curtains to see if the silhouette of the policeman was still there. A pair of eyes stared back at her from the darkness.

The racket started a few moments later as, frozen, she stood gazing at the curtains. There came the thump of footsteps on the lawn; then a thud against the window, as though someone had turned suddenly and hit the glass, followed by a man's shout and more running footsteps. The shouting came from some distance away. Her guards racing back from wherever the glass had been broken?

Confused, unidentifiable noises, more shouts, and then a cry of pain. Still she stood frozen. She shut her eyes tight and there in the dark-red darkness were the eyes. Suddenly there was a furious knocking on the door, the sound of a bell ringing.

She opened her eyes.

A man's voice: "Open the door, police."

She walked slowly and deliberately to the door, and looked through the peephole. There were two figures, one of them uniformed.

214

She opened the door and was in the arms of John Remick, who was standing beside the policeman. She stayed in his arms, felt his warmth, pressed her face hard against his shoulder, stayed there as he stroked her hair, stayed there as he raised her face and kissed her eyes, wanted to stay there forever.

*   *   *

The eyes belonged to a sullen, hollow-cheeked man named Joseph Campo, known to Staten Island police as both a voyeur-pervert and a small-time crook with a record of violence.

The question was: had he been operating tonight as hit-man or voyeur? He had been carrying a Walther P–38 and had drawn it when Remick, who had arrived to check that Helen was all right by herself, had hit him with a flying tackle.

But that didn't prove a thing, according to one of the police guards. Creeps like Campo always carried guns. What was more likely was that he had heard that there were two beautiful girls staying at the house and had decided to observe them in his special way. To do that he had created a diversion by lobbing a chunk of concrete through the window of a store at an intersection down the street; the impact had triggered the burglar alarm.

Privately Helen suspected the policeman was trying to minimise the danger to her, because neither he nor his colleague should have left the house. While he tried to explain their actions the other policeman, gun pointing at the handcuffed Campo, reported on the car radio. Within three minutes another police car drew up, siren wailing, roof light flashing.

Campo was taken away. Sheepishly the two policemen resumed their surveillance. And tentatively, facing each other across the empty fireplace, John Remick and Helen Fleming talked about everything except what was happening to them.

*   *   *

For a long time Tyler and Saul had tried to establish a connection between Frank Bruton, the dead hit-man, and either Carlos Cortoni or his father. From names culled from the transcript of Miguel Cortoni's trial, they had put out feelers. Without luck.

Levine, of Narcotics, had also tried unsuccessfully to establish a connection from his own contacts.

Now Tyler and Saul had Joseph Campo to work on. They interviewed him in a bleak room in the precinct in St George half an hour after he had been caught. "Well, Joe," Saul said, leaning against the wall and lighting a cigar, "things don't look too good for you, do they?"

"What the fuck am I supposed to say to that?"

Campo was sitting on a chair planted in the middle of the room; opposite him, behind a desk, sat Tyler. Campo had a twitch below one eye and from time to time he tried to smooth it away with the tips of his fingers.

Tyler and Saul stared at him.

"Okay, okay. So you caught me peeping again. Okay, it's my weakness, I admit it, I confess, so what's the big deal?"

"Do you always carry a gun when you look through ladies' windows?" Saul asked.

"Sometimes I carry a gun to protect myself."

"From naked ladies?" Saul blew smoke at Campo. "You got a licence for that thing?"

"You know I ain't. Okay, bust me for that too. I confess," hands held up, "so you got another conviction, congratulations." He paused. "Where you from anyway?"

"Homicide," Tyler said.

Campo put down his hands. The nerve below his eye danced. "Homicide? I didn't kill no-one."

Tyler said: "We're interested in the fact that you intended to."

"Intended. Are you kidding? I didn't want to kill no-one."

"Then why carry a gun?"

"Like I told you, to protect myself."

"Guns kill people," Saul said. "We've discovered that at Homicide."

"Homicide, Jesus!" Campo put a hand to his eye.

216

"Did you throw the concrete through the window?"

"Yeah. Is that homicide?"

Tyler said: "Who paid you to kill the girl?"

"Kill her? I only wanted to look at her, for fuck's sake. What the hell is this?"

"He usually pays five thousand bucks," Saul said. "Did he pay you five grand?"

"Nobody paid me nothing."

"You had the gun in your hand."

"So would you if some gorilla comes charging at you the way that guy did."

Tyler picked up a pencil, stuck it through the trigger-guard on Campo's Walther and delicately held up the gun. "Let's tot it all up," Tyler said, "just so you know the score. You were carrying this gun, right?"

Campo shrugged. "Right. So what's new?"

"You were trespassing on police property."

"Police property?"

"The house is police property," Tyler said. "Inside that house was a witness due to give evidence in a murder trial, right?"

"So she's a witness."

"Who's already been threatened."

"Not by me, Lieutenant."

"So you knew she'd been threatened?"

"I read the newspapers."

Tyler made a note. He then said: "So we bust you armed, gun in hand, on police property peering through the window at a witness in a murder trial who's already been threatened."

Saul said: "Then you make a run for it, asshole."

"And resist arrest," Tyler said.

"You poor, sad sonofabitch," Saul said.

Tyler picked up a manilla folder on the desk. "Plus this?"

"Plus what?"

"Your record," Tyler said.

"Ten years minimum," Saul said.

"Ten years? For having a little fun? Christ, she wasn't even stripped off . . ."

"Unless you co-operate," Tyler said, standing up. "Are you going to help us, Joe?"

Campo covered his face with his hands. "I can't," he said, "Don't you see? I can't. There ain't nothing I can help you with."

Tyler nodded at Saul who opened the door and called in a policeman from the precinct and said: "Okay, book him."

"Book him for what?" the policeman asked.

"Everything," Saul said.

*   *   *

Tyler and Saul departed on the ferry, across the dark bay surrounded by galaxies of light. They listened to the bows of the ship shouldering aside the water and Saul said: "You know, I reckon this tub would find its way home without a crew." He watched the light of an airplane moving through the thick stars. "Do you think he was going to kill the girl?"

But all Tyler said was: "Maybe Remick was right," and, without elaborating, he stood, arms folded, alone, watching the lights of Manhattan reach out across the water to the ferry.

XX

Tyler took the stand after Remick had given brief medical evidence. As always he excluded everyone in the court room from his mind except the lawyer questioning him and the judge.

In reply to Flores he described his actions on the morning the body was found and his subsequent interrogation of guests at the party.

Flores: "As a result of this questioning, did you ascertain who was the last to leave the party?"

"I did, sir." (Once Cortoni had been charged, Lodge, Winters and Padget had amended their statements and the chronology of their departures had emerged.)

Adler jumped to his feet. "Objection, Your Honour. Lieutenant Tyler is giving an opinion: these guests can surely testify themselves."

Flores said: "Lieutenant Tyler is giving a deduction not an opinion. He *is* a detective."

Adler shook his head. "As *I* understand the law – and as I'm sure Mr Flores understands it – a witness may not testify to conclusions drawn from his observations."

Judge Garvey removed his spectacles and snapped: "Will the two counsellors approach the bench please." And when they were standing in front of him, out of earshot of the jury, he said: "I want it clearly understood, gentlemen, at this early stage in what promises to be a long and arduous trial, that I will not tolerate either histrionics or improper examination in this court room. In particular," looking at Flores, "I will not tolerate the insertion of questions which, whether they are answered or not, influence the jury, even though I direct them to disregard such questions."

And to Adler he said: "You may re-adjust your halo, Mr Adler. I want no outbreaks in front of the jury. Please seek permission to approach the bench when you want to elaborate on an objection. Now, Mr Flores, do you have anything further to say?"

"Only that in this instance I submit that Lieutenant Tyler is excluded from the ruling on opinion, on the grounds that he is an expert witness."

The judge said: "Lieutenant Tyler may be an expert detective, Mr Flores, but this does not mean that he is any more expert than you or I or Mr Adler to determine on evidence not yet presented to this court who left the party first. Objection sustained."

Judge Garvey reminded Tyler of a movie director asserting his authority over two temperamental stars.

Flores asked Tyler: "As a result of your inquiries, did you mount a surveillance operation on the accused?"

"I did, sir."

"Who was responsible for the surveillance?"

"Officers from the Homicide Bureau and from Narcotics."

"As a result of that surveillance did you go to an address in Brooklyn?"

"I did, sir."

Tyler described how he and Kohl from Narcotics had visited the warehouse armed with a search warrant. He described the shoot-out involving Saul and the discovery of the heroin in Cortoni's briefcase.

He then explained how Cortoni had finally been charged with murder and described a subsequent interview at which, on the advice of his lawyer, Cortoni had said nothing.

Flores then questioned him about the hypnosis of Helen Fleming.

"What was the object of the exercise, Lieutenant?"

"To help her remember what she saw on the night of the murder."

"And did she remember?"

"Yes, sir, she did."

"I'm not going to ask you what she remembered – I'm going to leave that to Miss Fleming to tell the jury herself. But I am going to ask you whether, in your opinion, she was in a normal frame of mind after dehypnosis."

Adler was on his feet again. "Objection. Opinion."

Flores said: "May we approach the bench, Your Honour?"

"Certainly you may," Judge Garvey said. And when they both stood in front of him: "Well, Mr Flores?"

"In my submission a non-expert opinion is permissable when that opinion is founded on perception."

Adler said: "You just claimed Lieutenant Tyler *was* an expert!"

"He's not an expert on hypnosis."

"Then surely he can't give an opinion."

"Sustained," said the judge. "I suggest you re-phrase your question, Mr Flores."

Flores asked Tyler: "What was the condition of Miss Fleming after she had undergone hypnosis?"

"Just ordinary. Just the same as before she was hypnotised by Dr Hansom."

"She conducted herself quite . . ." Flores pulled at his ear ". . . happily?"

"She wasn't distressed in any way," Tyler said.

Tyler testified for another half an hour. When he had finished his direct evidence the judge recessed the court.

*　　*　　*

Tyler felt uncomfortable in his dark-grey lightweight suit. He and May had called it his Court Suit because in those days his other suits had been a little more colourful; these days there wasn't much to choose between them, except that the others were more comfortable. He wore a white shirt and a blue tie.

He looked around the corridor outside the court room, hoping that Saul would put in an appearance; he was due to give evidence after Tyler but, because they knew that Tyler's testimony would be a long haul, he had taken time off to interview some of the witnesses subpoenaed by Adler.

At the end of the corridor Tyler could see Flores talking to Adler. The public always enjoyed the spectacle of lawyers, bitterly hostile in court, talking amicably outside it; today they would have been disappointed – the two counsellors were arguing as heatedly as they had been in court.

When Flores came over he said: "If they ever make a movie of the life of Sir Laurence Olivier that guy should take the lead."

They were joined by Saul. He was sweating and he had unbuttoned his collar beneath his neck-tie. They looked at him expectantly.

"So I found Miss Betty Sawicki," he told them.

Flores looked interested. "She was balling Cortoni at the time of the murder?"

"Maybe she was but she's a very discreet lady. But stacked," Saul added.

"You mean discreet to you but not to the defence?"

Saul nodded. "Scared."

"If she's scared, then I'll scare her some more."

Tyler said: "Did you get anything from her?"

"Sure I got something." Saul consulted his notebook. "*I refuse to say anything until I've called my lawyer.*"

"Great," Tyler said. "And did she?"

Saul turned a page of the notebook. "*I have called my lawyer and he has advised me to say nothing.*"

"So," said Flores, "we have a witness who's willing to talk to the defence but not to the prosecution. We've got proven bias and if she's the sort of witness I think she is I should be able to impeach her on the stand."

Tyler asked: "What about the porter?"

"He'll testify to the time Cortoni allegedly got back. It doesn't mean a helluva lot because we haven't got an exact time of death."

Flores said: "Adler will try and get mileage out of it. Compare it with times given by our witnesses, ie Cortoni can't have been the last to leave."

"In any case," Tyler said, "he could have returned."

"What sort of guy is the porter?" Flores asked Saul.

"Moronic," Saul said.

"Good," Flores said. The crowd in the corridor was beginning to drift back to the court room. To Tyler he said: "Good luck, I don't think Adler will have any surprises for you."

He was wrong.

*　　*　　*

Sometimes Adler, immaculate in a dark blue mohair suit with a red rose in his buttonhole, silver hair falling across his tanned brow, paced the court room as he cross-examined; sometimes he stood facing the jury, dumbly eloquent when Tyler gave the reply he wanted; sometimes he approached the witness-stand.

Twice he clashed with Flores and once, up at the bench, Judge Garvey warned Flores that he was in danger of receiving a citation for contempt when he had audibly observed: "This is New York City, Mr Adler, not Hollywood."

The surprise came when Adler, standing close to Tyler, first raised the question of hypnosis.

Adler: "You were in charge of the investigation, were you not, Lieutenant?"

"In the field, yes."

"Did *you* suggest hypnosis as an investigatory technique?"

Tyler faltered and Adler said: "Speak up, Lieutenant, it's a perfectly straightforward question," glancing at the jury.

"No, sir."

"Then who did suggest it?"

Flores was on his feet. "This is totally irrelevant, Your Honour."

Adler spread wide his hands. "With respect, Your Honour, how can the counsellor possibly know that?"

"Perhaps you could tell us, Mr Adler," Judge Garvey said.

223

"I intend to show that the police officer in charge of this case viewed the use of hypnotism with extreme scepticism, Your Honour."

"Very well, Mr Adler, please continue."

Adler turned to Tyler: "Who did suggest it, Lieutenant?"

"I believe Dr Remick did."

"*Believe*, Lieutenant?"

"Yeah, he suggested it."

"Over your head?"

"He consulted Mr Knox, Chief of Homicide."

"I will repeat the question, Lieutenant. Over your head?"

"If you like to put it that way, yes."

"I do like to put it that way, Lieutenant," he said, smiling in the direction of the jury, "I really do."

Tyler felt sweat trickling down his chest beneath his shirt. It was the first time for a long while that he had been shaken on the witness-stand. How the hell did Adler know about the breach between Remick and himself? It was common knowledge in Homicide, so the inference was that Miguel Cortoni had a good informant there.

Adler said: "Why did Dr Remick feel it necessary to go over your head?"

"Because I wasn't in favour of hypnosis *at that stage in the investigation*."

"You considered routine police work to be more promising?"

"I felt that we would collect sufficient evidence that way, yes."

Adler moved away from the stand and, thumbs in the pockets of his vest, faced the jury. "But you didn't, did you, Lieutenant?"

"We reached a stage in the investigation where I agreed that hypnosis should be employed."

"When all else had failed?"

"No, sir, not when all else had failed."

"Then why did you suddenly agree to a process that had previously been abhorrent to you?"

"Not abhorrent. I figured it had its rightful place in an

224

investigation, but not at the outset."

"Because you didn't want to rely in court on a process that is still lacking in credibility and scientific foundation?"

Flores slapped the table with the palm of his hand, a lot of his brooding calm evaporating. "Objection. The counsellor is flagrantly leading the witness. If ever I heard a classic have-you-stopped-beating-your-wife that's it."

Judge Garvey looked sternly at Adler. "Sustained. Please remember what I said at the bench."

Adler inclined his head. "I'm sorry, Your Honour." And, changing track, he asked Tyler: "The first attempt to revive Miss Fleming's memory failed. Am I right?"

So they knew about that, too! "I don't believe there is any particular stage in hypnosis when recall is guaranteed."

Adler sighed. "Please answer the question, Lieutenant."

"I don't think failed is the right word."

"Did it succeed?"

"No, but –"

"Thank you, Lieutenant. Miss Fleming remembered nothing?"

"No, sir, not when she was dehypnotised."

"I'm obliged. You see, we haven't heard too much about this first attempt to find out what Miss Fleming remembered – or didn't remember. Were you disappointed at this negative response?"

"Sure, we had hoped that she would remember."

"Because without that you had nothing?"

"On the contrary, we had a helluva lot."

"But not enough to justify a murder charge?"

"Naturally an eye-witness account would have helped."

"You had changed your tune, hadn't you, Lieutenant?"

"No, sir."

"Had you previously interviewed Miss Fleming?"

"I had."

"Did you at any time suggest to Miss Fleming what she might have seen that fateful night?"

"I did not."

"You see, I'm going to call expert witnesses who will testify

225

that suggestion plays a great part in hypnosis. If a name is suggested a sufficient number of times then a subject in a trance may utter that name."

Tyler didn't reply.

"Had the accused's name been in the Press a great deal at this time?"

"Not when I interviewed Miss Fleming, no. Only to the effect that he had been at the party."

"And subsequently?"

"Yes, the Press gave considerable coverage to Cortoni's arrest."

"But not for murder, Lieutenant."

"No, sir, narcotics."

"But the two were linked in the media, were they not?"

"I believe they were, indirectly."

"So when Miss Fleming underwent hypnosis the name of the accused would have been in her mind?"

"Only if she read the newspapers."

"And watched television and listened to the radio . . . Come now, Lieutenant, if you had supposedly witnessed a crime, wouldn't you want to read every damn word written about it?"

"I've been involved in many crimes, sir, and although I've had to, I've never *wanted* to read a damn word about any of them."

Laughter rippled round the court. Tyler was surprised at himself: levity from a police witness was a mistake.

"You astonish me, Lieutenant. I read every damn word about cases I'm involved in."

Another flutter of laughter.

Adler said abruptly: "Tell me, Lieutenant, if a witness to a crime doesn't tell you what you want him to tell you, do you try, try again until he does?"

"No."

"But this is precisely what happened in the case of Miss Fleming, is it not?"

"No. She retained her memory of what happened that night on the second time she was questioned under hypnosis."

"In the normal way, the *routine* way, *your* way, Lieutenant, would you have subjected a witness to a second, identical interrogation within twenty-four hours?"

"It's possible."

"Would you agree that Miss Fleming was being subjected to pressure?"

"As I understand it, she was being put through a perfectly normal hypnotic procedure."

"Ah, as you see it." Adler prowled the court room, stopped in front of Tyler and, leaning forward, hand on one knee, asked: "What are your views on hypnotism, Lieutenant?"

"I believe it has a therapeutic value."

"And in the legal context?"

"It has been used to effect to help witnesses recall certain kinds of evidence."

"But when it comes to making an allegation of murder through hypnotic recall, then that's a very different kettle of fish . . . Are those your feelings, Lieutenant?"

"I've told you my feelings, sir. I believe that hypnosis may well have its place in an investigation but it also has its time."

"Why such emphasis on time?"

"Because I believe other steps should be taken first."

"Routine steps?"

"Routine steps."

"Even when you have an eye-witness to a murder?"

"We didn't know at the time that she was an eye-witness."

"A possible eye-witness then?"

"There were other avenues to explore."

"But they led nowhere?"

"I didn't say that."

"So you have a possible eye-witness and yet you prefer to go wandering down other avenues . . . Is that correct?"

"Not wandering, sir."

"I put it to you, Lieutenant, that you looked upon hypnosis only as a last resort because you believed that it could lead to a gross miscarriage of justice."

"No, sir," wondering if he was lying to himself.

As Flores rose to object, Adler said: "No further questions,"

227

and sat down, smelling the red rose on his lapel.

When Tyler left the witness-stand, after Flores had finished his redirect examination, he scanned the court.

Carlos Cortoni stared back at him, then looked away. Behind him his father, in a pearl-grey suit, smiled complacently because, Tyler thought, he reckoned Adler had scored during the cross-examination.

There was Earl Winters' monkish fringe; beside Winters sat a man Tyler didn't immediately recognise; then he had it – Marty Padget minus moustache. Beside him Peter Lodge, his features contained and watchful as always.

And behind them faces from the magazines, from television commercials, from hoardings; self-consciously serious here in court until they reached the cameras waiting outside the building in the June sunlight.

On the way to the parking lot during the lunch recess, Tyler asked Flores how he thought the case was going and when Flores said: "What you mean is how did you make out?" he said, yes, he supposed that was what he meant.

"I thought you were pretty good," Flores said.

Tyler was surprised: he had testified like a rookie.

"Adler threw the book at you and you reacted like any member of the jury would have done and that's what it's all about. You were a human being not a cop."

"You mean there's a difference?"

"I wonder how the hell Adler knew the girl had failed to remember the first time," Flores said.

"Because I figure there's a leak in Homicide. I've suspected it for some time. We'll have to set some bait."

Standing beside his car, a white Cadillac Seville, Flores said. "As I've said before, this case stands or falls on the testimony of Helen Fleming."

Tyler was silent.

Flores climbed into the driving seat. "And the testimony of Dr Hansom," he added switching on the ignition. "He takes the stand tomorrow."

And with a wave Flores backed up the Cadillac and drove off to lunch.

228

XXI

She didn't know how much more she could take.

Even now when she closed her eyes standing on the deck of the ferry, she saw the eyes staring at her through the window. The hand jammed in the door, fingers twitching. She opened her eyes and looked down at her own gloved hands; recently she had been neglecting them.

She was due to give evidence the day after tomorrow; until then her guards had been doubled. But they, whoever *they* were, could still reach her, she felt that. But if they still wanted to kill her why had they left her alone for so long? Perhaps the eyes *had* belonged to a mere voyeur. The thought comforted her a little. The comfort expanded when she thought about Remick, felt the cloth of his suit as she clung to him, heard the beat of his heart.

Peter Lodge said: "Only a few more days, then it will be all over."

"Yes," she said.

"How's that memory?" He squeezed her arm.

"It's fine."

"You were a long way away just then." The breeze blew his brown hair across his forehead.

"I was in the future, after all this."

Another squeeze. "I hope I was there too." A pause. "Well, was I?"

"Of course you were," she said.

"Good." He kissed her cheek. "I'm sorry I wasn't there last night. But at least you had a knight errant ready and waiting."

"If it hadn't been for Remick I might have been killed."

"Nonsense," Peter said, brushing at his hair with one hand. "The police are almost sure he was only a Peeping Tom."

"He had a gun."

Peter said: "So does half the population of the United States. By the way, in case you're wondering where your chauffeur is, I told Tyler that, as from today, I drive you home. I don't see why we should deprive the police department of the services of an up-and-coming surgeon."

A sightseeing helicopter hovered above them like a dragonfly, then slanted away towards Manhattan; a tug pulling a barge passed close by sounding its hooter.

If only she could be on that tug heading out to sea. She said: "The police chose his car because it wasn't conspicuous." She looked round the crowded deck for her bodyguards; there they were, two of them in plainclothes – uniformed police at night – leaning against the rail.

"Which is why I hired the compact," Peter said. "But what the hell was Remick doing outside the house disturbing prowlers at that time of night?"

"It was only ten," she said.

"So, what was he doing there at ten?"

"He'd come to see how I was. He knew I was alone –"

"I'll say!"

"He knew you had left me to do some business."

"Left you? For Chrissake I left you with Katy – how was I to know she was dining with Bally shoes? – and two cops."

"Peter," she said quietly, one hand on his shoulder, "why don't you forget it? It isn't anything."

Maybe it wasn't. Just circumstance. Emotion unleashed. "Okay," he said as the ferry nosed into St George, "it's forgotten."

*　　*　　*

230

That evening Tyler drove to a nautical-style bar on South Street to check out information that Frank Bruton, the hit-man, had been in the habit of meeting Carl Cortoni there.

Before he went he consulted several officers about the poss-ible leakage of information from within Homicide that was being fed to Cortoni's defence lawyers.

Several of them told Tyler that they had harboured suspi-cions, so vague that they hadn't acted upon them, about a detective named Sheehan. It was only when their suspicions were collated that they hardened.

Tyler told Saul to set a bait for Sheehan – the fact that he was investigating a possible link between Cortoni and Frank Bru-ton at the South Street bar. "Even if he does manage to tip off Miguel Cortoni it won't matter," Tyler said, "because I will have checked it out by then."

At 9 pm Saul went to a bar on Broadway where Sheehan drank. It was gloomy inside, lit by fluorescent strips that picked out white – shirt-fronts, cuffs, napkins . . . Saul was glad he was wearing a dark blue shirt.

"Hi, Phil," someone said, "what you having?"

Saul asked for a bourbon and water and moved close to Sheehan. When one of the detectives asked how the Trance Trial was progressing, Saul told him about the lead in the South Street bar.

Over the rim of his glass Saul watched Sheehan. Cop writ-ten all over him, he thought, and handsome with it, a TV cop. Except, of course, that he had stopped a bullet and wasn't as fit as he looked. Was that enough to make a man a rogue cop?

Sheehan finished his drink, glanced at his watch. He called out to the barman: "Set 'em up again, Tony, I'll be back," and headed for the corridor that led to the washrooms – and the telephone.

Saul watched his white, disembodied shirt-front disappear, then, sadly, followed.

The phone was on the wall beneath a hood that was sup-posed to insulate the speaker's voice but didn't. Sheehan's back was turned as Saul walked silently along the corridor.

"Hallo, Mr Cortoni, it's Brady."

231

Gun in hand, Saul tapped Sheehan on the shoulder and said: "No it isn't, asshole, it's Sheehan."

Slowly Sheehan replaced the receiver. When he turned, his face was oddly tranquil. "Thank God," he said.

While Saul searched him he wondered why Sheehan hadn't used a street booth, and it was only later that it occurred to him that Sheehan had deliberately led him to the telephone.

*   *   *

Remick circled the silver box lying on the coffee table in his cramped apartment. In it were three cigarettes, as dry as autumn leaves but smokeable. Tonight the craving was stronger than it had been since he had given up. Tension, he supposed. He opened the lid of the box and regarded the desiccated cigarettes, imagined the first catch in his throat as he inhaled.

If I can last out another three days, he thought, then I've kicked it. Because, although the trial wouldn't be over, they would know by then if they had won or lost. Not just this case but the battle against prejudice.

Three days. One for Hansom's testimony, according to Flores' calculations, and two for Helen's.

He smelled her perfume, saw the terror in her eyes. But she was in love with another man. Or was she?

He decided to have his second shave of the day (difficult to smoke with your face lathered) and go out to dinner. Perhaps Tyler would be in the Irish pub. He shook his head as he squirted aerosol foam; no, not Tyler. He drew the razor down one cheek, rinsed the foam from the blade. No doubt about it, shaving did exercise a certain tranquilising therapy. Carefully he negotiated the cleft in his chin.

Was it his imagination or had she lingered deliberately in his arms? More to the point, had he held her deliberately? No, she would probably marry Peter Lodge and have three kids; he cut himself on the chin and swore. He washed his face, applied after-shave, and went back into the living-room.

He took one of the cigarettes from the silver box, menthol

232

with low tar. He put it between his lips; he could taste the tobacco. Just one puff . . . Jesus, a doctor . . . one puff and you're hooked again. He looked around for a light. Not a match, not a lighter in sight. He took the cigarette from his mouth and tore it in half.

Just three more days.

*   *   *

The bar on South Street was *very* nautical. Nets drooped like hammocks from the ceiling, a ship's wheel stood behind the bar and the walls were hung with oil-paintings of schooners riding mountainous seas. The barman, wearing a battered yachting cap and smoking a stubby pipe, denied all knowledge of Carlos Cortoni or Frank Bruton. After questioning him for half an hour, Tyler believed him. He calculated that about one in five tips was genuine. Thank God the tip about Cortoni's drug-trafficking had been that one.

XXII

Dr Hansom's strengths were his self-effacing personality and the quiet, almost monotonous pitch of his voice. The voice neither lulled nor coaxed subjects into a trance; but neither did it distract them and so they became more responsive to his suggestions.

In court his voice proved to be equally effective, his modulated replies carrying conviction. At first the spectators strained to hear what he said; then they realised that this was unnecessary because, quietly, his replies reached them.

First Flores, swarthily elegant in a pale grey suit, took Hansom through the conditions that entitled him to be accepted as an expert witness – training, experience and qualifications. And when he had satisfied the court that he was expert and could therefore give opinions – on hypnosis only – as well as conventional testimony, Flores put to him general questions about his profession. As Hansom answered the questions Adler took notes, occasionally shooting out an errant white cuff on which diamond links glittered.

Hansom recalled the early days of hypnotism, *Mesmerism*, and traced its history briefly until 1958 when the Council on Mental Health of the American Medical Association had endorsed its use. He then loosely defined hypnosis, adding that, although authorities differed, he believed the hypnotic state could be separated into six levels, culminating in a condition where you could persuade a subject that an object in a room wasn't there. He also described the different types of amnesia and the methods used by hypnotherapists to restore memory.

"And what method did you employ, Dr Hansom?" Flores asked.

"Age regression, then mild post-hypnotic suggestion."

"The latter because Miss Fleming did not recall what she had remembered when you dehypnotised on the first occasion?"

"That is correct."

"A perfectly normal sequence of events in the context of hypnotic practise?"

"Oh yes," Hansom said, "perfectly. It can take many, many sessions before a patient is able to recall an event outside the hypnotic state. Especially if there is resistance to recall as there would be in a case involving a horrifying experience."

Flores stood beside the witness box. "Dr Hansom," he said, "I should like you to answer a few questions that normally puzzle laymen – people like the members of the jury and myself. Who knows, they may even puzzle the counsellor for the defence."

Adler raised one hand and continued writing.

Judge Garvey said: "I'm sure they're the sort of questions that puzzle judges."

Flores asked Hansom: "Can anyone be hypnotised, doctor?"

"Most people," Hansom said. "Figures differ but you can certainly say that more than eighty per cent of the population can be hypnotised. If they are willing, that is," he added.

"Who are the exceptions?"

"Children under the age of say six – but not always – and dizzy blondes."

Smiling, Flores asked him to elaborate.

"You have to be able to concentrate. Children aren't always capable of doing that. Nor are some hare-brained adults. In fact," said Dr Hansom, "the more intelligent you are, the more likely you are to be susceptible to hypnotism."

235

Flores asked: "Are you then saying, doctor, that everyone in this court room could be hypnotised?"

"At first glance, yes."

Said Judge Garvey: "I trust that glance embraced the bench."

Flores said: "This is perhaps the oldest query of them all, doctor. Can a subject be persuaded under hypnosis to commit an act that he knows is morally wrong? Or to put it more bluntly, could he, or she, be hypnotised into committing a crime?"

Hansom said: "You're quite right, it is one of the most common queries. And the answer, which surprises most people, is YES."

"You have surprised me," Flores remarked. "Could you elaborate?"

"The usual elaboration is: 'Can you persuade a woman in a hypnotic trance to take her clothes off?' "

Some of the jurors leaned forward and the judge said: "Judging by many of today's magazines and movies, hypnosis would be superfluous."

Hansom said: "Even if she were modestly inclined she *might* be persuaded to disrobe. To achieve this you would have to suggest to her, when a deep trance had been achieved, that she were in her bedroom and it was time to go to bed."

Adler said: "Why didn't someone tell me this when I was a young man?"

Hansom took a ten dollar bill from his pocket and held it aloft. "That's my money, right?" addressing the jury.

The jurors nodded.

"Under hypnosis I *might* be able to persuade some of you to steal it."

Most of the jurors shook their heads emphatically.

"If I suggested to you under deep hypnosis that this bill was rightfully yours then, on coming out of the trance, with a post-hypnotic suggestion implanted, it's quite possible that you would take the bill."

Flores said: "Let's move on before a crime is committed in front of the bench."

236

Hansom put the bill back in his pocket.

"Is there, in your opinion, any difference between hypnosis and the polygraph – the lie detector – and narco-analysis – truth drugs?"

Hansom raised his voice for the first time. "All the difference in the world. They are merely devices for ascertaining whether or not a witness is telling the truth. Hypnosis, in the legal context, is a method of ascertaining facts."

"Is there, in your opinion, any significant difference in the testimony of a witness who has been previously hypnotised into recalling an event, and a witness who has remembered without any such aid?"

Without looking up from his notes, Adler snapped: "Objection. If you want an expert opinion on testimony ask a lawyer not a hypnotist."

"Sustained," said Judge Garvey.

"Okay, forgetting the legal aspect then, is there any significant difference in the recall of a hypnotised and an un-hypnotised subject?"

Hansom nodded. "The hypnotised subject has a better memory."

Flores said: "I'm not allowed to ask you what Miss Fleming said under hypnosis, but am I right then in assuming that her memory of this particular event would be enhanced?"

Hansom hesitated. Adler stopped writing, leaned back in his chair, and stared at him speculatively.

Hansom said: "With respect, I don't think we should assume anything. I can only testify that Miss Fleming appeared to have achieved total recall. I cannot testify to its veracity."

Adler scribbled on his pad, underlining what he had written. He whispered to Carlos Cortoni, who smiled for the first time since the trial began and looked round at his father. Miguel Cortoni nodded expressively.

Flores said smoothly: "Of course not. No more than any of us can testify to the veracity of any witness."

Judge Garvey said: "I think, Mr Flores, that you are wandering into the realms that I am supposed to inhabit. Please

237

confine yourself to direct questioning."

Flores then asked Hansom what in his opinion had been the greatest disservice ever done to the cause of hypnosis. "In other words what has tended to distract laymen such as myself and members of the jury from its true value?"

Hansom answered promptly. "Without a doubt stage hypnotism."

"Could you explain, doctor?"

"In the first place, it has been used to make fools out of people and has made subjects scared of what they will do in a trance."

"You mean, Svengali, all that sort of stuff?"

"Precisely. In the second place, it has been practised by unqualified practitioners and this can endanger health. Even life."

"Life, doctor?"

"Sure, life. If a subject drawn from the audience proves to be difficult then the stage hypnotist often uses physical means to make him susceptible. He pretends to soothe and steady the subject with his hands on either side of his neck; he is actually pressing the blood vessels below the ears to cut off the oxygen supply to the brain. You may have seen such an exhibition," addressing the jury. "Then the hypnotist shouts: 'Now you are asleep,' and, not unnaturally, he is. I don't have to tell you that this procedure can be highly dangerous; in fact it could kill."

"This is all very interesting, Mr Flores," the judge said, "but what is its relevance to this case?"

Flores turned to him. "I want to banish every shred of prejudice that we laymen may harbour against hypnosis, Your Honour."

Judge Garvey shrugged: "Very well, Mr Flores, proceed."

"How else can it be harmful, Dr Hansom?"

"Post hypnotic-suggestion can be harmful if a hypnotist omits to remove the suggestion he has implanted. I once had a patient who became neurotic every time she saw a cat because a stage hypnotist had told her a cat was a lion on the rampage. He got a lot of laughs."

"Anything else, doctor?"

Hansom shrugged. "Of course, a lot of theatrical hypnotism is fraudulent. You know, when all those 'volunteers' rush onto the stage. The chances are that they have been previously hypnotised and their eagerness to volunteer is merely post-hypnotic suggestion."

"But the actual hypnotism isn't fraudulent?"

Hansom shook his head. "Hypnotism is a natural phenomenon: it is merely that over the years it has been abused."

"You obviously feel very strongly about this, doctor."

"I do. Just as any professional man resents seeing his calling prostituted. Hypnotism is today a recognised medical practise of immeasurable value, both therapeutically and legally."

Flores said: "No further questions," and sat down.

After the lunch recess Thornton Adler rose to cross-examine. He wore a fresh white rose in his lapel and he looked as though he had just visited a barber. In one hand he held a gold pencil with which he ticked points in his notes.

From the counsel table where Carlos Cortoni sat watching him, he walked to the area in front of the bench, turned and, pointing a gold pencil, asked Hansom: "Can a subject lie under hypnosis?"

"Oh yes," Hansom replied quietly.

"Under what circumstances, doctor?"

"In the first instance he can fake the actual hypnotic state."

"Is that easy?"

"For an actor, yes."

"Only for an actor, Dr Hansom?"

"Well, anyone with acting capabilities."

"And the hypnotist can't detect the . . . ah . . . act?"

"Not always. There are certain tests. Pain, for instance. A subject in a heavy trance can be told that he feels no pain but the fake will react to that pain."

"What you have described is a blatant attempt at deception. It is relevant, but what I asked you, or meant to ask you, is whether a subject who is truly hypnotised can still lie?"

"Unfortunately yes. His own defensive instincts can inspire a falsehood. That is the most difficult untruth for the hypnotist to determine. That and –"

"Yes, Dr Hansom?"

"That and the untruth prompted by the subject's reactions to the hypnotist himself. He may say what he believes the hypnotist *wants* him to say."

"Or her?"

"Or her," Hansom agreed.

"Without the hypnotist realising that he has, to use a legal term, led the witness?"

"It's possible," Hansom said.

"Ah." Adler marked his notes with his gold pencil. "Have you ever *led* a witness, Dr Hansom?"

"Not in that context. Obviously I have led, as you put it, when I've been regressing a subject or planting a post-hypnotic suggestion."

"Did you lead Miss Fleming?"

"Only in that context."

"But to an extent you did lead her?"

Flores said: "He's just told you that."

Ignoring the interruption, Adler paced the court room. "But you did know, did you not, doctor, that Miss Fleming wanted to remember. To purge her trauma. Would that be a fair way of putting it?"

"Catharsis? Yes, that would be a fair way of putting it when I regarded Miss Fleming as a patient."

"So she was patient *and* potential witness?"

"She was."

"And as a patient you would have urged her towards this . . . this catharsis?"

"Urged her towards it, but no farther."

"As far as the door of Daniel York's apartment?"

"I regressed her to events that evening."

"To the door of the apartment and beyond?"

"Objection," Flores snapped before Hansom could reply. "Counsellor is cross-examining on an aspect of this case which was not raised in direct."

240

Adler, looking pained, said: "On the contrary, Your Honour, the method of induction employed with Miss Fleming *was* raised in direct."

"But not," said the judge, "what she is alleged to have recollected as a result of that induction. Sustained."

"Very well," Adler said, "let us consider induction in general, doctor. If you, or any other hypnotist, continued to make one particular suggestion to a subject, is it possible that she would respond with that suggestion?"

"It's possible, yes."

"Did you persistently make suggestions to Miss Fleming?"

"I did not, sir."

Adler picked up his sheaf of notes. "But earlier today, Dr Hansom, you testified that you induced Miss Fleming into a trance by continually making suggestions that she should fall into a deep sleep. Is that not persistence?"

"It's part of induction, sir, not regression," an edge to Hansom's steady voice.

"But it was being persistent?"

"It was, yes."

"Had you read about the case in the papers, doctor?"

"The newspapers?"

Adler sighed. "Yes, doctor, the newspapers. And had you heard the radio and seen the television newscasts?"

"I had, yes."

"So you were well versed in those details known to the public."

"Yes, sir."

"You knew that Carlos Cortoni had been questioned about the party on the night of the murder?"

"I did, sir."

"And subsequently charged with a narcotics offence?"

"I had read that, yes."

"And you had read, seen or heard, that Daniel York had been a drug addict?"

"Yes."

Adler threw his papers onto the table. "It is possible, is it not, that Miss Fleming was in possession of the same facts?"

241

"It's possible."

"So we have a situation, have we not, where hypnotist and subject embark upon induction with the name of the man, accused here in court today, hanging between them?"

"I had certainly read about Carlos Cortoni," Hansom said. He took a handkerchief from his pocket and wiped his forehead. "I can't speak for Miss Fleming."

"But we do have a situation where a subject could have been influenced by factors drummed home in the media?"

"To an extent, perhaps. But she would still want to be guided towards the truth."

"And you, doctor, could also have been influenced?"

"Not during induction, no."

"Isn't it a fact that hypnotists have been known unwittingly to suggest a certain course to their patients?"

"It has happened, yes."

"Could it not unwittingly have occurred during your induction?"

"It's a possibility," Hansom said. "No more. I have induced thousands of subjects and to the best of my knowledge I have never deliberately suggested an outcome."

"I said *unwittingly*, doctor. If it was unwittingly, then you wouldn't know, would you?"

Flores jumped to his feet. "And if he doesn't know he can't answer the question. Your Honour, this is flagrant harrassment of the witness."

Judge Garvey removed his spectacles, polished them and said: "Really? I had the distinct impression that Dr Hansom is perfectly capable of taking care of himself." He pointed at Adler with his spectacles. "Objection overruled."

Adler said: "It is a fact, isn't it, doctor, that to a large extent successful hypnosis depends on the relationship between hypnotist and subject?"

"There must be rapport, yes."

"And respect?"

"And respect, yes."

"Did Miss Fleming respect you?"

Hansom said: "I hope so."

"Did she?"

"Well yes, I think she did."

"Is susceptibility heightened if both that rapport and that respect exist?"

"Without a doubt," Hansom replied.

"You understand what I'm suggesting, don't you, Dr Hansom?"

"I would have to be very unsusceptible not to," Hansom said. Laughter swept the court room.

"I am suggesting that, in your position of avuncular confessor," rolling his words, "you suggested to Miss Fleming, possibly unwittingly, perhaps because you yourself had been the unconscious victim of suggestibility through the media and your conversations with the police, that on the night in question she witnessed a certain sequence of events that in fact never occurred."

"I cannot agree, sir."

Adler moved closer to Hansom and said abruptly: "Memory is a fragile phenomenon, is it not, doctor?"

"Of course."

"Affected by many diverse factors?"

Hansom shrugged. "Sure, often people don't really remember what they claim to. For instance, a child will say it remembers a holiday in the Catskills when it is only remembering what it has subsequently been told."

"People tend to fill in gaps?"

"They do."

"And they do this to satisfy themselves? To complete a sequence, to make it acceptable?"

"That is correct. In fact, true memory is confined to exactly what the subject first saw. No more, no less."

"But if that initial sighting does not satisfy the subject then he or she might fill in the details?"

"Unwittingly, yes."

"In hypnosis just as in normal recall?"

"Hypnosis is not abnormal," Hansom said.

"I beg its pardon," Adler said. "We file away our memories, don't we, doctor?"

243

"You could say in this day and age that we feed them into a computer, the brain."

"A very advanced computer capable of processing those memories?"

"It does tend to classify."

"To amend?"

"It can certainly simplify. It can eliminate what it considers to be superfluous."

"And amend?"

"As I've said, details may be filled in to furnish a satisfactory account."

"That is, if prompted?"

"Several factors can influence the memory cells. For instance if the person considers an incident to be a part of a cycle of events, then events before and after the one in question may influence them."

"Ah." Adler paused, bent his head and smelled the rose in his lapel. "An interesting observation, doctor." Adler faced the jury. "So if a witness heard a quarrel before an event, that might affect her memory of that event?"

"It might, yes."

"And if she subsequently read that a murder had been committed, that might affect her memory?"

"If the brain classified the three events as a cycle, yes it's possible."

"She might invent the missing link?"

Hansom shook his head vigorously. "I didn't say that. You are manipulating my words. What I said –"

But Adler interrupted: "Is it a fact –"

Flores said: "Your Honour, could the witness please be given an opportunity to answer the question?"

The judge said mildly: "Mr Adler, you asked a question, let the witness answer it."

Adler inclined his head. "You were saying, Dr Hansom . . ."

"I was saying that I did not suggest that such a witness would invent a missing link. But she might adapt it slightly to slot in with what happened before and after."

"Not *invent* merely *adapt*. Thank you, doctor." Adler

244

paused to consult his notes. "Is it a fact that, in the legal context, hypnosis serves merely to cure amnesia?"

"Merely?" Hansom frowned.

"It doesn't guarantee that a subject tells the truth, does it, doctor?"

"I've already testified that, under some circumstances, a subject may lie –"

"Just answer the question, Dr Hansom."

"It doesn't provide a total guarantee, no."

From the counsel table Adler picked up a magazine and asked the judge if it could be marked as an exhibit. He then said: "This is a specialist magazine dealing with psychology and I am going to read to the witness one passage from it of a fairly lengthy article: *Hypnosis as a science is still in its infancy and must therefore still be regarded as fallible.*" Adler turned to Hansom. "Do you know who wrote that, doctor?"

"Of course. I did."

"No further questions," Adler said.

At the conclusion of his re-direct Flores said to Hansom: "You have testified to counsellor for the defence that in certain circumstances a hypnotised subject may lie?"

"Yes, sir."

"Be influenced by suggestions put to him?"

"Yes."

"Sketch in details to conform with a cycle of events, to satisfy his own anticipation?"

"Yes."

Flores paused, pulling at the lobe of his ear. Then he said: "Dr Hansom, don't these idiosyncrasies of memory apply equally to the subject who has been hypnotised and the subject who has not?"

"Oh yes, that is quite correct."

"And how does ordinary memory compare with memory revived by hypnosis?"

Hansom said: "Memory revived by hypnosis is often more accurate."

Flores sat down.

XXIII

The night was confused.

A man with a hearing aid like a telephone receiver, was chasing her through the cemetery. Long wet grass brushed her legs as she dodged between the gravestones and she knew that, beneath her feet, the dead were on the move. A gravestone opened and she waited for a face to emerge. Instead music issued forth. A Strauss waltz. *The Emperor*, wasn't it?

She stopped beside a gravestone. Hesitated. She stretched out a hand and touched the worn lettering. Traced the words with one finger. F . . R . . A . . N . . K. And then fresh and sharp-edged letters: BRUTON.

She turned and ran. Towards the man with the hearing aid. He held a knife in one hand. He was smiling.

In front of her was an open grave. She plunged into it . . .

"Hey," Katy Tanner said, "what was all that about?"

Helen sat up in bed; her nightgown was wringing wet. "A bad dream," she said.

"A very bad dream. You were whimpering."

"It's the last night," Helen said. "Tomorrow I testify."

"And then it will all be over. Do you want me to sleep with you?"

Helen shook her head. "The dream's over. I'll be okay now."

"Well, call if you want anything," Katy said as she went back to her room.

Helen looked at the bedside clock. 1 am. She took off the wet nightdress and switched off the light. The eyes were suspended in darkness. Yellow eyes. Cat's eyes. But they were disconnected. They wandered in the darkness seeking each other. Now they were pink eyes, now blood-red as they found each other and became one staring orb . . .

She awoke and switched on the light again. 2.30. She opened the drawer in the bedside table and took out a bottle of sleeping-tables, nitrazepam. No, she thought, I shouldn't take one because . . . Because of what? She put the bitter-tasting pill on her tongue. Because of what? She drank some water from a tumbler; the pill lodged in her throat; she swallowed hard and it was gone.

2.35. She switched out the light. Breathed deeply and waited for beautiful, tranquil, dream-free sleep to creep up on her.

She was making love. To Remick, not Peter. She awoke, aroused. It was 3.40.

She stayed awake for five minutes. When she closed her eyes Remick was the judge. She was on the witness-stand.

"Remember," thundered Remick. "REMEMBER!"

"Breakfast's ready," said Katy.

*　　*　　*

She smeared butter and honey on her toast and drank some orange juice.

"So," Katy said, sipping a mug of coffee, "today's the day." She wore a green robe over her nightdress and she looked ravishing, even at this time in the morning, red hair tumbling over her shoulders.

Sitting there in the poorly furnished kitchen, Helen felt surprisingly calm. Before the storm? She bit into the toast.

"Sorry it's burnt," Katy said. "I'll have to marry a chef."

The telephone rang in the hall. Katy answered it and called out: "It's for you."

It was Remick. He said: "I just called to wish you luck."

"That was sweet of you."

"Helen?"

247

"Yes?"

"I . . ."

"Yes?"

"Well, anyway," he said, "good luck."

"Thank you," she said.

"They figure you'll be testifying for about two days."

"That's not long," she said, "in a lifetime."

"Afterwards we'll celebrate. Just you and me," he added.

After he had hung up she kept the receiver to her ear staring out of the window. Down the street the sprinklers were already tossing their diamond-studded showers. The sky was blue and full of latent heat. In the driveways automobiles coughed blue smoke; wives and children waved to the bread-winners as, waving back, they drove away to work. A bird sang in the one tree in the garden, a mountain ash. Across the street stood the blue and white police car.

The phone rang again. Peter. His car had broken down, he said; she would have to go to court in the police car. He wished her luck. "See you in court," he said.

"So," Katy said when she returned to the table, "how was the good doctor?"

"Remick? Okay, I guess. That was Peter on the phone just now."

"I'm more interested in the good doctor." Katy drank some coffee. "You're falling in love with him, aren't you?"

The question startled Helen. But, after she had considered it, the answer came easily. "Yes," she said, "I am."

After breakfast Helen took a shower and attended to her hands. Standing naked before the floor-to-ceiling mirror, she remembered the dream. And smiled at her reflection.

She dressed simply in a navy skirt, yellow blazer and white chiffon blouse with wisp of blue silk at the neck. Katy, who was going to court for the first time to hear Helen, wore a green dress, vivid against her pale skin.

The plainclothes policeman who knocked at the front door whistled. "Sometimes," he said, "a policeman's lot ain't all that bad."

Katy sat in front of the car, Helen in the back with the

second policeman. They drove down Bay Street, onto Hylan Boulevard and the Verrazano-Narrows Bridge.

I mustn't be scared, Helen thought, and found that her hands inside her white gloves were tightly clenched. She said to Katy: "Just in case you didn't know, the bridge was named after the Italian who found the site for New York."

"Signor Narrows?"

"It's the longest suspension bridge in the world," Helen said, laughing.

Below them the water moved lazily in the sunlight. *Mustn't feel scared.* As they drove into Brooklyn, she silently rehearsed. *I took the elevator . . . I walked down the corridor . . . I saw –*

The driver said: "Here we go," as he drew up beside the courthouse. Photographers swarmed around the car.

"The biggest photo-call you ever had," Katy said, smoothing her stockings. "Smile please, Miss Fleming."

They climbed out of the car. Cameras clicked and rolled. "Just one more . . ."

Together Helen and Katy mounted the steps leading to the doors. Peter was among the spectators. Earl Winters, Marty Padget and a score or so of models, photographers, fashion editors . . . And Remick.

Helen heard her name called. And she was on the witness-stand. Facing Robert Flores.

XXIV

It was like those first interviews for jobs: after the initial
nervousness you settled down and had to resist the temptation
to be expansive.

The judge told her to sit down, saying:"I'm afraid you're
going to be there for a long time."

He reminded her of her history professor at college.

In front of her to her left she saw Carlos Cortoni wearing a
dark blue suit, striped tie and light blue shirt. The expression
on his face as he looked at her was . . . bleak; but there was
more to it than that, a nuance which she tried to catch but lost
as Flores began to question her.

Flores led her through the routine introductory testimony.
She answered him formally and precisely and thought: "How
calm I am," wondering if such tranquility could have anything
to do with the pill she had taken in the night.

At last Flores got round to the day of the party, December
23rd. She told the court about events leading up to the party
and about the party itself. She said she had seen Cortoni and
York having some sort of quarrel; she said she had seen guests
sniffing cocaine and had decided to leave but, because her
escort, Peter Lodge, was involved in a business discussion
with Cortoni, she had agreed to go home by herself.

In the lobby she had asked the porter to call her a cab and had
given him twenty dollars – because it was Christmas. The cab

had reached her block at 1.52 am.

"How can you be so certain of the time?" Flores asked.

"Because I had a shock."

"What sort of a shock?"

"I found I had left my purse behind at the party and I glanced at my wrist-watch. Instinctively, I guess, to make sure it was a reasonable sort of time to go back for it. Reasonable, that is, bearing in mind there had been a party."

Flores turned and addressed Judge Garvey. "It is here, Your Honour, that the witness's testimony departs from the norm. She will, in fact, give two versions of what happened after 1.52 that night, neither of which contradicts the other. In the first she will tell you that she was found wandering down Fifth Avenue at about three in the morning suffering from amnesia; in the second she will tell you exactly what happened during the interim period. The second version has been recalled by Miss Fleming under hypnosis but her account relies on *present memory*."

"And I shall, of course, object," Thornton Adler said, rising to his feet.

"I rather thought you would," Judge Garvey said. "I suggest we recess and adjourn to my chambers."

The legal argument in chambers lasted one and a half hours.

Adler, with a pink rose in his lapel this morning, submitted precedents in which testimony, initially recalled under hypnosis, had been ruled to be inadmissable. Flores cited case history in which such evidence had been allowed.

Adler concluded: "Your Honour, it is my submission that the court has no way of knowing whether the witness' resurrected memory was influenced by outside stimulus exerted intentionally or otherwise. Mr Flores claims that she is now talking from what he chooses to call present memory. But *present memory* of what? The actual event or what she was persuaded to recall in a trance? Furthermore, I submit that *if* she is recalling the actual event – and I certainly don't concede that she is – then, in Dr Hansom's own admission, she will remember it in greater detail than a witness relying on his

251

normal powers of recall. This surely is unfair to my client and against the spirit of the judicature."

Adler sat back and crossed his legs.

Judge Garvey leaned forward, elbows on his desk and said: "Mr Flores, do you have anything more to say?"

"Only this, Your Honour. Mr Adler claims that the court has no way of knowing whether the witness' memory has been tampered with under hypnosis. I would argue that the court has every way of finding out – through the legal prowess of Mr Adler who has never, in my experience, been found lacking in the art of cross-examination."

"You're very kind," Adler said.

"You see, what I am suggesting is that any memory, natural or hypno-induced, is fallible and, in the context of testimony, there is little to choose between them. As we all know hypnotism is not the only method employed to jog a memory. Leading questions have been permitted to refresh memory as have memoranda and other devices.

"Finally, I would suggest, Your Honour, that an eyewitness account, revived through hypnotism and subsequently submitted as testimony, is not that different from *any* eye-witness account which at best can be plagued with inaccuracy and at worst be beset with falsehood."

Judge Garvey took off his spectacles. "An interesting case," he said. "Very interesting. I have, of course, been studying precedents prior to today."

Flores and Adler looked at him expectantly.

"And, generally speaking, it seems that testimony from a witness suffering from amnesia, whose memory has been nudged by hypnosis, has been permitted. It would, of course, be a very different matter if the witness' memory had been revived during hypnosis only to be lost again in the posthypnotic state. In that case I would have no hesitation, provided there were no special circumstances, in refusing to admit such testimony. However, in the cases I have studied three conditions seem to have evolved: One, that the hypnotist should tell the jury how he performed the induction – and how reliable the technique is; two, that the witness should be testifying from existing memory; and three, that the lawyer representing the other side – in this case the defence – should be able to cross-examine both the facts elicited through existing memory and the techniques employed to revive them.

"I find myself in agreement with these conditions and, as it seems that we are complying with these conditions, I see no reason why Mr Flores should not directly examine the witness on her existing memory."

The three of them returned to the court room.

"And what happened after the police found you wandering down Fifth Avenue?"

"I was taken to hospital and then driven home."

"Could you at that time remember anything of what had happened after you had discovered the loss of your purse?"

Helen shook her head. "Not a thing. I didn't even remember that."

Flores said: "We have heard that you subsequently visited a hypnotist. Did you do that of your own free will?"

"The police advised me to go and I took their advice. It was good advice."

"And now," Flores said, "I want to take you through what happened during your sessions with Dr Hansom."

By the time she had finished describing the hypnotic procedures it was time for lunch. When she resumed afterwards she still felt calm; but the expression on Miguel Cortoni's face disturbed her; it was appraising . . . no, more than that. When Flores started questioning her again she forgot him.

"And now," Flores said, "I want you to tell the jury what happened when you found you had lost your purse. What you recalled after Dr Hansom had refreshed your memory."

She saw the snow falling outside the cab window and suddenly felt cold.

"Did you hear me, Miss Fleming?"

"Yes,' she said, "I heard you."

The judge leaned forward, staring at her intently. Cortoni was also staring at her. And Adler. And all the faces floating in the background.

"Well?"

"It was snowing," she said. The snow was blowing in her face, blinding her, but that was crazy because the windows of the taxi were closed.

"And what happened?"

"I told the driver to take me back to Daniel York's apartment."

Flores nodded impatiently.

"This was going to be my last trip," the bearded cab driver said. He seemed more menacing this time.

Flores said: "Go on, Miss Fleming."

Adler said: "Please, Your Honour, the witness shouldn't need prompting if she is speaking from *existing memory*."

The judge said, "Let her say it her way, Mr Flores," And then to Helen: "Take your time. Everyone in this court understands what an ordeal you've been through."

She blinked away the snowflakes and described the journey back to York's block She told them how, surprisingly, the street doors had opened. She stopped.

Flores, pulling at his ear, looked inquiringly at Judge Garvey who said gently: "And in the lobby . . .?"

"I waited for the elevator," Helen said. "It took some time."

In the elevator the snow on her hair was melting and water was streaming into her eyes.

The elevator stopped at the tenth and she walked down the corridor. The water was pressing her lids against her eyes and she couldn't open them.

She brushed at her eyes with her hands, brushed away the tears. The court room was quiet. An airplane passed overhead. Somewhere a clock chimed.

Softly, the judge asked: "And what happened then?"

She stared at him, at Flores, at Adler, at Cortoni, at spectators. "I forget," she said.

It was a few seconds before Flores spoke. When he finally turned away from Helen, sitting with her head bowed, he said to Judge Garvey: "Without a doubt, what I am about to suggest will be highly controversial."

Judge Garvey said: "If it's what I think it is, Mr Flores, then I'm inclined to agree with you." He beckoned Flores and Adler to the bench. "Well, Mr Flores?"

"As I'm sure you've guessed, I'm going to ask you to rule that the witness should be hypnotised in court."

"And as I'm sure you've also guessed," Adler said tightly, "I shall fight such a preposterous notion all the way to the Supreme Court in Washington."

Judge Garvey said: "Perhaps, Mr Adler, you will be good enough to permit me to give my ruling first. I'm going to recess the court while we adjourn to chambers."

In his chambers Judge Garvey motioned Flores and Adler to two chairs and sat down behind his desk.

Flores said: "Frankly, Your Honour, I am appealing to your progressive instincts. I believe that, in the interests of justice, hypnosis should play a greater part in our judicial system and I believe that this case represents a watershed in our thinking."

"You really want to create legal history, don't you, Mr Flores," Judge Garvey said, taking a blackened pipe from an ashtray and stuffing it with tobacco.

Flores said: "There are precedents."

"State versus Nebb?" When Flores nodded Judge Garvey addressed Adler: "Are you familiar with that case?"

"No, Your Honour," Adler said flatly.

"Interesting case." Judge Garvey lit a match, sucked the flame into the bowl of the pipe and blew out smoke from the corner of his mouth. "Wasn't it, Mr Flores?"

"It was a long time ago," Flores said. "In 1962, I think. A lot of people assumed it would open the way to acceptance of hypnosis in the courts. But the idea faded away."

"I'm not surprised," Adler remarked.

Judge Garvey told Adler that State versus Nebb was a murder trial in Ohio. The jury was excluded from the court and a hypnotist was allowed to put the defendant into a trance. His account under hypnosis of the killing was so convincing that the murder charge was thrown out and he was convicted of manslaughter.

Flores said: "I don't suggest that hypnosis in court should become the rule rather than the exception. What I do suggest is that when a witness loses his memory on the stand – a not infrequent occurrence – then he should be hypnotised."

"In the interests of justice, of course," Adler said.

"Of course," Flores said.

"Or injustice," Adler snapped. "For Chrissake, Flores, what are you trying to do, turn the courts into vaudeville theatres?"

Judge Garvey sucked on his pipe. "The theatre has frequently drawn on the courts for material." He blew out a thin jet of smoke. "However . . . Could you phrase your objections a little more precisely, Mr Adler?"

Adler said: "I'm beginning to wonder if there's any point."

"Take care, Mr Adler," Judge Garvey said.

Adler spread his hands. "Okay, so you've heard my previous objections. They still apply. What I want to know is, how the hell do I cross-examine a witness who's hypno-induced?"

Flores said crisply: "You don't. We're merely refreshing a memory as a continuing part of the trial. You cross-examine when she's been dehypnotised. When, hopefully, her memory has returned."

"Returned yet again," Adler said. "How many times do you have to jog it to get the testimony you want?"

Judge Garvey said thoughtfully: "In certain circumstances – not in this case – I can envisage a witness still in a trance being cross-examined. But the questions would have to be posed through the hypnotist who would understand how to phrase them . . . Do you have anything more to say, Mr Adler?"

Adler shrugged. What's the use? the shrug implied.

From the top pocket of his vest Judge Garvey took a gold pill-box, extracted a white tablet, placed it on his tongue and swallowed it with a draught of water. He patted his chest. "Heart," he explained. "And this doesn't help," holding up the pipe. "So, gentlemen, I figure that if I'm ever to make any impact on our legislature then it's high time I did it now."

To Adler he said: "You know, I really can't see any reason why Miss Fleming should not have her memory jogged in

256

court. After all, we frequently use other methods." He put away his box of pills, laid his pipe down on the ashtray. "But doubtless you will argue otherwise in the appellate court."

*   *   *

She sat on a chair beneath the bench, between the court reporter and the clerk, and prepared herself for the third time to be escorted under hypnosis on a journey that led to death.

She didn't know why she had suddenly forgotten; but Hansom had always warned her that it might happen. If the stress of a particular moment was too great, if she was asked to remember in the presence of the man she had named . . . If I had dulled my brain with a tranquiliser, she thought. She smoothed her eyelids with her fingertips. No melted snowflakes. But she was trembling.

Hansom sat opposite her. The court room had been cleared of the jury and all spectators except police, because Hansom had said he wanted the setting to be as peaceful as possible.

Carlos Cortoni had also been excluded in case his presence affected Helen's recollection. But Adler remained, and Flores, and court officials.

Hansom smiled one of his warm, brown smiles. "Don't worry," he said, "we'll show them."

She smiled back uncertainly and he looked into her eyes and began to talk in his measured way, and once again she was returning to that night, although all the time she was aware of everyone in court. Not only that but she could also think and reason in the present. Because I am in a light trance, she thought; because the conditions aren't right. As she walked down the corridor.

"And now," Hansom said, "you are in front of the door but there's nothing to be frightened of and when you awake you will remember . . . you will remember."

At the end of the corridor she turned. The door was ajar, held on the inside by the chain.

The judge leaned forward, head cocked to one side. Tyler sat motionless, eyes narrowed. Adler's hand froze at the rose

257

on his lapel. Flores' hand strayed to the knife which he had been going to show to Helen Fleming if she had remembered. Instinctively, his fingers closed on the handle. He picked it up.

Helen peered into York's room and saw the knife in Flores' hand. *In his hand.* Her whole body shook.

"Now tell me," Hansom said very gently, "what you see."

She closed her eyes, opened them again.

"Who do you see?"

She was aware of Hansom, aware of the knife in Flores' hand, aware of what lay beyond the door.

"I can't see anyone." Her voice was harsh.

"Very well, you can't see anyone. What *can* you see, Helen?"

Still aware of Hansom, she said: "I never could see anyone."

"Then what did you see, Helen?"

She stared around the court room. They were waiting, predators. She looked back into the room. Her voice was suddenly loud: "I saw a hand. A hand holding a knife, that's all I saw."

"Whose hand, Helen?"

"Just a hand, a terrible hand, covered with sores."

Tyler was first into the corridor outside the court room. He scanned the spectators waiting there expectantly. But Earl Winters wasn't one of them.

Tyler grabbed Marty Padget's arm. "What sort of a car does Winters drive?"

"Winters? I don't know. Why? Hey, what happened in there?"

Tyler tightened his grip on Padget's arm. "Winters' car. Think."

"Winters' car?" Padget frowned. Then: "Got it – a new Chev compact, two-tone, tan and cream. Why . . .?"

But Tyler was running down the corridor followed by Saul. Saul caught up with him as he turned into an office.

Tyler, shield in hand, snapped, "Police," at the girl clerk, and said to Saul; "Put out an alert for a tan and cream Chev compact. Cover the airports and all exits out of Long Island –

my guess is he's heading for Manhattan or Brooklyn or Manhattan Bridge, possibly Williamsburg or Battery Tunnel. Give a description of Winters, tell them to check out the licence plate number and tell them to move it."

Saul grabbed the telephone on the desk; the girl backed her chair away.

"I also want stake-outs on Winters' apartment, his wife's shop and his wholesale business in the Garment Center. West Thirty-Eighth, isn't it?"

Saul nodded and began to speak urgently on the 'phone.

Tyler took the elevator to the lobby, and then ran to the parking lot. "Sure I saw a Chevvy compact," the attendant told him. "Bald guy with a fringe at the wheel. Seemed like he was in a hurry . . ."

Tyler drove his tan Caprice out of the lot, crossed the river on Brooklyn Bridge, heading north on the Franklin D. Roosevelt Drive. He crossed to the west side at Fifty-Seventh and reached Winters' block on Central Park West via Columbus Circle.

Immediately he saw the stake-out cops in a battered cab owned by the New York Police Department, one at the wheel and one in the passenger seat. So nothing had moved here. He called Homicide on the radio. Saul had just called in. He was at the Garment Center – and so was Winters' car!

Tyler swung the Caprice round in a U–turn in the driveway and drove away, tyres spitting gravel at the police cab.

The Garment Center lies south of West Fortieth Street between Broadway and Ninth Avenue. It is a great sprawling area devoted to the manufacture of clothes; it has been estimated that if you enter a crowded room anywhere in the United States; one in every three women will be wearing clothes made in the Garment Center.

Factories, outlets, warehouses line the streets and at noon, or at factory-closing time, the area is swept by an army of more than 300,000 workers fleeing their electric cutters, sewing machines, presses and button-makers. When they have departed in the evening, it is a deserted and dangerous place.

259

When Tyler joined Saul outside Winters' wholesale premises on West Thirty-Eighth in the late afternoon, the street was in a tumultuous disarray and a tourist might have imagined a riot was taking place. Youths raced racks of clothes as though pursued by a forest fire; trucks and vans pushed their way through the crowds, horns blaring. The clothes on the racks, destined for marketing in the autumn and winter, were thick and heavy and they made the humid day seem hotter.

Saul loosened his tie, wiped his forehead with the sleeve of his jacket. "The miracle," he said, "is that he managed to park his car at all," pointing at the tan and cream compact standing between two vans, one loaded with denim skirts, the other with topcoats with imitation fur collars.

Glancing at the fur-collared coats, Tyler began to sweat. "How are we covered?" he asked.

"We got cops at each corner of the block and some behind on Thirty-Ninth."

A youth racing a handtruck carrying a rack of chiffon dresses against another truck, loaded with pale blue track-suits, charged between them. A few blobs of rain fell from sky which had become dark and bruised.

"What's he got in there?" Tyler asked, nodding towards the grimy shop-window adorned with faded bills and discount prices sprayed with red and blue aerosol.

"Beachware," said Saul. "Not *Vogue* material. You know, Hawaain shirts, leopard-skin swim-suits, stuff like that. Winters has got two floors, I reckon he's up on the second floor right now."

"Staff?"

"Just a couple of guys. They were both on the ground floor."

"Did they know you were a cop?"

Saul shook his head. "I was a buyer from Miami. I figure I look more like a rag-trade rep than a cop."

"Access?"

"Just the main door and a fire-escape leading to an exit at the rear." The rain was thickening and the air smelled of wet dust. "So what the hell do you figure this is all about?"

"I figure that Winters has got more than beachware in there," Tyler said. "You don't kill a man over swim-suits."

"So you believe what Helen Fleming said in court?"

"Sure, who else has hands covered with sores? Who else got the hell out of that courthouse because he figured she might change her story under hypnosis?"

"But he can't know that the girl *did* identify him. Identified his hands," Saul corrected himself.

"He doesn't. He's merely taking precautions just in case."

"So up till now we fucked up?"

"But not this time," Tyler said. He walked towards the store. "Did the two guys in there see Winters go up to the second floor?"

"No, but they sure as hell missed him," Saul shouted excitedly, "because here he comes."

Winters, wearing a crumpled beige suit, stood at the entrance to the store stooping from the weight of two large, olive-green suitcases he held in his black-gloved hands. He looked warily from side to side, searching the rain-soaked crowds, the vans, the racks of clothing now covered with plastic.

Guns in hands, Tyler and Saul ran towards him; but as Tyler shouted: "Hold it right there," a rack of blue and pink dressing-gowns shot in front of them, momentarily obscuring Winters. When it had passed, only the two suitcases stood outside the entrance.

Saul spotted Winters dodging behind a battered blue van to their left. He shouted to Tyler and they ran down either side of the van.. The crowds parted before them.

Saul raised his .38 Special and fired a shot into the air. Winters ducked, ran, fell as someone pushed him from behind. Then he was on his feet again. As Tyler and Saul converged on him he pushed a stationary rack of suits at them. They dodged it, but lost time.

Despite his weight, Winters was running fast.

Ahead of him, the crowd closed into a phalanx stretching across the street. There was only one escape route – the entrance to a clothing factory.

Winters disappeared inside followed by Tyler and Saul thrusting their way through the crowds. Inside the factory, machinery throbbed rhythmically. Women in green overalls leapt back as Winters ran between two lines of machines cutting, stitching, pressing.

Again Saul raised his gun, aiming this time at Winters' legs. As he squeezed the trigger, his foot slipped on a patch of machine-oil, he felt the barrel of the gun jerk up. Too high.

Winters flung up his arms. Stumbled. Fell sideways across a stationary electric saw, its guards removed for repairs, as the mechanic on the other side of the machine pressed the ON switch.

Winters' wrists fell across the blade of the saw as it began to move. The saw, Tyler and Saul learned later, was capable of cutting five hundred thicknesses of cloth in one operation.

XXV

The waiter in the Irish pub on East Forty-Fifth Street was surpassing himself for the benefit of Helen Fleming. His brogue was as thick as Guinness and his smile was roguish, as he balanced his laden tray above his head on one hand. With a flourish he set down the drinks on the chequered tablecloth. A glass of Californian white for Helen, a bottle of Guinness for Remick, a bourbon on the rocks for Saul, a Scotch and water for Levine.

"There you are, ladies and gentlemen," said the waiter, smiling at Helen. "When you want another just be after giving me the wink."

They touched glasses and drank and Saul said to Remick: "Maybe Tyler will be along later, he's got a few loose ends to tie up."

But Remick shook his head.

Helen said tentatively to Remick: "You said you thought you'd be able to explain everything tonight."

It was forty-eight hours since Carlos Cortoni had been formally acquitted of murder and released on bail on the narcotics charge, and thirty-six hours since Earl Winters had died in Bellevue – without hands and a bullet in his back.

Saul said: "John wanted Tyler to be here."

But Remick said tersely: "We can forget about that," and to Helen: "I'll do my best, but Phillip here and Lieutenant Levine will have to fill in the details."

"First," Saul said, "I'll be giving Paddy the wink. They tell me," he said as the waiter took his empty glass to the bar, "that he dyed his hair green on St Patrick's Day."

"Well," Remick said to Helen, "let's start with you. You see, a lot of what Adler suggested in court was correct. You had been hammered with Cortoni for days in the media – and elsewhere. And your brain responded to that stimulus in the hypnotic state."

"The 'elsewhere' is interesting too," Saul said, but when Helen looked puzzled Remick told her: "We'll come to that later."

Levine said: "Time I caught Paddy's eye," and ordered another Scotch as the waiter brought Saul's bourbon.

"The problem of outside suggestion is something hypnotherapists employed by the police will have to work on," Remick said. He turned to Levine. "Maybe you'd better tell Helen about Winters."

Levine sipped his Scotch, rubbed his beaky nose. "To put it briefly," he said, "Homicide gave us the break of the year. We had been looking for the wholesaler selling dope to the pushers operating in high society circles for a long time. As I expect you know by now, the wholesaler was your trusted friend and agent, Earl Winters."

Levine warmed to his subject. "You see, more often than not the pusher doesn't know the identity of the wholesaler who, in his turn, doesn't know the identity of the importer."

"So Cortoni was pushing drugs but didn't know his source was Winters?"

"Right. A wholesaler like Winters will use couriers, drops, phoney names . . . anything so that the peddlars can't identify him."

Saul said: "But Winters blew the whole thing as he was dying." He caught Helen's expression and said: "Don't mourn for him, he was a bastard. And a mean one – that lousy apartment . . ."

Levine said quietly: "Winters killed a whole lot of people in his time. Young people . . ."

"Anyway," Remick said, beckoning the waiter, "I was in

the hospital with Tyler and Saul when Winters told us a little about what happened. He told us that after the party that night he went to the bathroom to fix his hands – to wash them and put some sort of ointment on them because they were irritating. When everyone else had gone he planned to scare the hell out of York who had got wind that he was wholesaling drugs."

"How did York find that out?" Helen asked.

Saul lit a cigar and told her: "He was sleeping with Winters' wife. No taste, but it paid off. Winters' wife didn't know how deep her old man was into drugs, but she knew enough to alert York's suspicions. But York was stupid. He didn't realise just how ruthless dear old Friar Tuck was. He should have left well alone; instead, he suggested some time before the party that Winters might like to give him a little financial help. That night Winters was going to tell him that, if he didn't lay off, he would be shot and dumped in the river. As a criminal York was an amateur: Winters was a pro."

Helen stared across the saloon at the leprechaun on the bar. The pub was filling up with cocktail-hour drinkers. It was a hot evening and when they first encountered the air-conditioning they shivered.

She looked at Remick, thinking that he needed a shave, and said: "You must tell me everything. Now, for the last time." His eyes looked very green in the sunlight streaming through the window.

Remick spoke softly. "The rest is largely conjecture because after a while Winters stopped making any real sense. But we do know that by the time the other guests had left – while Winters was still in the bathroom – York was desperate for a fix. We figure that, before Winters had put on his gloves again, York burst into the bathroom screaming for money to buy a fix. Winters' own dope," Remick explained, "wouldn't have been prepared for an injection."

"And then?"

"Again, it's largely guess-work. But Winters probably decided there was no point in threatening York when he was out of his mind so he made for the door leading to the corridor and opened it. But before he could release the chain, York came at him still yelling for money. Winters probably escaped into the kitchen and picked up the carving knife. York, strong and desperate, then went for his throat with his hands. Winters must have managed to back off into the living-room, but York caught him by the door. There was a struggle and Winters plunged the knife into his back . . ."

Helen was silent. She saw the hand covered with sores. She understood why, when she had subsequently been in Winters' presence, her memory hadn't been jolted. Why should it? She associated him with *gloved* hands.

Saul said: "We figure Winters heard you outside. He looked through the peephole and saw you but you must have got away pretty damn quick. By the time he reached the end of the corridor, you were in the elevator on the way down. And then he had to get back to the apartment to get rid of his finger-prints. The smears on the knife-handle were just beautiful for him: old Earl, we assumed, wouldn't have to wipe off his prints because he would have been wearing gloves!"

The waiter brought Remick his drink.

Helen said: "That day in the forest, Boxing Day –"

"Winters must have paid Frank Bruton to kill you," Saul told her bluntly. "He can't have known what you saw in the corridor that night, but he had seen you through the peephole and that was enough. So he wanted you dead as soon as possible. But when we interviewed him on Boxing Day, it must have been obvious to him that we didn't suspect him anymore than we did anyone else. In other words, you hadn't identified him. So he told Bruton to lay off."

Levine asked: "So what happened at Miss Fleming's apart-ment bock when the porter fell down the well of the elevator?"

Saul drew on his cigar. "I can only give you an educated guess. You see we figure that Winters hoped Helen's amnesia would be permanent. But when she told him that she was going to be hypnotised, he had to renew the contract on her life. Bruton was interrupted by the porter – and got rid of him. Having screwed up there, he went on the rampage at the Metropolitan when time was really running out. Then the miracle occurred for Winters: Helen named Carl Cortoni."

Helen remembered the eyes. She began to tremble. She drank some wine. The trembling subsided. "What about Staten Island?" she asked.

Remick said: "Winters didn't have anything to do with that. He wouldn't have wanted to kill you when it was Cortoni who was facing the murder charge. And Tyler doesn't reckon Miguel Cortoni employed him, because Cortoni figured Adler would win the case. Tyler reckons that Campo was what he said he was: a gun-toting pervert."

Helen said: "Even if I had identified Winters in the first place, couldn't he have pleaded self-defence? Wouldn't that have been better than deliberately setting out to . . . to kill me?" she finished.

"No way," Levine said. "He couldn't risk a penetrating scrutiny of his affairs. As it was he knew some inquiries would be made, but nothing like the investigation that would have been launched if he had admitted killing a junkie. What we have to do now is find out where he stashed all the bread because he was a classic miser."

Helen said: "I still can't believe that he wanted to kill me."

"You've got to believe," Levine said. "Any guy who sells dope on that scale is capable of genocide. You were just *one* obstacle in his path."

Helen turned to Saul. "What was that you said just now? *The elsewhere is interesting too?*"

Remick said:"I'd better explain." He patted his pockets, instinctively searching for a pack of cigarettes.

But she stopped him, then said: "It's about Peter, isn't it?"

Remick folded his arms. "I said you'd been hammered about Cortoni in the media – and elsewhere The 'elsewhere' was Peter Lodge."

"I don't understand," she said.

"In the hospital Tyler asked Winters if he had tipped off the police that Cortoni was a drug-pusher. It was one of Winters' few lucid moments but the question puzzled him. He said no, the last thing he wanted was a narcotics connection with the killing."

Remick drained his drink; Helen waited calmly.

"But just before he died," Remick went on, "he said something like: 'Now who would benefit most if Cortoni went to jail? Think about it.' Well, we did think about it and the guy who would have benefited most – Winters apart – was Peter Lodge."

"Because Cortoni was trying to buy him out?"

"Yesterday Tyler and Saul discovered that Cortoni was doing more than that. He was threatening to wreck Peter's stock and terrorise his staff, generally making it impossible for him to operate, if he didn't sell out – for peanuts, of course. The whole operation had old man Cortoni's backing. But I doubt if we can prove any of it."

"Who told you?" Helen asked.

"Peter Lodge," Saul said, "under pressure. Apparently Daniel York told him that Cortoni was pushing dope, so he tipped us off anonymously."

"Poor Peter," Helen said, thinking about his limp and his occasional moods.

"Poor, devious Peter," Saul said. "Tell me, Miss Fleming, at the time you were so desperately trying to remember what you saw after the party, did Lodge keep plugging Cortoni's name?"

Of course he had. She nodded and was sad because another strand of her life had been severed. Snip, just like that.

"So all that time he was helping the media to plant the name in your sub-conscious," Saul said. He crushed out his cigar butt in the ashtray. "Boy oh boy, was poor Peter devious. In the first place he played the good Samaritan, pretending to forget the names of the last guests at the party, knowing all the time that he'd have to tell us. Then, of course, he comes on strong with Cortoni."

"But he did try to protect me," Helen said, "when he thought I might have killed York."

"Maybe," Saul said flatly, "he didn't want you charged with murder when he planned to implicate Cortoni."

Remick said: "Isn't that a bit strong?"

Saul shrugged. "Maybe. The police mind. But what a hell of

268

a quartet that was – Winters, Cortoni, Lodge and Padget. Each claiming they left first because they were scared of being investigated. Well, I guess they each had something to be scared of because, with the notable exception of Earl Winters, they'll all be busted. For possession of narcotics, for tax evasion, for sexual offences against juveniles. Nice people."

Helen said: "And I suppose the business discussion at the party –"

" – Was monkey business," Saul said. "Cortoni threatening Lodge, Lodge playing for time."

Levine said: "In the end the sonofabitch almost had it all ways. The guy who was blackmailing him over tax evasion dead, and every chance that the guy who was trying to strong-arm him out of business in jail for the murder."

Realising that she had been living with a man who was prepared to use her, to use her mind, to frame a man he wanted out of the way, Helen felt sorry for Peter Lodge for the last time.

She looked up from her drink to see if Remick understood. But he wasn't even looking at her. Tyler had just entered the bar.

The waiter wiped his hands on his green apron, shook Tyler's hand and said: "It's a pleasure to have you back, sor."

Tyler sat down between Helen and Saul and said: "So no-one won. We got the wrong guy through hypnotism, we got the right guy through hypnotism."

"What matters," Remick said, "is we got *someone* through hypnotism. As Hansom wrote: *Hypnosis as a science is still in its infancy and must therefore still be regarded as fallible.*" He grinned at Tyler. "Which doesn't mean to say it isn't here to stay."

"Okay," Tyler said, "let me put it another way. We both won."

Levine said:"As an outsider, I'll put it yet another way. Progress won. How about that?"

"Safeguarded by proven techniques," Tyler said.

"Here we go again," Saul said, but Remick shook his head: "Not tonight, I've got a date."

Helen stood up. "With a hypnotist," she said. "He's going to stop him wanting to smoke."

Remick and Helen walked to the door followed by Tyler. As he watched them walk away in the evening sunshine mingling with the homeward crowds, he thought: "May would have approved."

Just before they turned a corner Helen looked behind her and waved at him, then tucked her hand under Remick's arm. Together they disappeared round the corner.

* * *

The nightmare continued for several weeks after Winters' death.

At night she saw the hands and woke up screaming. Even during sunlit moments during the day, the hands reached for her. Sometimes they were severed, sometimes not.

One warm July evening she and Remick dined with Hansom in his apartment adjoining his consulting rooms. They entered the block by the entrance which she remembered and for a while as she sat, drink in hand, listening to Remick and Hansom discussing hypnosis it seemed to her as though she were lying on the couch.

Hansom's voice took over. Monotonous, soothing. "Relax," she heard him say to Remick as he described a particular method of induction. Then from a garble of words: "Sleep . . . relax . . . sleep . . ."

And she was walking down the corridor. Peering round the half-open door. She saw Marty Padget poised to plunge the knife into Daniel York.

She closed her eyes tight. Opened them again. Saw the knife sinking into York's body. Held this time by Peter Lodge.

She saw her own hands – and began to tremble violently.

"Hey," said John Remick, "you're day-dreaming. Was it the usual bad dream?"

She took his hand and placed it against her cheek. "I forget," she said.

270